P9-DUB-621

PEOPLES

PEOPLES

BY ROBERT C. S. DOWNS

THE BOBBS-MERRILL COMPANY, INC.
INDIANAPOLIS NEW YORK

Published by The Bobbs-Merrill Company, Inc.
Indianapolis New York
ISBN 0-672-51900-3
Library of Congress catalog card number: 73-10704
Designed by Jack Jaget
Manufactured in the United States of America
First printing

For Lou Renza

PEOPLES

SUMMER

MONDAY

They just told me to sit down here with you for a while, an' they be along soon to orientate me to the system they usin'.

So what you do 'fore you was brought here? Any good tricks or like that? Or you just the kind what eats an' sleeps an' lives off you people? You know, it look to me like you got it made in you own way. You got all you need right here in this room. I mean, you warm, you eatin' good; they don't cut you up too bad, only when they got to. But they told me that you don't feel it so much like we would. If some cat went an' cut me like that I'd have to kill him. But you cats don't complain 'cause you know it won't do no good howsoever. You could howl an' howl an' howl an' you know nobody goin' to hear you, an' if they do they ain't goin' to listen to you. You all closed off from everythin', an' you best to get one thing straight: all you got is me. An', yeah, I know, all I got is you, leastways for a while. Like the white priest he told my ma, "Mrs. Peoples, Billy has got to crawl before he can walk." Whatever that mean.

An' you over there, why you cut up diff'rent from this one? He cut all 'long the side an' you got it in the belly. Don't make no sense to me. If they goin' to cut you all why ain't they no system for it? An' that black an' white cat over there he cut in two places 'long the neck. Look now, if they goin' to cut you why don't they do it right? Look at that line there. That no real cut at all. It look to me like they cut you slow. That ain't no way to cut. You got to do it quick, flash like, an' they don't feel nothin'. They just drop easy an' funny like they doin' it in slow motion, an' they lookin' at you like it didn't happen to them. The cat what cut you he don't know nothin' 'bout a blade. An' you know what? They told me upstairs that they goin' to teach *me* how to do it.

Man, you cats should see this here layout. It got tunnels an' rooms an' more tunnels an' bigger rooms with them high silver tables all polished like fine new chrome. An' all them cats in they fine white coats. They told me I be gettin' a white coat soon. But it be short for a while, not down to the floor like that doctor have who take me 'round. That come after I prove myself solid for the place. An' they told me that all I got to do is this here job an' they take care a everythin'. If I get sick like you cats I don't pay nothin' for no hospital or anythin'. That good. My ma she goin' to like that. But they don't tell me what they doin' to you or why. I s'pose I find that out. My ma she told me you don't ask them kinda questions a white folk. She say if you do they think right 'way you tryin' to take over. Now maybe what ought to happen is that you cats take over. That'd be somethin' else.

An' you know that big white doctor what took me 'round, he told me I get used to the smell. I don't smell nothin' bad, not real bad. It just like the hallway in the buildin'. Been smellin' that smell for years. But he told me I get *a*ccustom to it, an' when I tell him it don't bother me he look funny at me like I lyin' to him. Then he tell me he goin' to do somethin' to Number Twenny-six an' I s'pose to get him ready. I don't know what he goin' to do to you, Twenny-six, but he 'splained it all to me. First thing we do is we go for a walk an' then I got to weigh you. Weighin' you important he say. I never weighed no dog 'fore. He say you a nice dog, Twenny-six. I hope you a nice dog, 'cause if an' you ain't he say I got to bust you one on the nose. That the place it hurt most, he say. Then after we walk an' I weighs you I got to bring you to that there room down the hall, the one with the sign that say, KEEP OUT. Then he say he's goin' to put you down. I got to help with that, the man say, an' when they finish with you I take over 'gain an' see to it that you all right. An' someday the white doctor told me I goin' to be made Spec'men Supervisor. I s'pose that's when I get the long white coat.

I don't know 'bout this here job, no*how*. You know what they doin' to Twenny-six? They cuttin' him. I didn't see them begin but I knows they doin' it. I helped put him down, an' when the white doctor say down he mean *down*. What I did was to walk Twenny-six an' he like that fine, an' when we come back in I puts that dog on that big scale they got. He wrigglin' 'round an' he upset like, an' fin'ly I scratch his ears an' he calm down. Then I looks to the scale an' it say fourteen. That dog no fourteen anythin'. Scale busted. An' I tell the white doctor scale busted an' he give me his smile an' he say, "What did it read, Mr. Peoples?" I tell him fourteen an' he look at Twenny-six an' he say that 'bout right. I tell him that dog a lot more than fourteen. Then he say kilograms, an' he turn 'way an' he gets the needle all set to stick in Twenny-six's leg. I don't know what they slip him, but man, it work fast in that leg. Just quick like an' that dog fall over easy with his eyes not seein' nothin' an' his tongue hangin' out the side a his mouth an' he breathin' real slow. Then 'nother white doctor who be there he say somethin' 'bout tube, an' then he shoves this little rubber hose right down that dog's throat. It remind me a Jimmy Jackson when he have hisself the overdose an' the doctors come an' they did the same thing to him. 'Cept he die, an' they tell me Twenny-six he goin' to be all right. Then I ask what they goin' to do, an' the white doctor he smile 'gain at me an' he say "spleen-ec-toe-me." I say fine, what that, an' he say they goin' to take out that dog's spleen. I say fine 'gain, an' I ask him why an' he say that where that dog he keepin' his blood all stored an' they got to have the volume a blood all constant like for the 'speriments.

Man, then we go to work on Twenny-six. Onto that table, tie down his arms an' legs, hook that little rubber hose into that machine that pumpin' like little bicycle wheels, an' then the white doctor he give me this here razor, like the barber use on my neck, an' he say, "Shave the abdomen, Mr. Peoples," an' he put his hand on Twenny-six's belly. You know, maybe I be me a barber 'stead of a doctor 'cause I shave that abdomen good, he say. An' when I finish with the big 'lectric razor he give me one for you face an' he say, "Now right down to the skin, Mr. Peoples." By the time I done my back an' feet they hurtin' bad an' I can't feel nothin' in the toes on this here foot. Then the man he take this big bottle a red stuff—it look like wine to me—but it smell like doctors all right, an' he pour it all over that dog's belly, an' then he take alcohol an' he do the same. Then he say to the other white doctor, "Drape him." I watch while they layin' all the green sheets an' stuff on Twenny-six an' they go an' clip them sheets right to the skin with what look to me like them little scissors my ma she use on her toes sometimes, only these got little curved ends what look like claws. They hold them sheets tight, all right. Then they tell me it okay for me to go, they send for me when they finish.

Now lookit this here dog. All you cats take a big lesson from this. They goin' to cut you just like they cut Twenny-six here. Course some a you knows 'bout that already. How it feel not to have no more spleen, dog? Man, you lyin' there in you cage like you got a belly full a hurt. An' you sleepin' like you never goin' to see tomorrow. That doctor he told me you goin' to sleep till way late tonight. Then you goin' to wake up an' they ain't goin' to be nobody here to say it all right, you goin' to be all right. I could stay but I don't get but the min'mum, an' I don't think it do no good. The man say it don't hurt you, but any cat what cut clean 'cross his belly, he hurtin'. I knows. Now you get some good sleep, hear, Twenny-six dog?

Now for the rest a you cats it gettin' late an' you s'posed to get you food now. Then I goin' to fill them water dishes an' then I goin' home. An' you know what I goin' to do? I goin' to have me a fine big drink a Scotch whisky. I got a bottle in my room my ma she don't know nothin' 'bout. It for special occasions, an' my first day on the job it special.

There, that the last a you. Now listen up, you cats. I goin', but I be back tomorrow. Soon I be the Spec'men Supervisor, an' then I goes to the school an' then I gets to be me a doctor. Then *I* gets to cut you up an' some other cat he be in here supervisin' you spec'mens.

TUESDAY

You know, Twenny-six, I couldn't do nothin' last night 'cept worry 'bout you. My ma she told me they ain't no good in the world when a young man pass an evenin' agitatin' over some mongrel dog. I s'pose you can see from that the kinda trouble we got with our women. So you ain't lookin' too bad now 'cept they told me you be up an' 'round by now. You still lyin' 'xackly like I left you last night only now you 'wake an' you givin' me the bad eye. Well, I didn't do that thing to you. But I s'pose you be all right after a bit.

Now lemme get to these here water dishes, an' then I be tellin' you 'bout my night. An' then I goin' to clean out that mess you all made there an' then I hose down the cages. I got to take it slow today 'cause this here leg a mine it hurtin' bad from all that standin' 'round yesterday. You know, this here leg a mine it got no muscle like from the knee down. An' I ain't got no kinda toes on this foot neither. They all just big lumps what go together an' come all loose like they takin' orders from some other brain. Now I don't s'pose if an' I told you like when I was at my high school I was a high jumper you'd believe me. But it true, an' you know I was good, man, good. This other leg a mine one time it measure twenny-eight inches 'round the biggest part. It my take-off leg, you know, an' I had me plenty a what they call lift. I mean I could go up, y'understand. Trouble was, I couldn't never get more an' like 'bout five ten 'cause I couldn't get no speed comin' at the bar. But if they still had that there standin' high jump, man, I be the champ of the whole world in that. Nobody ever beat Billy Peoples in the standin' high jump. But all that business it fi' years ago now, like when I was in the tenth grade, an' other things goin' now, like you cats an' these cages. But I figure the first few days on the job be like them first few days a high jumpin' every year. I be stiff for a while an' then them other muscles they come 'round an' I gets my rhythm down just so.

So, like 'bout last night. First thing I do is have my drink a Scotch whisky, an' then I waits for my ma to come home from the job. She work in the cleaners all day, you know, but 'fore she go in the mornin' she go to Mass an' 'fore she come home in the evenin' she makes her 'nother visit an' lights herself one a them candles. I used to go with her all the time when I was a kid an' didn't have no say in nothin'. An' then I tells her one day that goin' to church it for the women an' she look at me like I one ter'ble lost soul an' she say, "Billy, I got to go double now for you soul. But it don't matter none," she say, "I bring you through with my prayers to the Jesus baby." An' she start crossin' herself like a couple hundred times an' I just standin' there thinkin' to myself good, that business all over an' done with.

So like there I am waitin' for her to come home an' after a bit I hear her runnin' up the stairs an' she done blow in that door like I Christ hisself handin' out special favors. First thing she ain't even got her breath an' she askin' me did I spend the whole day here an' didn't quit or nothin'. I told her everythin' it fine an' I didn't quit or nothin'. She cross herself an' she look up to the ceilin' an' she say, "Billy, I pray for you all the time an' the sweet Jesus baby he gonna keep you on the job." You know, she even pray all day long on the job. Everytime she check a pocket, that all she do is check pockets, she sayin' one a them beatitudes 'bout the meek takin' over when Jesus come down on his throne an' the big end come. That all she do all day long. Man, if the meek wants it, that fine with me.

Then after she quit prayin' I told her 'bout you cats an' how everythin' here it 'ranged. I told her I got me this big room with you cages all 'round the walls, two dishes in front a each, an' how they all diff'rent kinds a you dogs here. I told her they's long-eared cats like you two over there, one all white, a couple a fine-bred dogs that the white doctor told me just got lost from they homes. An' I told her that you cats come from the pound an' that most a you just run off from bad homes an' end up here. An' she say, "No matter what, you always got to stay with you people." I don't say nothin', man. I just tell her what the doctors told me. An' I told her that this here buildin' it not really a part of the medical school or hospital. Then she ask me what they doin' to you dogs here, an' I told her that so far I couldn't make out 'xackly what it was but it look to me like they takin' out spleens. She say that a good thing for me to be learnin' an' I 'bout to ask her why she think so when I 'members that there shore ain't no use in askin' her nothin' like that no more. Then she ask me if anythin' wrong with the place an' I tell her the floor hurt my leg 'cause it slope to the center drain there. An' then I think for a second more an' I tells her only one other thing wrong. This here room got no window.

Then after a while I goes down to the bar an' I shoots some pool an' mix myself up a little on the wine. But I slept good when I got home, like my ma said I would when I got a good job that goin' to take me some place. I s'pose she right 'bout that.

But this mornin' it somethin' else 'gain. It rainin' out, you know. No, I guess you don't know 'cause every day it just the same in here for you. So when I comin' down Hundred Twenny-fifth Street to the subway everybody he hurryin' to cram hisself down them stairs. An' right at the top a the stairs is one a the brothers who all uptight 'bout goin' back t'Africa an' you could see he high on somethin'. He just standin' there 'gainst the wall yellin' over an' over, "You all too close together, you all too close together." He right, you know. But I don't 'spect that he be sayin' all that business if an' he could get hisself a look at you cats here.

Now did you take some notice a that? Don't seem to me to be no way for a man to conduct hisself. The big white doctor, you know, he come to the door just now an' he all shaved an' smellin' like he fit for jazzin' an he say to me, "Good morning, Mr. Peoples."

"Mornin', doctor," I says nice like.

"What is the condition of Twenty-six?" he ask.

"Cages ain't clean yet," I tell him, "but you can have you a look if you want."

"Oh, no, thank you," he say polite like an' he pull back from the door like the smell it killin' him. So I tell him it look to me like Twenny-six he still got hisself a fuzzy head, an' the doctor he say, "That's to be expected." Then he pull back some more an' he say, "Afternoon splenectomy on Twenty-seven." Now what I don't like 'bout that man is he don't want to come in here. He actin' like this place not made for his kind. What I wanted to say to him was that the trouble with you, y'understand, is that you got a nice sens'tive nose. It also one a the biggest noses I ever seen.

Now for these here cages. First thing to do, they said, was to take out the tray under each a them an' then stack them trays in that big sink over there. My, Thirteen, it look to me like you eatin' too much. How come a little dog like you put out so much in just one night? An' you, Fifteen, how come you ain't keepin' pace? I s'pose you could use youself a run. They say that clean a dog out good. Now into the sink an' you know maybe that doctor he right. This don't give out no real bad stink till you gets too close. An' then it somethin' else, man. I see now why they say yesterday they havin' trouble keepin' men for this here job. I don't mind talkin' to you an' takin' care a you after they cuts you up, but this here part a the job it ain't for me. It ain't even for people.

Les see now. I got eighteen a you dogs in all, an' the missin' numbers is from the dogs what died on the table, they say. Top number now it twenny-seven. Eighteen from twenny-seven it leave 'bout eleven dogs they kill or there'bouts. This cage-cleanin' business it okay for now, but they told me that after a while when the 'speriments get goin' they goin' t'have 'bout fifty a you dogs in here. Now if I got to clean up after fifty dogs, how I goin' to have time to learn all they say they goin' to teach me? I s'pose I goin' to have to streamline this here job.

Now to put the 'monia on the trays an' then hook up the hose an' get the hot water goin'. Hot water an' 'monia all over the cages it take care a the smell all right. You know, with this here big drain in the middle a the floor it remind me a that drunk tank last summer. All the cats in there they vomitin' all over the floor all night long, an' in the mornin' the cat in the overalls he come in with the hose, just like me now, an' he clean that place out fast. Everythin' slide right down the drain easy like. Maybe I try that with you cats. This here place just like the drunk tank. Leastways I don't see no diff'rence.

There, now all that mess done for today. You know, if I don't show up one mornin' it goin' to be 'cause I got to thinkin' 'bout cleanin' up an' I just couldn't take it no more, y'understand. So if you don't see me you knows I be in the bar early like tryin' to forget I should be here.

Now les see, Twenny-seven. You a fine young dog. You a cocker spaniel an' I goin' to let you out a you cage for a little run 'fore I goes for my dinner. Seems to me that with the system they usin' here they ought to be some time set aside for you cats to have youself some fun. There, the cage open, Twenny-seven. Come on, now, why you crouched back in there cryin' like an' carryin' on like I's 'bout to hurt you? You a strange dog. If I close the door you comes right up an' sticks you head through the hole an' you seem all happy like at the door bein' closed. I got to find out 'bout that later. That don't make no sense to me.

Well there, Twenny-seven, you wasn't jivin' me after all. I knows 'bout you now. I was goin' through the line in the cafeteria an' behind me 'nother cat an' he say to me, "Hey, man, you new here, huh?"

"My second day," I tell him.

"Where you work?" he ask.

"Research Center," I tell him. He say that a good job to have, an' I ask him why an' he say 'cause that where they payin'. I tell him they payin' only the min'mum an' he say that okay for now, but if I work out for the place the bread it get good quick. He say they can't keep nobody in this here job. I tell him I believe that, 'cause this no good at all 'cept it better maybe than bein' in the street. He say yeah, he know, he on parole. "What they bust you for?" I ask.

"'Bout everythin'," he say an' he laugh. You know, dogs, when they bust you for one thing an' you gets in front a the judge you got to listen to a whole list a things they said you done an' it don't sound like you the cat s'posed to be standin' there *a*-tall.

"Where you workin'?" I asks.

"Diet 'speriments," he say, an' then he look at me, an' he say, "Drag, baby. Don't do nothin' all day 'cept weigh out this here special food like an' write down what they eatin' an' what they ain't eatin'. Then come five o'clock I substracts the whole mess an' takes it to the doctor. That the whole problem, you know, the substractin'."

"What they tryin' to prove?" I asks.

"Don't know," he say. "But I been doin' it for 'bout a year now. Just finish with a whole batch a dogs, they a year old now an' no good for the 'speriments."

"How young you start them dogs?" I asks.

"Soon as we can get them off the tit," he say, an' he laugh 'gain.

"What you do with them when you finish?" I asks.

"Give them 'round to other places. Like we gave you one last Friday. He a cocker spaniel." That you, Twenny-seven, an' I tell him you won't leave you cage an' you scared when I opens the door. "That dog won't ever leave no cage," he say.

"How come?" I asks.

" 'Cause he born in one an' he live there his whole life now. He don't know nothin' but a cage," he say. Well, you be leavin' you cage s'afternoon, dog, 'cause you havin' you spleen out.

WEDNESDAY

Now that what I like to see. Twenny-six, you lookin' fine, you know, all up an' 'round like an' you pantin' after the water an' the food like them doctors never done nothin' to you. They told me 'cause you a big boxer dog you the kind what strong an' can take it. But old Twenny-seven cocker spaniel here, he look like he havin' a bad time. Hold on now, Twenny-seven, you bleedin'. You ain't s'posed to be bleedin'. Lemme open this here cage an' get me a look. It all runnin' down the cage an' spillin' onto Twenny-six. *Hey,* dog! You bit me when I just tryin' to help you. You went an' raise up you head an' you bit me best you could, an' now you just layin' back with you eyes hangin' an' you dead, ain't you, Twenny-seven? You dead as hell. I knows the look. I can't blame you none for bitin' me. What you know 'bout the whole thing anyhow?

Now I got to go an' find out what I do with a dead dog. Two days now an' I been dreadin' findin' out what I do with a dead dog.

I s'pose I got to tell you where you all goin' to end up. I knows you all is goin' there 'cause the white doctor he told me that you goin' to be tested an' tested till you die. First place you goin' is into one a them heavy brown paper sacks like what I put Twenny-seven in. An' then, if the incinerator ain't workin' you goes straight to the freezer box. That where I put Twenny-seven just now an' they told me that after a while he be rock hard an' then they can incinerate him when it *con*-venient. So that's it, man, this here the end a the line for you. 'Cept you don't know what goin' to happen an' I don't s'pose you even knows 'bout dyin'. That make all the difference.

An' you know I ask that doctor why Twenny-seven he die,

an' he say it all an accident. He say Twenny-seven get hisself a he-ma-toe-ma, whatever that is, an' that what kill him. An' he say that the hematoma it begin right under that *in*-cision he made an' sometime last night that dog he woke up an' he start to lick at them stitches an' he break them open. Then he in trouble, the doctor say, 'cause that when Twenny-seven's hematoma it open up. That why Twenny-seven he bleed to death. But you know what I think? I think that big white doctor's a jive cat an' he just tryin' to cover up what he done wrong. I don't think he really know what he doin'.

Well, now, I finally know what's goin' on here. 'Member the old white doctor what come in just 'fore I goin' for my dinner? Yeah, well, he a fine man, a fine man. You know what he done? He bought me my dinner in the cafeteria. He told me when he come in that he want to sit me down an' give me the whole plan a what they doin' here. He say I goin' to be a 'portant part a the team. Now that sound good to me, y'understand. Sound like I needed. An' he told me all 'bout what goin' on here an' all 'bout the 'speriments. He so smart he somethin' else. Now here's what they goin' to do to you. Takin' out spleens ain't but one small part of what he call that there to-tal-it-ty. Dig it, man, if I be learnin' words like that. An' I got to learn them, see, 'cause that's how you makes it with the white folk.

So they goin' to take out you spleens as part one, y'understand. Two is to cut you open again so we can make you hearts like if you had a human heart. I think that what he say. See, you problem is that you got good hearts, an' 'fore we can do 'speriments to help you bad hearts we got to give you a bad heart. So they goin' to cut you open an' go right into you heart an' make it like you was a human bein' what got hisself the heart disease. You got valves in you hearts, you know, like little doors what openin' an' closin' all the time to let the blood go where it got to. Well, if an' you was a human bein' with the heart disease then these little valves sometimes they don't work just so. They wouldn't open or close just right, see, an' then the drugs would work on you good.

Seem like they sayin' that you problem be all solved if you was just a human bein'.

An' you know what he went an' done? He gave me his Jell-O for dessert. He say he been overeatin' lately an' that ain't no good for you heart. An' he say this afternoon I begin to watch the splenectomies so I can learn how to do them. Hear that, you dogs? After a bit I be takin' out you spleens.

Man, splenectomy it somethin' else. *Man,* it somethin' else. It just like I see on the doctor show on the television. Man, all them cats there just like that. They got the masks an' them little caps an' them rubber gloves an' gowns. An' them doctors they so cool while they doin' the cuttin'. Oh, *yeah,* they so cool. They tellin' jokes, man, the whole time they tellin' jokes an' stories 'bout when they in the medical school. An' they talkin' 'bout the chicks they been jazzin', an' some a them other doctors at the hospital who ain't doin' like too good a job. That one big white doctor he a funny cat. He talkin' for the longest time, you know, 'bout one time when he at the medical school an' he lyin' in bed one mornin' an' some cat come to him an' offer him fi' dollars for his seed for some 'speriment. An' he laughin' like crazy an' he tell them other doctors he need that fi' dollars bad, but he jazz some chick three, four times night 'fore an' he laugh at the cat who want his seed. I don't know what the whole thing it comin' to when people be buyin' other people's seed an' doin' 'speriments on it. Seed, it ain't for that.

An' all the time, you know, they takin' out Twenny-eight's spleen. The spleen it a big organ you have in you body. An' it got all kinds a thick blood veins an' such that go into it an' come back out. 'Fore they cut them lines the doctor he take that spleen an' he squeeze an' squeeze till it get real small like, an' I ask him why he do that an' he say he pushin' all the blood in the spleen back into Twenny-eight's body. Then quick like, he snip everythin' right 'long 'tween them big clamps he put on the blood veins an' he drop that dead spleen into this dish what shaped like that bedpan my grandma she use all the time 'fore she die. Then the cat take the thread an' he begin to sew an' tie, an' my he good at that. I know he good 'cause he fast. That cat's fingers they movin' like a magician I once saw. An' them fingers they makin' little squeaky sounds from the dried blood what stuck to them gloves. Then that doctor he begin to stitch that dog's skin, an' you know what he done? 'Fore he cut him in the beginnin' he make two little cuts in the skin an' then he make the big cut right through the little cuts. He say that for bein' able to match up the two sides of the big cut so the skin it grow back together just right an' it look good. I don't know what they worryin' 'bout you lookin' good for, dog. You ain't goin' no place.

Well, I got to be gettin' 'long now 'cause tonight I starts the school. I goes from six till 'bout nine-thirty, they say, an' after I sharpen up in a few subjects I goin' to take me that there *E*-quivlancy *di*-ploma 'xamination. Yeah, man. An' after that I goin' onto the program at the City University. That program it called SEEK, 'cause they lookin' for cats like me, you know, what they call dis'vantaged an' from the black ghetto an' all that boo. So I goin' to be learnin' 'bout readin' which I don't do too good at like, an' math'matics, an' what that white cat what signed me up he call 'self-wareness.' But dig this. They payin' me to go to the school. Nobody did that 'fore. If an' they had, man, I never leave. They payin' me forty-fi' dollars a week just to go an' get the skills. Course they ask me if I got a job, 'cause if I got a job they shore ain't payin' me. I tells them, no, sir, I can't get no job, an' the white cat he say he understand an' all. So right 'way, man, I beatin' the gov'ment for forty-fi' dollars every week. Then they gave me these here tests, an', man, I don't do so good, but they say that fine, lower you score better the gov'ment like you 'cause then they can help you more. They say I readin' like I was in the third grade an' my 'rithmatic it like somewhere 'round grade number four point fi'. They say that fine too 'cause now they know 'xackly where to start me. I told the man what signed me up that I didn't get but to the tenth grade an' he say, "That's fine, Mr. Peoples. There are many young men here such as you are." He seem all right, you know, an' I just 'bout ready to tell him that I want to become a doctor when he look over my shoulder an' he say, "Next." He give me this here card an' told me come tonight six sharp.

THURSDAY

Now this here school it goin' to be the answer to a whole lot a things. Course last night they just orientatin' the cats an' they say like tonight we begin. But I tell you cats one thing. It seem like everybody I ever knew was there last night. Sidney, Ernest, Harmon, George—all the cats, an' they lookin' cool all right. They look like they there just to beat the gov'ment for forty-fi' dollars every week. An' Harmon, man, he got hisself some fine threads on an' he jivin' the white cat what signin' him up till no one know for shore if Harmon ever got no Social Security number. He say he don't even know where he born or if he had hisself any sickness when he was a kid. He just sayin', "Look, man, when do you pass out the forty-fi' dollars?"

"Well, of course," the white man say, "we have to process the forms through the proper channels to Albany."

"I know all 'bout that, man," Harmon say, "but like when do I begin to collect?"

"About two to three weeks," the white man say.

"Man, you tell me when you sign me up that I be collectin' right soon. In two weeks, man, I can be in the street takin' down three, four C's."

"Legally?" the white cat say.

"You a parole officer?" Harmon shoot back at him. White man he know he got hisself trouble. "Then why you askin' questions ain't none a you business?" An' Harmon he gets up an' he move off to the door where I'm sittin' an' I ask him if he stayin' an' he say, "All just jive cats, man. I got to go downtown an' take care of business, y'understand." Well, that's when I see that Harmon he flyin'. He take off his shades slow like an' you can see he finish for the night. Then I see his hand comin' out from under the jacket an' I say, "Harmon, you bleedin'."

"Yeah, I know," he say, an' he just keep right on goin' out the door.

Then they take Sidney an' he so meek that white cat like to love him to death,'specially after Harmon. Sidney tell them he want that there *e*-quivlancy *di*-ploma an' he goin' to work, oh my oh my is he goin' to work. Then Ernest he do the same an' finally George sit down with the man. You could see George gonna be trouble. "What kinda buildin' this here anyway?" George ask.

"A converted Y.M.C.A., " the white man say.

"I s'pose you got a swimmin' pool I can use?" George say, an' cool like he begin to file his nails. He always proud a the nails on his left hand, an' he put that clear polish on them all the time, you know.

"The swimming pool is not for use by the trainees," the white cat say.

"Who goin' to use it?" George ask.

"No one," the man answer. You can see he gettin' uptight like 'cause he mess up his desk with the carbon paper.

"I s'pose it full," George say.

"Security guards are posted by the pool to see that the trainees do not enter," the cat say.

"The gov'ment it own this place, right?" George say, an' he look up at the man. "An' this here is Harlem, right? An' it August in Harlem, right?" The white cat just keep noddin'. "An' the gov'ment it own a pool right here in this buildin' an' it payin' security guards to keep us out, right?"

"Yes," the man say.

"Dig it," George say, "that sound like the gov'ment, all right."

But then George ease up on the man an' the white cat he glad all over, an' he sign George up right quick an' he come to me. "Mr. Peoples," he say, "I need certain information in order to complete your registration." I gives him all he needs an' he seem happy t'have me sittin' there. Then he say, "What is your purpose in coming to NEW?"

"I goin' to be a doctor," I says.

"Fine, Mr. Peoples, fine," he say. An' he write somethin' down on the folder he got an' he look past me just like the first time, an' he say, "Next."

So I leaves the table an' goes into the main room where all the cats just sittin' 'round on them green plastic couches an' like they waitin' for they don't know what. They waitin' 'cause they ain't nothin' to do. It still light out in the street, you know, an' they ain't no action when it still light out. After a while a just sittin' like, 'long come this security guard in his *po*-lice uniform an' he swingin' his stick cool like. "All right, gentlemen," he say, "this building is closing. Report tomorrow night at six p.m." An' he said it just like he some white cat. If I hadn't been lookin' at him I woulda thought a white cat for shore. Put a uniform on a cat an' right 'way he sound white. But 'cept for the cat what signed us up everybody they colored. Leastways, the big cats in the place is colored. George told me that some a the teachers they gonna be white. If they is they gonna have theyselves a time, 'cause it's them white teachers what got us in this mess in the first place.

I got to cut the jivin' here an' get me to work. Lookit all the stuff in them cages. Only cat who don't mess up nothin' is Twenny-eight an' that 'cause he still out from the splenectomy. Twenny-nine he comin' in later, the doctor told me this mornin', an' the doctor say we got to take special care of Twenny-nine 'cause he a big collie dog. Big dogs they hard to come by an' they needed bad by the doctor 'cause a big dog he got a big heart like a human bein'. That doctor say that someday he hope he can work on sheep 'cause they got 'proximately a human heart.

But here now, I runnin' off the mouth an' all you got on you minds is you dinner. Lemme get to them there dishes an' the like, an' then I be tellin' you all 'bout *Doctor* Peoples' first *o*-peration.

Course first thing we do is put Twenny-nine down an' get him set an' then I starts to make up the pack like, an' that took near a hour 'cause the big white doctor he take me through step by step an' show me what got to be in the pack. In the beginnin' I don't see how we goin' to use so much 'quipment, but we did all right. An' I wrap all that stuff up in the towels like an' the doctor he show me how to tape the pack just so an' then we goes to the aw-toe-clave, which look like one a them machines at the cleaners, you know, with all them dials an' the big old black handles, an' it hiss somethin' fierce 'fore it get itself workin' right. When somethin' come out a the autoclave it sterile an' you got to treat it just so. You touch it wrong an' you blow the whole thing an' back it all got to go. But if an' you touch it right you don't contam'nate nothin'. I ain't got that part 'xackly straight yet.

Then come the part I don't like. It call scrubbbin', an' the doctor an' me we got separate ideas like on what clean is. To me like clean is when you wash you hands 'fore you goin' to eat you dinner. To *that* man, clean is when you just 'bout ready to bleed from you hands an' arms from that little hard scrub brush. Oh, man, but did he make me scrub an' scrub. An' after I wash for a few minutes he say, "Let me see your hands, Mr. Peoples." I show him an' he say that no good, plenty a dirt still under the fingernails. I 'bout ready to tell him so what did he 'spect with the kinda job I got when he say, "It takes at least fifteen minutes of hard scrubbing before you begin to approach a sterile condition." Fine, I say, an' like when I finish my fifteen minutes I 'bout ready to be bandaged. An' I thinkin' this doctorin' business it ain't for me. But then, you know, all of a sudden like, my hands they start to feelin' good, like they ain't never felt before. It like they all sudden real senst'tive, you know, an' they ready to do the job.

Then come the best part a the whole thing. That when you put on the mask an' the gown an' the gloves. I already had my hat on, so that no problem, an' the mask it lyin' cool 'round my neck. So up that go over my head an' gets tied, an' then we open up the pack an' out come them long green gowns. The doctor he hold mine for me an' I slips into it, an' he tie it up tight in the back like, an' then, all a sudden, you know, I begins to feel important. I feel like I could do anythin', you know, an' I'm not uptight no more, heart it beatin' slow like, an' I know I'm ready. Then I reach for the gloves an' then the doctor he stop me an' show me how to put the powder on my hands so them gloves they slide on real easy like. Then that it, man, I'm set.

Now all the time Twenny-nine he down on the table, you know, all shaved nice like, all tied down, and he breathin' on the machine. The doctor he get on one side of the table an' I'm on the other. Then he open the pack up some more an' takes out the small square green towels. He lay the first one 'cross Twenny-nine's belly flip like, an' then he take what he call the clip, that the little thing what look like manicure scissors, an' he clip the towel right to Twenny-nine's skin. Then he show me how to turn the towel so that the clip it under the towel an' the field, that what he call it, is clear. Then he take three more towels an' he makes hisself a nice little square out a the skin, the towels lappin' over each other. An' you know what happen all a sudden? Right there quick like it don't look to me like it Twenny-nine's belly we gettin' set to cut. It don't look like nothin' live there, only like it was some kind a 'speriment. That 'cause the dog he all covered up an' he don't look like no dog no more.

Then the doctor he take one a them clips an' he hand it to me. "You try this one, now," he say, an' he show me how to handle the clip first, you know, by takin' the thumb an' the ring finger an' stickin' them in the handle a the clip. Course, I tried it first time an' I did it all wrong. I tried to use my goosin' finger but the doctor he stop me quick. An' you know the way he told me it feel funny at first, but then like I say I got the hands for it an' after a couple a seconds it feel natural to me. Course, when I clips the skin I do a bad job of it. 'Stead a takin' just a bit a it, y'understand, I grabs a whole mess a it with the prongs an' the doctor he say, "Mr. Peoples, you're not going to hang the dog up by that thing." An' I say I be gettin' on to it after a bit. He laugh an' he say he do the same thing first he operate, only he say that was on a human bein'.

Then after he feel 'round for a bit he say, "We'll cut under this nipple," an' he give it a little tweak like. Then the cat reach for the knife an' he say, "Get ready with the clamps and sponges." I just look at him thinkin' what he talkin' 'bout. He stop an' he show me the clamps an' the sponges an' he say, "Now when you hand them to me be fast." Then all a sudden he just stop an' step back an' look at me. Then he say, "Mr. Peoples, I've got to apologize to you. I keep thinking you should know all of this terminology. And you don't." That the truth I tell him. So he pick up one a them clamps, an' he tell me it a he-mo-stat an' it used for clampin' off the little blood veins he cut through. An' the sponge it really ain't no sponge at all. Sponge, it just a little piece a gauze like. So he say that what I need to know for the beginnin', an' he picks up the knife an' *zoom* he cut quick like. Straight, deep an' solid, an' the blood from Twenny-nine it spurt up out the incision.

Now that doctor he keep cuttin' an' clampin' an' tyin' an' 'fore you know it he right down through them muscles to what he call the per-it-o-ne-um, which he say we all got, an' it a big sack that dog keepin' all his insides in. Doctor he cut through that an' then he reach into the pack an' take out what look to me like two little silver rakes. He put both pullin' ends into the dog an' then he give me the handles. "Here," he say to me, "pull back on these. Gently." An' I starts to pull back an' he say, "Just right," an' I holdin' them good. Then all of a sudden he say, "Okay, where are you, you bastard?" an' I think he talkin' to me but really he speakin' directly to the spleen. Then he slip his hand into the gut an' he begin to feel 'bout for the spleen. He push the intestines here an' he push them there, an' then he put the other hand in an' lift up slow like. Out pop the spleen. It look all shiny like an' even me could tell it full a blood. Then the doctor turn it over an' I sees the big blood veins runnin' in an' out, an' I knows them's the ones to cut. I give him the thread when he ask an' he starts to tie the big blood veins. That way nobody get sprayed in the face. Then, when he all done with the tyin' an' he ready to cut he pick up them scissors an' he hand them to me. "Time to get your feet wet," he say, an' I just stand there lookin' at him like he crazy. "Come on," he say, "you snip this thing out yourself." 'Fore I know it my hand it movin' up to take them scissors, an' he show me where to cut. I only takes a little bit the first time, but then he tell me, "Go ahead, cut the bastard right off." An' I feel my stomach goin' up an' down like I ridin' an el'vator. But you know cuttin' through that it nothin'. It just ain't nothin'. It so easy, man, any cat could do it.

An' I cut all the way through an' the doctor he tell me nice job, but that don't finish it for me, see. I reach for the big pan all cool like an' I picks up that dead spleen an' drops it right in there.

After the doctor he free up the clamp come the sewin'. That mostly a drag, y'understand. I mean once you done a layer or two a the muscle an' the ad-i-pose tissue like, all the rest it the same. He do somethin' like cross-stitchin' an' some fast tyin' but didn't take me no time 'tall to get them knots down, an' 'fore you know it we got that dog all freed up like an' we untie his paws an' take him off the breathin' machine. 'Cept he don't start to breathe right 'way on his own. The doctor he see this an' he start to swear like some mama who check don't come from the welfare. He somethin' else when he swear, man. So what he do is give Twenny-nine collie dog there a punch in the chest, but that don't do no good. Then he give him 'nother an' fin'ly he end up slammin' both hands down on that dog's chest an' all the time he sayin', "Come on, you bastard, *breathe*." An' after a time, shore 'nough Twenny-nine there he begin to twitch an' throw his head 'bout on the table, an' then his big old chest it start up an' down slow but sure. Then I picks him off the table an' brings him back here with you cats an' he sleepin' good now.

So there, that's it, all right. Doctor Peoples he done his first splenectomy an' the patient done live. That all right, I thinkin', that all right.

FRIDAY

'Fore I do anythin' today, I got to tell you 'bout the readin' lady at the school. She just full a what I got to thinkin' last night in bed is just a whole lot a nice warm curves an' lumps. Now I tell you, if I had my pick a chicks I'd take her an' treat her to the right kind a jazzin'. Her skin it so nice, you know, like a chocolate bar, an' I bet it taste just as good. What happen was that I was late last night an' when I tell her I didn't mean no harm an' I stick out the blue card the guard gave me she read it an' say, "Are you always going to sleep through reading class?"

"No, ma'am," I say, an' I look her up an' down good an' gives her a nice smile like.

"Sit over there," she tell me, an' I look 'round an' I see an empty seat next to George. He all tied up inside from laughin' at me an' when I sit next to him he give me the palm, an' everythin' then it cool.

I watch her turn 'round an' begin to write somethin' on the board an' over in one corner of the board I see where she done write her name, "Miss Beverley," an' next to it is her office number an' when she be there. On the board she writin', "Exercise Number Two," an' when she done she turn back to the class an' she say, "Exercise Number Two is for everyone except Mr. Peoples," an' George he turn to me an' he say, "Yeah, man, you can't do number two till you done number one. What you got in your head, anyway?" I look over at George's paper an' I see that out a the ten questions in number one he got but one right, an' I say to him, "You be doin' the gov'ment a big-size favor if you go home now."

"I s'pose you goin' to do better," George say.

"You only got to watch," I say, an' I reach over to the middle of the table an' gets myself one a them booklets what called, "Beginning Reading," an' gets goin'.

Man, like there's a whole lotta things wrong with exercise number one. First thing is the words they usin'. Mostly white people's words, but they got pictures a colored cats all over to make you think that the way we s'posed to talk. Well, exercise number one it a story 'bout this cat called Chuck Brown who is just gettin' hisself out a high school an' is readyin' hisself to go to his college. But what this cat do, it all wrong. See, he live in a nice white house with trees all 'round an' he got hisself one a them sweaters with the big letter on the front, an' course he got hisself a real nice chick who always cheerin' him on when he *com*-pete in the athletics an' such. So I readin' on an' I 'bout ready to bust up like 'cause I never seen no cat like this before. Oh, he somethin' else, man. Whatever he do he smilin'. He run for a touchdown he smilin' like crazy. He take his girl home an' he still smilin'. Course he don't smoke no stuff an' he only drink root beer an' you know he never jazz no chick in his life. He too busy runnin' for touchdowns. But that all right, I s'pose. I mean they got to put somethin' into the books. If an' they put in how it really is they have theyselves some trouble. But one thing it kill me right there. There this one little drawin' a Chuck Brown an' he s'posed to be high jumpin'. Course he smilin' like all the time when he goin' over the bar an' he make the height by 'bout two feet. But the cat who drew the picture he don't know nothin' 'bout high jumpin'. He got the bar on the wrong side a the standards what hold it up.

When I get done with the questions at the end I give them to Miss Beverley. "Mr. Peoples," she say nice like, "did you understand the story?"

"Yes, ma'am," I say.

"And what do you think of Chuck Brown?" she ask.

"He just 'nother jive cat like all the rest," I say. "Nobody ever do the kinda things he do."

"The purpose of these stories is to show the ghetto child how other people live and to try to prepare him for when he is ready to leave." Dig that, dogs, she call me ghetto child when I be nineteen years old an' been jazzin' for like seven, eight years. An' you know what I think? I thinkin' she never been jazzed, that the whole problem right there. She never bothered to try her some good wood. It a shame, you know, but I 'spect it true.

So I says to her, "Chuck Brown he don't live on my block, y'understand?"

"Mr. Peoples," she say, "you've got to learn vocabulary." I pick up the book an' I show her the trouble with the high-jumpin' standards an' how the cat drew the bar on the wrong side. "This doesn't make any difference," she say. "It's only representational." Oh, my, I thinkin' here come the message. She goin' to start soundin' like the white priest an' shoot her mouth off 'bout overcomin' everythin' an' the like. So I just takes the book back to my seat an' sits there an' looks up the right answers an' tries to mem'rize what they should be.

You know, you lookin' good now, Twenny-nine collie dog. Not like Twenny-six there 'cause you ain't near as strong as a boxer dog. Can you stand up in that cage for you surgeon—Doctor Peoples? Ain't movin' for no one, huh? Can't say's I blame you. Man, but didn't we move you insides 'round. Leastways with you bein' operated on I don't got to clean you cage. But with the rest a you cats it still somethin' else. Sometimes I thinkin' you ain't dogs *a*-tall, you just crappin' machines.

So lemme get to you dishes an' these cages like an' then I be tellin' you 'bout the math'matics class.

I got to get used to the 'monia smell. It ter'ble. So what happened was that George an' me we move out a the readin' class an' goes to the toilet for a smoke. Well, some a them other cats they in there an' some them I knows from the neighb'hood an' some them I never seen 'fore. An' the toilet it in bad shape, man. School ain't been open but two days now an' already the mirror it busted, two doors they off the stalls, an' one toilet it don't work at all. The urinals they workin' okay, but you can tell they 'bout set to back up from the butts. An' the writin' it beginnin' to 'pear on the walls. Oh, man, there all kinds a stuff writ on the walls. First thing course is the number a the man to see for some stuff. How his number always get on the toilet wall first I don't know, but there it is. An' there a number an 'dress where you can jazz for like two dollars. An' course some cat make his fist sign, an' he write next to it 'bout the black power business, an' Elija he get hisself some space too.

Well, George he relieve hisself an' then he take out some grass an' he makes hisself a joint an' lights up. "Man, you can't go to the math'matics high," I tell him.

"No?" he say an' he look cool at me.

"They find you high they goin' to throw you out," I say.

"Man, they don't throw no cats outa this here program," he say. "The big men who runnin' this place they gettin' paid by the number of us trainees they got on the rolls. The program it get so much from the state for each cat an' for each hour the cat spend here. Come on, man, they throw a cat out, they throwin' they own money with him." He hand me the smoke an' I takes me a long drag an' right 'way things begin to look fine to me. But I only gets the one drag 'cause George he take it back right 'way. Then the bell go off, an' George he curse an' flick the head a the roach into the urinal an' the rest a it go in his pocket.

"What room we in?" I say.

"Same one for the math'matics as for the readin'," he say. "An' goin' to be the same one for the Self-Wareness boo." Then George say slow like, "Man, let's you an' me split from this jazz. This business it ain't for me. Let's us go downtown like an' see us a couple a chicks. I know one who go big for you." I 'bout ready to split with George when into the toilet come one a them teachers. He a big strong cat sportin' hisself one a them big Afro jobs an' he move to the urinal without speakin'. Then while he relievin' hisself he say to the wall like, "Anybody need himself a boost?" I looks to George an' he back to me an' I know then it the teacher who writ the number a the junkman on the wall. He may be hisself a teacher, dogs, an' 'pear very proper like, but he a pusher all the same.

Then I gets the cold palms an' my heart it start racin' like crazy an' my breathin' start up fast like, an' I knows I gots to get outa there or just like that I be back on the stuff. George look at me an' he see me gettin' uptight, an' he say, "Come on, man, we late for the math'matics," an' he sorta take my arm an' lead me outa there. He know 'bout me an' the junk an' he do a good thing to take me out. If an' I was there 'lone I be flyin' right now, dogs, an' I never be comin' back here.

But I make it fine to the room an' we sittin' there an' they ain't no teacher. Then me an' George we start playin' 'round on the table arm wrestlin' an' the like until suddenly the whole room it get quiet like a funeral. That when I looks 'round an' sees the math'matics man. He white, an' right there I thinks the man in trouble. He just standin' there lookin' over the room an' you could see he wonderin' what *he* doin' there. Sidney who sittin' 'cross the table from me an' George he study the math'matics man an' then he look 'way from the cat an' he say, "Oh, no, man, not a white cat for the math." Then he look to George an' he say, "How do a white cat get into a place like this? Everywhere I go there a white cat messin' me up." The math'matics man he drop his books hard on the end of the table an' he look down to Sidney. "I'm not going to give you a lot of crap that says I'm here to help you," he say. "I'm teaching here because the money's a hell of a lot better than the public schools." Sidney look down to the table an' he don't say nothin'. The white cat he seem straight to me an' he look cool as he move his eyes 'bout the room. "Let's get one thing straight right away," he say. "If you want to learn math I'm the guy who can teach it to you." He stop an' he look at each one a us an' you can tell he winnin', man. "There isn't black math or white math, there's only math. You've got a lot of it to learn and let's get going." With that he whip 'round to the board an' he shove up a string a numbers like a mile long. "You," he say, an' he point to George, "let's count these numbers off. What is the first number to the left of the decimal point called?"

"Units," George say, an' he say it like he mean it.

"And the next one," he say, pointin' to me.

"Tens," I tell him. An' he move 'round the table quick like till he get to Sidney an' he ask him what the sixth number out it called. Sidney don't answer an' he don't even look up. "Do you know?" the math'matics man say. Sidney shake his head slow. "Did you ever know?" Sidney still shake his head.

"That's not your fault," the white cat say. "Okay, it's called hundreds of thousands. Write it down. Remember it, you'll need it." An' you know what, dogs, Sidney open up his book an' he begin to write it all down like the man say.

So the man he take us up to trillions like an' then he do it again quick, an' 'fore you know it we all chantin' long with him an' we begins to know 'bout what the numbers is called. That take but a few minutes, you know, an' then he put up a addition problem. It just two numbers, seven an' nine, an' he say, "Who knows the answer?" Six of the cats they put up they hands, but the white cat he don't go for one a us. He go for the cat who don't have his hand up, an' he work on him till he get it down. Then he say, "Addition's no big problem for you, is it?" an' he throw up a bunch a numbers an' we s'posed to add them up. An' we do it fine, you know, an' the white cat say, "But how about subtracting them?" an' he smile like he know that the beginnin' a the problem right there. Ain't one cat in that room ever learn how to do the subtractin' problems. He turn 'round an' he write 100 on the board an' 'neath it he put 69. "Subtract that," he say, an' we all start lookin' one to the other. "Can't do it, right?" he say.

"That the picture," George tell him.

"Never done it?" the man say.

"Never done it right," George say.

"Want to bet you can do it?" the man say directly to George, "and do it without pencil and paper?"

"In my *head?*" George say. "Yeah, I wanna bet on that. It a sure thing." The man reach in his pocket quick like an' he throw a dollar bill on the table.

"Say you're running a newsstand," he say to George, "and I just bought a newspaper and two magazines from you. With tax it comes to 69 cents. Make change." George reach in his pocket an' quick like he count out the bread for the man.

"There," George say, "thirty-one cents back."

"That's subtracting," the man say.

An' you know, dogs, all of a sudden like the cats begin to see that they been subtractin' all 'long an' doin' it right an' they just never knowed it was subtractin'. Then the white cat say, "You guys been in the street for a long time, right?" an' the cats nod to each other. "And in the street you're always beating some guy for this or that, right?" an' he smile like he know what he talkin' 'bout. "And I'll make another bet that the number of times somebody has cheated you is damn few."

"Dig it," Sidney say.

"Well," he say, "that's what mathematics is all about."

White cat he all right.

I don't s'pose you 'ware a this, dogs, but this whole buildin' here it air condition. All but this room, that is, an' everybody he uptight an' runnin' 'round complainin' 'cause it broke down while I havin' my dinner. There's them technicians upstairs an' they sayin' they can't poss'bly do no work when the air conditionin' it busted. An' the doctors sayin' they ain't goin' to be no operations s'afternoon 'cause it so hot. Man, what these cats know 'bout heat, anyway? This here it August an' the place it New York City. That say to me that it so hot the tar on the roofs it move under you feet. But the heat it don't bother us, now does it, dogs? Not a bit, man, 'cause we used to it all the way. Sometimes it get to me at night when I can't sleep, an' me an' my ma we got to go to the fire 'scape.

Man, I goin' to get me a soda.

My, but it truly hot out there in the buildin'. An' most a the technicians they gone home for the day. I don't know why, but it seem to me that the air conditionin' it always bust itself on the day that the hottest. This here a grape soda an' I got it from the machine upstairs. This the last soda in the machine; all the others they been drunk up by the technicians. Man, but it hot an' steamy upstairs. I mean, like you can see the heat just hangin' in them empty hallways. It look to me like it goin' to be a bad night at home. It a good thing it Friday night. A workin' cat he don't have to get hisself to bed on Friday night.

An' the school, man, it goin' to be somethin' else in the heat tonight. That buildin' it old an' them walls they so thick that it take a few days for the heat to build itself up in there. Well, it had its few days now, an' it built up, all right. In a buildin' like that once the heat built up it stay. An' you know what, dogs? They got themselves air conditioners in all them rooms they usin' for teachin' but none a them work. An' you know why they don't work? 'Cause the knobs for turnin' them on they just never come from the place they s'posed to. Them big old air conditioners they just sittin' there in them windows an' they ain't no way to turn them on. That make you hotter, you know.

You know, I 'most forgot the last part of the school last night. I s'pose that 'cause I don't want to 'member it. It the part called Self-Wareness, an' the man who teach that, he the biggest jive cat of all. He like to think he in the army or somethin' an' we the troops an' he some kinda gen'ral. An' talk, my, he never shut his fat mouth from the time he walk in till that bell ring. He walk in the class an' right way he talkin'. "All right, now, be with it," he say, "everybody be with it." I looks to George an' he to me an' we can't make the cat nohow. "Be with it," he sayin' as he makin' it to the table, an' under his arm he got like fifteen copies of *The New York Times*. "Be with it," he say an' he start to pass them 'round. "Yeah," George say to me, "be with it, man. That's you whole trouble, you know, you got to be with it." I give him a punch on the arm, an' then George he pick up his newspaper an' he turn it upside down an' he start to make like he readin'. He rub his chin like he concentratin' hard an' all the time he sayin', "Hmmm, hmmm, yeah, man, dig. Course, the world sit-*she*-ation it bad. Any cat know that." An' George he glance up at the man a few times an' fin'ly the cat buy it. "The paper's upside down there, fella," the Self-Wareness cat say.

"Don't make no difference to me," George say, an' the cat right way start to get uptight. His big old eyes they begin to look like they 'bout set to pop outa his head, an' the sweat it start to pop out on his forehead.

"Be with it," he say to George.

"All the way, man," George say.

"All right, men," the Self-Wareness cat say to us, an' he

don't pay no 'tention to George. "Self-awareness means exactly that. We're going to be discussing the important issues of the day so that you might have a better picture of the world and your place in it."

"Oh, my," George say to me quiet like, "do you smell somethin' very bad?"

"I shore do," I tell him.

"An' it a familiar smell, huh?" he go on.

"Most certainly," I say.

"What you think it is?" he ask.

"I think it this here jive cat," I say, "an' I think if an' he keep this mess up they goin' t'have to fumigate the room."

"Keep quiet there," the Self-Wareness cat say to us. Then he turn back to the class an' he say, "All right, men, we're all black here, and it's certainly the time in America's history to discuss the black man's identity." He slow up his speech an' he look 'round the room to pick a cat for a question. He pick the wrong cat. He say to Leonard, "What do you think it means to be black in our American society?"

"Dun't know mawn," Leonard say, "not U.S.A., Trinidad." An' he give the Self-Wareness cat a big old smile, an' he look 'round the room like he want all of us on his side. But he from Trinidad, an' the rest a us cats we don't dig no island boo. So Leonard he all 'lone an' the Self-Wareness cat he start in on him. "What is the proportion of black to white in Trinidad?"

"Dum small, mawn," Leonard say quick like, an' his voice it sound so funny all the cats they start laughin'.

"Tell the other trainees what your life has been like in Trinidad," the cat say. The hole he standin' in it gettin' deeper an' deeper.

"Dum good life, mawn," Leonard say, "U.S.A. no good place for me, mawn. That sure."

"And what may I ask is wrong with this country?" the cat ask.

"Whole dum country stink," Leonard say. "No nigger in 'Dad, just only folk. White people nice, black nice too."

"Why then did you come to this country?" the Self-Wareness cat ask.

"Dum me if I know, mawn," Leonard say. He give his shoulders a little shrug, you know, like he don't care, an' he say, "My mum she hire out to rich famly an' I come 'long. That all."

"Why did you join NEW?" the cat ask.

"My school 'ploma it no good in States, you know. So I come to practice m' sums, that all, mawn."

"All right," the teacher say to us, "here's a good example of a place where prejudice is at a minimum. How can we effect these changes in our society today?" Like clockwork, from the back a the room come, "Kill whitey." That Millard talkin' an' you just knowed that was comin'. Millard been sittin' 'way from the table in all the classes, an' he quiet in the back just readin' like, an' he been waitin' his turn. But the teacher he got hold a the class pretty tight, or so he think. "And what do you think an all-out war with the white man is going to accomplish?" he ask Millard.

Millard he twirl his beret cool like on his finger. "I killed me 'bout thirty, thirty-five V.C., that on a sure count, man, an' I got whitey all figured out. If every black brother he kill hisself just ten white folk, then they all be gone. An' you don't have to do it in the open like. It come quiet at night, see. You get youself one, two of them in the night, an' then you lay quiet for a while an' then you gets youself a few more. An' if we be operatin' like that, inside a month the white folk be all dead, y'understand."

"That's crazy talk," the Self-Wareness cat say, an' I watch him close as he look 'round to each a us to see how we takin' it. An' a lot a the cats they turned an' lookin' at Millard now 'stead a the teacher. They waitin' for Millard to go on.

"I goin' to the toilet," Millard say, an' he walk to the door.

"It's polite if you *ask* a teacher if you may be excused from the room," he say to Millard.

"Come on, man," Millard say to him, an' he cock his head a bit to the side cool like, "when you goin' to stop actin' like a lootenant?"

So that my first day a learnin', dogs, an' you know it not so bad as I figured. An' tonight, man, after the school it close, me an' George an' some a the cats we goin' downtown t'have us some a the relaxation. George say he know a couple a chicks who do it an' do it, an' they don't care *who* on the other end a the jazzin'. That my kinda chick, man, 'specially after one whole long week a workin'. This truly a drag, you know, sittin' in here most a the time on this stool with nothin' to do 'cept cut you up an' then take care a you. But if an' there wasn't some cat like me, you know, a cat who care 'bout you, where you be anyway?

Les see now, it near to goin' home an' I s'posed to give you all extra chow tonight 'cause you ain't goin' to have no one in here for the whole weekend. So what I gives you, you eats slow, y'understand?—leavin' some for Sat'day night an' Sunday night too. An' don't go lappin' up all you water right quick after I leaves. You do that an' you goin' to be very thirsty dogs come Monday mornin'. An' I 'spect this place goin' to be the end a the world come Monday what with no one cleanin' up in here for like two days. But it for shore I ain't comin' in here on no weekend just to tend to some dogs' mess. Weekend it ain't for that. Weekend it for forgettin' who you is an' what you been doin' for the week. It for jazzin' an' spendin' some time high on one thing or 'nother, but mainly it just for makin' sure you cool.

I gots just 'nough time to finish you up here an' get on up to the payroll office where the cat hand out the digits. Then I gets it cashed an' I gots just 'nough time to get to the cleaners 'fore it close. I s'pose I goin' to have to part with twenny, thirty dollars at the cleaners. Cleanin' suede an' the like it very 'spensive.

MONDAY

Now I hopes you don't take no 'fense, dogs, but it necessary for me to be wearin' this here nose clip 'cause this room it smell worse than like a hundred sewers all backed up. I s'pose it smell so bad 'cause they ain't no way for the air to get itself outa here. No fan, no vents, no nothin', just old stale air what thick with the bad smell. There also 'nother reason I wearin' this: Deeborah she give it to me like it some kinda joke, you know, an' I goin' to wear it every Monday when the smell it ter'ble in here. An' I do believe that you Spec'men Supervisor-to-be he went an' got hisself messed up over a chick. Oh, man, all last night I lyin' in the bed thinkin' an' I gets me such an ache for her it hurt all way from my belly to my knees, it seem. Deeborah so fine, man, just so fine, not like mosta the other chicks who jazz you for a joint or two or who do it 'cause they need the bread for some junk. Not Deeborah, 'cause she class, man, all the way class.

But I gettin' way 'head a myself, you know. First thing I gots to do here is get the 'monia open an' start the pourin'. The smell it don't bother my nose none, see, but this breathin' through my mouth business it startin' to turn my belly.

Well, dogs, you be gettin' youself some company s'afternoon 'cause the big white doctor he told me just now that a whole new batch a dogs be comin' in from the pound. I got to get the tape out now an' put the numbers on the cages. Place it goin' to be jumpin' s'afternoon. An' the doctor he told me that he an' me we goin' to be doin' *two* splenectomies today. Oh, man, my leg an' foot goin' to be hurtin' tonight. But the man say that once we gets it down right we be doin' splenectomies like mass production. He say when you knows how, it don't take but forty-fi' minutes to take out a spleen. That I got to see, man.

There now, you cages they fin'ly all clean for you, an' you dishes they full an' I 'bout set to go for my dinner. But 'fore I does that I got to tell you 'bout Deeborah.

When me an' George an' Sidney we split from the school Friday night we heads downtown to like Hundred Twenny-fifth Street an' we starts cruisin'. We ain't out to start no real action, y'understand, but we ready to take what come our way. After a time Sidney meet one a his friends an' he say he know where there a party, an' right quick like we takes off for it. Sidney say it got to be a good party 'cause everybody he be high on somethin' if an' he know his friend. But the party it way up on Hundred Thirty-eighth Street, an' it seem to take us forever to get up there an' find the place.

But we do an' it seem like a all-right place. Cat who we goin' to see he live in one a them new developments like, where they used to be the ten'ments an' such. Them old ten'-ments they mostly made outa wood, you know, but where this cat live it a beautiful new buildin' what go up thirty, forty floors. That ain't no cold-water walkup, man. It got cool, fast el'vators an' mostly good lightin' all 'bout, an' Sidney he tell us on the way that they even got machines in the basement for the peoples to do they laundry. But you know, dogs, that place still takin' a fair beatin' 'spite of everythin'. Most a the back a the el'vator it been kicked out, an' they's the busted light bulbs sittin' inside them wire cages they put 'round them so's nobody can bust them. An' the mirrors they got 'round the place so's people they can see 'round the corners, they all busted too. An' when we gets outa the el'vator, Sidney, who been there 'fore, show us the incinerator. He say all you garbage it go right down that chute like, an' that's all you do with it. 'Cept he say it busted now an' he right, you know, 'cause them hallways they stacked halfway to the ceilin' with the people's garbage.

So we turn a few corners an' right way I knows we close to gettin' there 'cause I can smell the stuff blowin' in the hallway. An' we get down to the door an' it standin' half open. Inside I see it mostly dark 'cept for a couple a blue lights comin' soft outa the corners. "This the place, man," Sidney say, an' he say he goin' in to see the man an' he say for us to wait where we is. When he come back he say, "The man say it two dollars each for everythin' you want."

"You think it be worth it?" George ask.

"All the way," Sidney tell him.

"I don't know," George say, an' he look to me. "What you think, man?" he say.

"It gettin' late," I tell him, an' it 'pear to me it goin' to be the only action all night.

"Can I hold two dollars?" George ask meek like, an' I

knowed right way George he don't want to go in 'cause he ain't got the price. I peel off two for him, an' Sidney say he need seventy-fi' cents an' I gives him that 'long with my two dollars an' we go on in.

Well, there 'bout twenny cats in the big room, a few more sittin' on the floor in the small kitchen there, an' I don't know how many in the bedroom an' the toilet. Then this short little cat wearin' a Malcolm goatee an' shades come up an' say somethin' to Sidney in what Sidney tell me later it that Swahili boo, an' Sidney answer him an' give him the bread an' then the little cat he break out some joints an' we gets started. But the stuff it not very good, you know, an' the high it take a long time comin'. I think the cat he musta cut it up with sawdust, it so bad. But after a time I don't care.

So when my eyes they get used to the dark an' my mind it ease up a bit, I looks 'bout the room an' it seem to me they all kinds a cats there. Chinks an' P.R.'s an' the Afro cats, an' there even a few white cats here an' there. An' I see right 'way that the white chicks they with a couple a colored cats, an' one a the white guys he gettin' stoned bad, man. He sittin' with 'nother white guy in the corner an' the one who stoned he got his mouth open an' he tryin' to speak, but they ain't no words comin' outa his mouth. Other white cat he sittin' for the tripper, who 'pear to me to be all strung out on acid. Very few a us colored cats fly on acid, you know. That mainly the white cats' stuff. The white chicks they ain't on no acid, though. They just blowin' theyselves some grass so's they can get warm, I s'pose.

After a time the high it start to fade, an' I lookin' 'round for some better stuff to get me goin' 'gain, an' that when I first see Deeborah. She sittin' in a big chair in the darkest corner a the place in this beautiful white dress. An' man, she don't 'pear to me like she belong there. She sittin' so proper like, you know, with her legs crossed at the ankles an' her hands they folded in her lap like she in church or somethin'. So very easy like I begins to make my way over to her, you know, cool like, lookin' in cigarette boxes an' glancin' 'round the place. An' fin'ly I gets me a joint an' sits down on the floor next to her. I light up cool, see, an' then I hands the joint up to her without lookin' at her. She take it from me an' then I looks up to watch her drag. Only she don't take no real drag. Only a little puff, you know, an' then she blow it outa her mouth without inhalin'. So I says to her, "If an' you don't want the smoke, say so, but man, don't go wastin' it."

"It makes me cough," she say, an' she hand it back to me. She watch while I takes me a long drag an' pulls it in an' holds it. After 'bout twenny seconds I blow it out an' looks to her. "So what you get high on?" I asks.

"Glue," she say, an' I break up right there front a her, an' I start to laugh an' cough all at the same time.

"What kinda glue you partial to?" I asks, an' she know I puttin' her on but she go 'long with it.

"Don't make no difference," she say, an' she look 'way with her head in the air.

"You live here?" I asks, an' I change the sound a my voice so's she know I mean what I sayin'.

"No," she say, "Newark."

"So how you get here?" I asks.

"With him," she say, an' she point to this jive cat lyin' half under a chair 'bout fi' feet 'way an' he stoned out *com*-pletely. I could see that the cat had hisself the good bread though, 'cause he wearin' very 'spensive threads. Next to his hand is a bottle a all diff'rent-colored pills, an' I asks her what they is. "Everythin'," she say, "he take anythin' he can swallow."

"How long he been out?" I asks.

"Couple of hours now," she say. "Most of the time, you know, he a very nice man, but when he come to town he always come here an' mess hisself up."

"You go with him?" I asks.

"When he don't have his head on the wrong way," she say.

"He good to you?" I ask her.

"He drive a convertible," she tell me. "You do that?"

"I can't even get me no license," I tell her.

"You been in jail?" she ask quick like.

"No, man, I ain't been in no jail," I say back to her, an' that a big lie, you know, dogs, but a little lie to a chick ain't no harm. An' sometimes they pay off, you know. "It 'cause of my leg here," I tell her. "Can't drive with no leg like this, you know."

"I don't s'pose you been in the army," she say, an' look 'way from me. "I like men who been in the army. They older."

"Closest I ever got to the army was when they wrote me an' told me come down so's they 'xamine my leg."

"You work?" she say, an' she look close at me like she truly want to know the answer. An' I kinda been waitin' for her t'ask me, you know, 'cause not many a the cats they got steady work.

"Course I got a job," I say cool, like I always had me one, you know.

"What you do?" she ask, an' she ask it like she still don't believe I workin'.

"I have me a very good situation," I tell her. "An' like in a month or two I be gettin' me a fine raise."

"What you do?" she ask again. "It reliable work?"

"Nine to five," I says.

"Where?" she say, an' she beginnin' to sound like the fuzz with her questions. So I tells her 'bout the Research Center here right 'tween the hospital an' the medical school. An' then I lays 'nother little lie on her. I tells her I Spec'men Supervisor already, an' you know, dogs, she like that fine. She say it sound to her like I got a fine job.

"I do," I tells her, an' then I goes on a bit 'bout what me an' the doctors doin' here an' I tells her at some length 'bout the operations an' the like. Course I don't tell her I got to clean the animal room an' you cages. I tell her only that I got to come in here now an' 'gain, an' 'bout the smell, an' she laugh good at that. An' that when she reach into this big straw basket she got, an' she fish 'round for somethin'. "Herbert an' me we been swimmin' out in Rockaway today, an' I got just the thing for you." That when she pull out this here nose clip. "You wear it every time you got to be in there," she say.

Then she ask me for the time an' I tell her it near one

o'clock, an' she start to get all uptight lookin' at Herbert. "I got to be at my job in the mornin'," she say.

"What you do you got to be workin' on a Sat'day?" I asks.

"I'm in trainin' for the phone people," she say, "an' we all got to come in two times on the weekend durin' the trainin' time."

"What you goin' to do for them?" I asks.

"Don't know," she say, an' she shrug her shoulders like it don't make no diff'rence to her.

"Op'rator?" I asks.

"First I be a recessionist some place," she say, "an' then they say I can move me on up to bein' a op'rator."

"It good to work for the phone people," I tell her.

"It all right," she say.

"You got all the ben'fits," I tells her.

"Yeah," she say, "but Herbert tell me I wastin' my time. He say I should be waitressin' some place where they pay good. He say you can't eat none of them ben'fits." I tell her that true, but you has the ben'fits for you people, not youself. She say I'm right, protectin' you own the way to do it today.

Right then some cat put on some crazy Indian music or somethin' that don't make no sense, an' I say to Deeborah, "Come on, s'pose you an' me we cut."

"I can't just leave Herbert," she say.

"What *he* goin' to know 'bout it?" I say, an' I takes her hand an' she stand up. That when I see her body it so fine, man. She shaped on the order a Miss Beverley, an' only diff'rence is Miss Beverley she got Deeborah beat in the chest all the way. But that all right, I go for the chicks who shape up on the thin side. So she standin' there an' she holdin' my hand tight an' lookin' down at Herbert. Then all a sudden, you know, she let go my hand an' she bend down an' try to wake the cat up. Well, Herbert he stoned out so bad he look half-dead anyway. She see this an' she turn to me an' she say, "I'll write a note for him." I 'bout ready then to tell her cut the jivin' over this cat an' lets us get goin', when I see in her face that she truly concern 'bout him. An' I think to myself that it be nice she get that way for me, you know. So she write the note an' she tell Herbert that she all right, that she got home fine. Then she finish the note with, "And you forget tomorrow night!!" An' right then I feels I got it made with her. I figure she write that there 'cause she want to open the door for me. She take the note an' she pin it to Herbert's coat an' then she look to me an' she say, "I'm ready now. Let's go," an' she take my hand 'gain. At the door I see Sidney sittin' on the floor an' he in very bad shape. His eyes they rollin' 'round in his head an' he talkin' to hisself 'bout how bad things they been for him in the world. "Sidney," I say, "you flyin' very high, you know."

"Ohhh, man," he say, an' he raise his hands up an' he flap them slow like front a his face an' he try to smile, but his face it only get screwed up like. "He your friend?" Deeborah say.

"Yeah," I tell her.

"He got no self-respect," she say an' she turn an' start out the door like Sidney insult her or somethin'.

"Be cool," I say to Sidney. He look up at me with what seem like only one eye an' he lift his hand. "Ohhh, man," he say an' he slump over 'gainst the door.

In the hallway I asks her what she mean Sidney got no self-respect, an' she say that any man who go 'round takin' stuff like that he don't have nothin' to look to in his life.

"Sidney he all right," I tell her.

"Don't know what a man like you be doin' with his kind," she say. "It look to me like you doin' somethin' with youself, but that Sidney he goin' to 'mount to nothin'."

"A man got to fly for hisself sometimes," I say, an' she don't say nothin' till we gets down in the el'vator an' starts for the door. "You take me down to the tubes?" she ask.

"I do that," I tell her, an' we go out the door an' into the street. Man, it hot, but Deeborah she don't take no notice of the heat. Right 'way she take herself a couple quick steps an' she go into the street an' stops herself a taxi. Dig it, dogs, a *taxi.* That class all the way, but it easy to be class on some other cat's bread. A taxicab all the way from Hundred Thirty-eighth Street to them Hudson River tubes. I 'bout ready to bust her one when we gets into the cab, but she all a sudden like starts to lean over on me, an' that cab ride it somethin' else, man. It worth every penny a the six dollars. Right outa nowhere, man, Deeborah's body it seem to come 'live, you know, an' she start movin' 'gainst me an' sighin' so pretty like. An' she kiss me all over my face an' on the mouth so's you wouldn't believe it. She got herself a firm wiry body, you know, an' just when I 'bout set to let my hands loose on they own, we gets to the tubes.

Inside the buildin' while we waitin' for her train she say to me, "What's your name?" An' I tells her an' she say she like my name but she goin' to call me William. I say that fine with me, an' I find out her name an' I tells her I likes it. Then I puts my arm 'round her, you know, but she pull'way quick like, an' she say, "What you tryin' to do, man, this is a public place." I thinkin' a taxicab it public too but I don't say nothin'. Then we just stands there an' after a time she ask for a smoke an' we both lights up. Then I say, "You comin' in town tomorrow night?"

"You want me to?" she say.

"Well, yeah, course I do," I say, but I say it cool like I could take it or leave it.

"What we do?" she ask.

"What you want to do?" I say.

"Eat some place," she tell me.

"An' after that?" I ask, waitin' to see what she 'spectin'.

"I have a girl friend who live up on Amsterdam Avenue," she say. "We go up an' see her." She stop an' she think for a minute. "Can you get a man for her?" she ask.

"Depend on what she look like," I tell her. I ain't goin' to be hangin' up George or Sidney with a ugly, you know.

"She a very nice young lady," Deeborah say like I hurt her or somethin', an' right 'way I knowed this friend here she a ugly. But I tells her I see what come up, an' then the train it come in an' she say, "I meet you here 'bout six o'clock."

"I be here all right," I tell her.

"You're a very nice young man, Mr. Peoples," she say, an' then she give me a good kiss, you know, an' it the kind that make you feel good all up an' down an' it get me set for Sat'day night.

You know, dogs, that cafeteria food it gettin' to be like a big drag. Every Monday they havin' the spaghetti an' it always goin' to be fill up with water an' taste like it spend its whole life in that pot. An' man it don't do nothin' for you gut 'cept it sit there like couple a hours an' then leastways in me it start to move itself fast an' I got to go to the toilet for some reason or 'nother.

So, like 'bout Sat'day night. It a all right time, you know. Everythin' it work itself out just fine.

I goes by an' collects George an' he 'bout ready as he can be, you know, 'cause George he at the end of the line when it come to the threads. He can buy hisself the best there is an' when he put them on nothin' happen to him. He still just George an' he could go 'bout in tore-up sneakers an' a red bandanna an' he look just the same. "You look all right s'evenin'," he say to me, an' I know he diggin' my duds.

"I ready for what come," I tell him very cool like.

"You best to start watchin' out for youself, man," he say to me, "you startin' to look like you gettin' ideas 'bout things."

"What you mean?" I say.

"Man, here you is with a job like, a *job*, an' you goin' to the school for the *di*-ploma, an' now you sportin' 'round in the finery for some chick. Sound to me like you headin' for trouble."

"Everythin' cool," I tell him, "don't you go worryin' 'bout me."

"Man, it seem to me like all of a sudden you tryin' to be somebody," George say.

"An' what wrong with that?" I asks, an' I makes it sound like I gettin' angry.

"Nothin' man," he say, "nothin' wrong with that." An' right quick he drop it an' he leave it there.

You know, dogs, trouble with George is he don't want to be nothin' 'cept what he is. He very happy 'bout goin' 'round couple times a month on mother's day an' collectin' some bread off the welfare chicks. All he want is to get 'long, that all. But George he a funny cat, all right, an' maybe someday he get hisself straight an' hold a job.

So we go down to the tubes like, an' George he don't like that trip nohow. Not too many a the cats they like to leave the neighb'hood. Make them uptight, you know. But we make it fine an' we waitin' for Deeborah an' when she get off her train she look 'bout as fine as a man could ask. An' while she walkin' to where we is George say, "Very nice, man. She all right." George he know the class when he see it. Deeborah she get close to us an' she say, "Good evenin', William," an' then she look to George an' she say to me, "This the young man for Violet?"

"Yeah," I say, "this here is George."

"How do you do, George?" she say an' she put out her hand to him.

"Well, all right," George say, an' he grab her hand like he 'bout to shake it off.

"You lookin' fine tonight," I say to her.

"Thank you, William," she say, an' I see George look to her an' then to me, an' I know he thinkin' what this here William boo.

We goes outa the buildin' an' right 'way she get herself 'nother taxicab an' quick like I subtracts the six dollars from the twenny-eight I got left from my digit. That leave me twenny-two an' we ain't even eat yet. But in the cab she hold my hand tight, an' I don't care nothin' for the six dollars no more.

Movin' all these here new animals 'round it like t'exhaust a man. There now, that the last a you. Ten fine new dogs for me an' the doctors. 'Cept for Thirty-four an' Thirty-fi' there, you all small dogs, an' even you two just mutts like with no breedin'. But you got youself big hearts an' that what count, they say. From what I seen here they ain't no chance that none a you small dogs even goin' to get past the splenectomies, let 'lone the rest a the business when they opens up you chest.

Thirty-four, there, you lookin' a bit fat through you middle like you had youself a fine home with some good food. So how come you run off? *Hey,* dog! Don't you go growlin' at me or I bust you one so's you won't forget who the boss in this here place. I ain't had to bust no one yet, but if an' you'd like to be the first I oblige you, all right. An' Thirty-fi', what wrong with you? I put you in you cage an' you actin' so meek like, an' you lie down right 'way an' it don't look to me like you care 'bout movin' or nothin'. You lyin' there on you side all bunched up like you scared a the whole world. Would you take youself some water here or some a this food I put out right next to you? What the matter with you, Thirty-fi', you won't even smell it? An' when I touch you an' rubs you belly you won't even look at me. I wonder what you thinkin' 'bout, dog. I s'pose it some kinda nice home where maybe you had you own old chair an' where everythin' it fine for you. Well, you ain't nothin' no more 'cept Number Thirty-fi' now, an' you goin' t'have to be doin' without you spleen soon.

Now like I was 'bout to say with Deeborah. We fin'ly gets up to Violet's, you know, an' George I can tell he gettin' uptight 'bout meetin' the ugly. An' just 'fore we go into the place he turn to me an' he give me a look that like to cut me up. So I turns on him an' I say, "Who bust you arm to make you come?" An' he give me a punch on the shoulder that tell me he goin' to make the best a it. An' he do, too. Only far as I concern it take a lotta nerve, 'cause Violet she a ugly all the way. An' on top a she bein' ugly she fat, an' she fat all over her body. It ain't just her belly that fat: her legs is fat, her arms is fat, her fingers is fat, an' even her *head* is fat. An' when I get me a good look at her it 'pear to me George he ain't never goin' to be speakin' to me 'gain after what I done to him. But George he got things figured diff'rent. The two chicks quick like they cuts to the toilet an' George he turn to look at me, an' I put my hands up like I surrenderin', you know, an' I say, "What can I tell you, man?"

"Nothin'," George say.

"How you goin' to pass an evenin' with that?" I asks.

"Everythin' be all right, you know," he say to me, an' he go right to the kitchen an' he open one a them cabinets an' he say, "There the answer, man," an' he take down a big old jug a Thunderbird. Now if there one cat who can walk in a place an' find the grape right 'way, it be George. He take the top off an' he put the jug to his mouth an' he take several drinks an' then he stop. "Fine, man," he say an' he wipe his mouth with his hand an' he say, "All I goin' to do is empty this here bottle. An' I going to do it with the lights off. You give me a gallon or so a the grape an' I be fine with any chick." An' he take hisself 'nother long drink an' then he put it back quick like 'cause the chicks they comin' in the room.

Deeborah she come up to me an' she say she gots to talk private like with me, an' so we goes into the bedroom. She tell me that Violet can't go to no rest'rant 'cause she on some special diet like an' she ain't 'lowed to eat almost nothin'. Deeborah she say it ain't right for us to be eatin' when Violet can't. So I say it fine with me if an' just her an' me we go an' she say, "Don't worry none 'bout George, Violet fix him somethin' right here."

"George like that fine," I tell her. "George ain't got no money anyhow."

"We go soon as I tells Violet it all right," she say, an' then she give me little kiss on the cheek, you know, an' she say, "We goin' to have us a fine time."

"Where you want to go?" I asks. An' she give me the name a this little place couple blocks 'way that don't serve nothin' but the soul food. "Why you want to eat there?" I asks.

"Herbert says soul food is good for you once in a while," she say. Personally, dogs, I hates soul food. First thing it got wrong with it is the kind they be sellin' in them new rest'rants it not the true soul food. Second thing it got wrong with it is how long it take a cat to eat it. You can't get youself no quick meal a the soul food. An' anyway most a the time it burn my belly like bad wine sometime do. Soul food it ain't for me, dogs. But Deeborah she want to go, an' after she clear herself with Violet we leaves, an' George he give me the sign that everythin' it all right with him, an' just as I goin' out the door I see Violet handin' him the Thunderbird an' I know he goin' to be all right.

Now like I told you, dogs, Deeborah she a thin chick, but when it come to eatin' she do that like she Violet or somethin'. She have herself a mess a food, an' I wonderin' where she keepin' it all. An' she talk while she eat, you know, like maybe she want to cover up how much she puttin' 'way. But she just keep pushin' the food into her mouth an' down it go. I 'spect she have herself close to twenny ribs, an' when she get done there a pile a bones picked clean as you please sittin' to one side a her plate. An' me I eatin' them ham hocks with the beans an' it ter'ble, man. Just a lotta bone an' gristle like an' all they done is let it sit in some old hot sauce for what seem like couple a weeks. So I have one a the hocks an' I finish it an' Deeborah she reach over to my plate an' she take the other. I tell her go right 'head 'cause that kinda food it ain't for me. So she 'tack that hock like it a Porterhouse or somethin' an' she hack an' carve at that thing till she get herself all there possibly is t'eat off'n it. The bill it come to fourteen dollars an' 'bout eighty cents.

I lay down a dollar for a tip an' I looks at Deeborah. "Two," she say, an' so's I lay down 'nother. "That's better, William," she say. An' I 'bout to bust her one right there for givin' 'way my bread, but she smile cool at me an' I forgets 'bout the bread.

On the way back to Violet's we stop an' buy some wine an' that come to a few more dollars, but I thinkin' it all goin' to be worth it. An' it was, you know, it truly was. 'Cept for George. He somethin' else, man. When we walks into Violet's I hear George holler, "Don't turn on no lights, man," an' I figure George he jazzin' Violet. Deeborah she must a figure the same 'cause cool like she take my hand an' she lead me to the bedroom. She turn on a soft light by the bed, an' then she sit down on the bed while I opens the wine. We get high real quick, it seem, an' then she say to me, "Come over here, William," an' she pat the bed with her hand. I look at her an' all a sudden I tremblin'. She stretch out so cool like I 'bout to lose it all on the spot. "Now you gives Deeborah a kiss," she say to me, an' then quick like we goin' very heavy on the bed, an' my hands they workin' on they own. I s'pose you should know, dogs, that I a very cool cat with the women. I smooth, an' I gots all the good moves a cat should have hisself. I can work me a chick till she be doin' anythin', a chick who don't mean nothin' to me, that is. But you give me a chick like Deeborah, a chick that like to drive my motor all by itself, an' I ain't nothin', man, nothin'. I what you call the *o*-riginal ten-second man. I got no control howsoever. An' I think Deeborah she know that 'cause right 'way she put her hand on it an' *pop,* that it for me, man, I finish. But that seem all right to her, dogs, 'cause she just like to lie there an' hug for a time an' I feelin' so good.

Then after a bit I hears the toilet flush an' I knowed George he finish too, an' then when we hear some music from the livin' room I gets up an' goes to the toilet an' gets together. Then me an' Deeborah we go on in.

Well, George he see the wine we got an' he starts hisself on 'nother bottle, an' Deeborah she start talkin' to Violet in the kitchen an' soon, you know, George an' me we very high. Deeborah see this an' she tell me an' George it time for us to be goin'. She give us 'nother bottle a wine an' she show us the door. But 'fore we leaves I square myself for next Sat'day night an' she give me little kiss an' we cut.

So that it, dogs, that my Sat'day night. 'Cept for George an' me we take that bottle an' we goes to his place where we sit on the stoop an' drink it. Then I goes home.

On Sunday I didn't do *nothin'*.

FALL

MONDAY

There you go now, Sevenny-eight, you sleep off that old splenectomy right there 'long with Sevenny-seven. Two a you's done in a hour an' fi' minutes. I gettin' very good, you know. Shorter the time you under the anesthetic sooner you wakes up an' less danger they is a you dyin'.

Hush you up there, old Number Thirty-Four. Cut you whinin'. You oughts to know after two months that it shore ain't goin' to be doin' you no good. An' with all's been done to you I s'prised you gots the spark even to be whinin'. Hush you up, dog, I be there in a second after I tends to these two cats.

Now what seem to be you trouble in there? You carryin' on like you gots a paw caught in the cage wire or somethin'. *Holy be-Jesus,* Thirty-four, you havin' puppies! Holy be-Jesus, you havin' youself puppies! What do I do, man, what do I *do?* This business shore ain't my line, you know. Lookit that, lookit that! *Puppies!* One, two, there's three. An' here come number four. Dog, you needs a doctor....

I can't find no one, Thirty-four. I sorry, but all the cats they havin' dinner an' they ain't no one here 'cept me. But you look like you finishin' up on you own just fine. S'pose you could be usin' youself some water, though. Here, this make it a bit better. You lookin' 'xhausted, you know, an' no wonder. You oughts to be right proud a youself, an' you still with the energy to flop you old tail on the wire there. Good for you. Now I goin' to get you some kinda coverin' for the bottom a the cage there. You can'ts have you puppies lyin' 'round on the cold metal like. Here, you use this old lab coat. I get me 'nother. I just spread it out like an' 'range the little cats right here side a you belly. There, now you looks like a happy mother, you know.

What I can'ts figure out, Thirty-four, is how you gots past the doctors. But I don't s'pose they lookin' for no dog to be havin' puppies. But Thirty-four, I promise you somethin' all right. They ain't goin' to be no 'sperimentin' on you for a long time, not with you havin' youself four puppies like. I am personally takin' you outa the 'speriments myself. An' from now on you goin' to be gettin' youself some milk an' all the rest a what you needs.

Thirty-four, you goin' to be travelin' first class with Mr. Peoples.

Now can you truly be believin' youself? You gettin' to be quite the big old cat in this here place. All the technician chicks from upstairs they got wind a you havin' youself some puppies, an' they flockin' down here to have theyselves a look. My, but you a obligin' dog. But them chicks what was just in here I takes me some offense at them, you know. They come in here with them hank'chiefs over they noses an' they lookin' 'round like they scared a the place. They ain't nothin' wrong with the animal room that they gots to be conductin' theyselves that way, you know.

An' it seem to me that the big doctor got no feelin's in him nohow. When I told him 'bout you an' you puppies here he just curse an' say somethin' 'bout everythin' always gettin' delayed on him. He keep that up, he turn out to be a bad cat.

Now you goin' t'have to 'scuse me, Thirty-four, 'cause I still got me three spleens to take out 'fore I go home. If an' I have the time 'fore I goes 'long to the school I be back to check you out.

So how you doin', Mother? Seem to me like I runnin' in out here the whole day now, an' I ain't been payin' much 'tention to you. You puppies they lookin' fine, you know, all 'cept for the little cat there who all messed up under the lab coat. I just fix that there. Ain't no bad accidents goin' to be happenin' in the animal room when I be in charge. Lemme get my stool an' visit with you. Leastways much as I can, what with the time bein' short now.

Ter'ble thing happen Friday night at the school. Anyway all the teachers they say it was ter'ble. The *po*-lice they come an' they busted Jerry right at the school. They bust him in the hallway 'tween the toilet an' 401, right when the man was on his way to readin' class. But it a smooth bust an' Jerry he didn't fight or nothin'. There was two cops, one colored an' one white, which is the way they takin' to travelin' 'round now, an' there was the two white detectives with them. But the detectives they don't do nothin' 'cept hold a man's arm an' walk him 'way. Trouble is, Mother, when you sees the detectives with the off'cers you know some cat got hisself in big trouble all right. If an' it's just a couple a patrolmen what come 'long you knows you ain't got no real problem, they ain't goin' to lay nothin' heavy on you. But when them detectives shows up, it usually somethin' big. An' Jerry he no 'ception. An' you know, dog, it seem to me that the bigger the thing they bustin' you for the nicer they is. If an' you just gettin' called down for havin' some stuff or for runnin' a number they get very mean, you know. They curse you out, they say they goin' to lock you up forever an' jazz like that. But if an' they think they get you for somethin' big, somethin' that like to be in the paper maybe, then they so nice it like they be takin' you to a party or somethin'. An' that the way they treat Jerry. First the cops they rubs him up an' down for a weapon, an' when he clean they check his name an' he nod.

Then the detectives they come walkin' down the hall, an' they lookin' like they in church or somethin', they so serious. They check his name 'gain, an' then they put the handcuffs on him an' lead him to the stairs. An' you know, Mother, whole time that goin' on all the rest a the cats they just goin' 'bout they business takin' no notice a what goin' on. They just pass the whole thing by like they don't wants nothin' to do with it. Which is *'xackly* the way to conduct youself.

So I ask 'round an' fin'ly the Self-Wareness cat he tell me that they sayin' Jerry kill hisself a couple a his brothers from his organization. Now you'd think that if an' a cat go killin' other cats that be Millard, you know, 'cause he forever runnin' off the mouth 'bout it. But the cats who do it they like Jerry, all right. Course I ain't sayin' he done it for shore, 'cause Jerry he don't tell me hisself, y'understand. But Jerry he seem 'most like he too sweet 'bout everythin', an' that the cat to be watchin'. If an' you's too sweet all the time you don't never blow off none, an' if you like Jerry when you let youself go, you do it all the way.

TUESDAY

Now here it is already with half the day gone an' I just gettin' in. An' the place here it startin' to stink like it a weekend or somethin'. I sorry to be late, dogs, but it ain't my fault. Last night right after the school I walkin' home an' my teeth they begin to hurt somethin' ter'ble. They ain't nothin' like you teeth hurtin' to mess you up. So I stops into the bar an' has some wine, you know, but that don't help matters none. All it do is it make it hurt more. So I spend the whole night walkin' 'round in the house an' listenin' to my ma who all the time sayin' it just God's way a punishin' me for playin' 'round all the time. She gettin' to be somethin' else with that God business.

So I gots me to a dentist this mornin', an' I very relieve when I sittin' there in his chair, you know. He look in my mouth an' he say, "You've got some troubles there." I's 'bout set to tell him I knows that else I wouldn't be sittin' in no chair with him peerin' down my throat, but 'course I can't say nothin' with that big old metal stick he got in my mouth. "Just make the hurtin' stop," I tell him when he take the stick outa my mouth. Then he give me a needle fulla somethin' an' right 'way things they begins to ease up. That when he start to talk to me. "When was the last time you consulted a dentist?" he ask.

"Never been," I tell him.

"It looks like it," he tell me, an' then he ask why I never been to no dentist an' I tell him 'cause my teeth they never hurt before. Then he start in on me with his jive 'bout you s'posed to all the time be takin' care a you mouth like maybe it somethin' extra special, an' fin'ly I tells him just to fix the tooth, man, 'cause I gots me a job to get to. He tell me to fix up my mouth it goin' to take maybe six months an' cost me like four, fi' hundred dollars. I tell him I ain't got that kinda bread to be spendin' on no teeth, an' he tell me he can take them all out an' give me some fake ones that last a long time. I tell him 'gain just to fix up the bad one I got an' I be thinkin' 'bout havin' the fake ones. I 'spect he got hisself some angle he workin' wantin' to take out a cat's teeth an' put in them fake ones. He a jive cat like all the rest.

I bring you some milk this mornin', Mother, 'cause I know you need it. Lookit them little cats squirmin' 'round you belly there. They lookin' mighty hungry.

Hey, you over there, Number Forty-three. You ready for s'afternoon? I hopes you is 'cause you goin' to be the first cat we do the heart work on. S'afternoon the doctors they goin' right into you heart an' they goin' to mess with it till it like a human heart what got itself the heart disease.

Takin' out a spleen it ain't nothin' compare with this here heart business. This goin' to be somethin' else, man. I just got done with puttin' Forty-three shepherd dog down an' gettin' him all set, an' the big white doctor he there supervisin' me, an' the big doctor there an' it look to me like he supervisin' the other doctor. The big man he say that everythin' it got to be 'xackly right for this here operation. Everythin' he say it got to go off smooth like 'cause they havin' in some special cat to do hisself the heart work. Doctor who goin' to mess up Forty-three he a real heart doctor who all the time workin' on human bein's.

So I do everythin' to the letter, you know. I sets up the pack just so, an' when I gets it outa the autoclave I sets it near the end a the table kinda right 'tween Forty-three's legs, an' then I sets to work preppin' the dog. Now workin' on his chest there it much more diff'cult than doin' his belly 'cause a them there ribs always gettin' in the way a the razor. An' course I ain't never shaved me no ribs 'fore an' I cut the dog up in a few places. But the big white doctor say it don't matter none long as the hair it gone right down to the skin. He tell me it got to be done like if an' Forty-three there he a human bein', 'cause the man who comin' to do it he a very partic'lar cat. So just when everythin' it get itself fine, you know, the partic'lar cat he call the lab an' he say he goin' to be a while 'cause he havin' some trouble with one a his sick people in the hospital. Big white doctor ask him how long he think he be, an' he say he don't know but it be soon if the cat die an' long time if an' he lives. That when the big white doctor he told me I could come back in here an' take me a rest 'cause this operation it goin' to take a long time. Messin' with a cat's heart it ain't like whippin' out no spleen, you know.

You know, dogs, there a lotta things I don't like 'bout this here job, but there one thing that all right, you know, an' that the fact that you all so friendly. I can tells you anythin' I want an' all you do is just sit back an' wag you tails like I the best cat in the whole world an' the only friend you ever had youself. Nice thing 'bout you is that you don't gives no advice. Not that I be needin' any, y'understand. I takes care a my own self, an' most a the time I just needs to hear myself talk to get a diff'culty straight. Most time, that is. But I gots me a diff'culty now that I shore wish it just go 'way by itself. Deeborah she tell me she think she goin' to have herself a baby. Now that no kinda thing for a cat to have happen to hisself when he gots a job that takin' him some place an' when he gettin' set to start makin' his mark at the school.

She told me last night at Violet's that she findin' out from a doctor today an' she tell me tonight. If an' she goin' to have herself a baby I tell you I one unlucky cat, dogs, 'cause I only jazz her but two times an' both times she say she sure it all right. An' you better know Deeborah she the kinda chick who goin' to be on my back 'bout gettin' married. Mosta the other chicks they wouldn't be carin' nothin' 'bout it, but Deeborah she diff'rent, you know. She have herself the class an' she ain't goin' to be takin' no for a answer. She have the class in everythin' she do, man, even right down to jazzin' itself. She ain't like a lot a chicks, you know, who when you go to jazz them they lie down 'bout where they is an' all you got to do is raise up the dress an' be 'bout you business. No, man, she ain't like that at all. She 'range everythin' an plan it out so it a good thing that got some respect to it, you know, somethin' that it be nice to 'member when you finish. I didn't tell you this, dogs, but first time we jazz it somethin' else. We do it a couple a months 'go at Violet's an' Deeborah she got everythin' set just so. Violet she out for the evenin' an' when I go there Deeborah she have some wine ready, an' it good wine, no cheap grape, y'understand. An' she make us a little somethin' to eat an' we talks close like for a long time after we done eatin', an' then so cool an' sweet like we moves off to the bedroom. The lights in there already on soft like, an' Deeborah she put one a them nightgowns you see through 'cross the bed. Man, I gettin' all 'cited just thinkin' how it was. An' she told me she want to make it nice for me, that makin' love it the best thing two people they can do for theyselves long as they straight 'bout the whole thing. She take off her clothes in kind of a dark corner so's I can't see me too much, an' then we gets into the bed an' we have us long talk 'bout one 'nother. She tell me she sorry I ain't the first, but they only one other an' that be Herbert some months 'fore. An' she kid me 'long, you know, while we kissin' an' huggin' 'bout how many chicks I musta had myself, an' she say she 'spect it a consid'rable number. So who am I to tell her it ain't, you know.

So then we make us some love an' it the first time in my life I ever knowed there a diff'rence 'tween jazzin' an' makin' love. Jazzin's when you all the time thinkin' 'bout what you doin'. Lovin' is when you ain't. An' 'fore I know what goin' on everythin' it over, an' we lyin' there like it the most 'portant thing in the whole world. That when she tell me she love me, you know, an' them's the words to make a cat uptight all right. Lovin' up a chick it a all right thing to do, but when you start tellin' them you loves them, that when the trouble begin. So I don't say nothin' back to her, I just gives her a couple a kisses an' she don't press it none that I should be tellin' her I be in love too.

An' man, I tell you one thing. If an' she goin' to have herself a baby I goin' to have to make me some very fine moves so's I don't marry her. I know she goin' to be on my back 'bout that, an' she ain't never goin' to get off. So I see what happen, you know.

I gots to go now, man, 'cause the heart doctor he here now, an' I got to watch him an' see what he do to Forty-three's heart.

WEDNESDAY

Forty-three, man, what you doin' standin' up? After a operation like you had youself yesterday how you got the energy to be standin' up? An' lookit the way you hangin' you head. Man, it 'bout down to the floor an' you tongue it hangin' outa you mouth an' you breathin' so hard it like you been out for a run or somethin'. Could you be usin' youself some water like, or some a this food I puttin' here? You can have all the water you want, but you got to take it easy on the food 'cause they say too much it ain't good for you heart. You shore don't look like no big strong shepherd dog no more. But you 'cision there it comin' 'long very good, you know, an' you look like you goin' to be all right for the rest a the 'speriments. Take it easy on the food, dog, 'cause too much it ain't good for you heart.

Oh, man, lookit Eighty-seven over there. I was 'fraid that happen first time he come in here. I think he fin'ly dead, you know. An' we didn't even do nothin' to him yet. He like

Thirty-fi', I 'member, who when he come in he have his tail way up 'tween his legs an' he too meek to want to do nothin'. Thirty-fi' he just got in his cage an' he lay hisself down an' he didn't move or nothin'. He just like Eighty-seven. Both them dogs they don't do nothin' 'cept lie down there till they die. Ain't nothin' wrong with them, that for shore, an' they ain't nothin' a cat could do for them. Now I gots to get me a incineratin' bag an' put Eighty-seven where he go. You know, dogs, when Thirty-fi' he die I think maybe it me that do somethin' wrong, but I knows diff'rent now. It the dog who do somethin' wrong. They get theyselves in here an' I 'spect they knows what goin' to happen to them. I s'pose they just knowed this here it the end a the line. So they lies down an' they don't change no position for a couple days an' they don't eat or drink nothin' an' then one mornin' they's just dead....

Eighty-seven he in the freezer now, an' I can takes the tape with his number writ on it off his cage an' put it here right 'long side all the rest. Now there, that done. Now I got to get me to the 'monia business.

Like things they beginnin' to get theyselves straight at the school. Least some a the things. You know, dogs, dec'mals really so cool when you gets them down. Dec'mals just like makin' change for a cat, only you got to 'member where to have that dec'mal point. That what make a number mean somethin'. F'rinstance, dogs, if an' you take youself the fraction ¼ it really mean .25 if an' you be messin' with the dec'mals. An' that true 'cause to gets you a dec'mal from the fraction like you divide the numerator there into the denominator. Or maybe it the other way 'round. Yeah, man, numerator it on the top an' denominator it on the bottom. Dig, that right. So if an' you divides the bottom *in*-to the top there it be the denominator *in*-to the numerator. Now it when you does the dividin' that you gets the dec'mal, y'understand. But the math'matics man he say it ain't no real answer you be gettin', it just the same thing. Boo, man, to me it a answer all right.

Now most a the cats they diggin' that all the way, but

things they begin' to mess up a bit when the math'matics man he start throwin' some diff'cult problems at us. Like 33⅓. That mess up my mind for a while till I see that the ⅓ it don't matter none. It just a third a some number that so small it don't make no diff'rence if you writes it down. An' 'nother that mess me up good it that there ⅛. Oh, man, when that cat say to change that to a dec'mal I forget everythin' I learned. But I work on it an' after a time I get me .125. So I know that .125 it 'proximately the same thing as that there ⅛.

Then he throw 'nother bad-awful problem at us. "Now that you've got .125 for a decimal from one-eighth," he say, "how do we change that decimal to a percent?"

"Oh, man," Sidney say, an' he drop his pencil on the table there, "ease up, man. Dec'mals they hard 'nough."

"Watch," the math'matics man say, an' he just move that dec'mal point there two places over to the right. "There," he say, "now you've got your percent."

"That all?" Sidney say, an' he lookin' like he don't believe the mathematics man.

"On the Equivalency Examination," the man say, "you just remember to do that."

"What 'bout puttin' the whole mess over a hundred or somethin'?" George ask.

"Those steps aren't necessary," the math'matics man say, an' then he stop an' look 'bout. Fin'ly he say, "Now how do you change a percent to a decimal?"

"Move the point two places to the left," Sidney say, like he all sudden so cool, "that all, man." Right then George lean over to me an' he say, "See, man, I told you it easy. Stop your complainin' all the time." Course I ain't said nothin', you know.

"Now how about this one," the math'matics man say, an' he write on the board, .00125, an' he turn 'round an' he look at us. Then he turn back quick like an' he put a percent thing after the dec'mal.

"Oh, man," Sidney say, an' he drop his pencil again.

"What is it?" the man ask George.

"It a dec'mal per-*cent*," George say slow, like he very proud a what he know.

"Is it a large number or a small one?" the man ask.

"Small, man," George tell him. "It just a very small part a one percent."

"And how would you make this percent into a decimal?" the math'matics man ask George.

"You s'posed to move the thing two places to the . . ." an' he stop there to think an' fin'ly he say, "*left*."

"But you don't have two places to the left of .00125," the man say.

"Yeah," George say slow like an' he start to rub his chin, "I sees what you mean." He know the mathematics man got him then.

"I 'member," Sidney say quick like, "you just goes an' gets you two more noughts from some place, that all."

"Oh, yeah," George say, "that right. I 'member now."

"*Jive*," Sidney say, but George he don't take no notice.

You know, dogs, math'matics man say that it all just a matter a us cats practicin' with numbers. That's why I got me this here book. I goin' to work on it an' see if he right.

Now, man, it's 'bout this here Deeborah business. She carry on somethin' ter'ble last night. When I get to Violet's I 'spectin' the very worse thing, you know, but she all cool when she open the door an' I see she dress so fine an' when I walk in I smells the perfume. An' dig, dogs, right then she take my arm so cool like, an' she walk me to the livin' room where she sits me down on the sofa right front a big jug a the grape. She pour me some an' then she take herself a small glass, an' then she sit herself right down close to me an' she start to lean on me like she gettin' herself all set for a night a jazzin'. So I haves me a touch or two a the grape an' I ask her how she feelin', an' then she look up at me an' she say, "You my man, you know."

"All right," I say.

"I glad you're reliable, William," she say.

"I ain't missed me a day on the job," I tell her.

"A man goin' someplace is the kind a girl should have herself," she say.

"What you talkin' 'bout?" I ask her.

"You an' me we goin' to be gettin' married," she say, an' she lean her head on my shoulder.

"What you talkin' 'bout this marryin' business for?" I ask her, an' I beginnin' to get angry, you know.

"We goin' to get married," she say soft.

"I only heard one a us sayin' that," I tell her, an' that when she sit up straight an' she put her glass down hard like on the table, an' her eyes they start gettin' big in her head, an' I sees one little blood vein stick itself out on her forehead. "Now you listen up here, *mister*," she say, an' when you hear them begin like that you know the big trouble it still ahead. "Is you a *man* or what is you?"

"What kinda boo you talkin'?" I asks.

"Mister, you the father of the child I carryin'," an' she make it sound like she readin' the Declaration Independence or somethin'.

"So how I know if I be the man?" I asks, an' I knows what the answer it goin' to be, but I needs the time to think.

"How do you *know*?" she yell at me. "What you think I do, make room for any stud who just happen down the block?"

"No," I say easy like, an' quick I looks to the floor like I sorry 'bout the whole thing.

"That's better," she say, an' she take herself a little pull on the wine. "Now we got to talk tonight 'bout when we gettin' married."

"Why we got to get married up?" I ask, an' that set her mouth off 'gain.

" 'Cause my child he goin' to have himself a father, y'understand? An' he goin' to have himself a name people can call him. My mama she don't raise me up right to be havin' no bastard child."

"Ain't nothin' wrong in not havin' no father," I tell her. "The kid he get here he be all right."

"Say, where your pride, *mister*?" she say.

"Never you mind where I keepin' my pride like," I tell

her, "I got me plenty." But I don't see what somethin' like that there pride got to do with a man gettin' hisself married up.

"Ain't you proud you're goin' to be a father?" she ask.

"I never thought 'bout it," I tell her, an' it the truth, you know. But then I see her startin' to get all uptight, man, an' I say, "I s'pose it all right." But she don't take no notice, an' her mouth it start 'gain.

"There it is," she say, an' she start talkin' like she lookin' at some other cat 'cross the room, "that the trouble with the men right there, all right. They got but two things on their minds, an' that be gettin' high as you please an' takin' care of what they carryin' 'round in their trousers. That all," she say, an' she wave her hand like she finish with the whole thing an' it time for me to leave. But then she say, "But I thought you were a diff'rent young man, William," an' then I begins to feel very small, you know. But now I thinkin' 'bout it, it don't seem to me that feelin' small it be near as bad as feelin' married. Dogs, all the cats I know they tellin' me that when you marry up it finish for you. That nice little piece you marry youself up with she right 'way down to the furniture store buyin' this an' buyin' that on the time an' doin' it with bread you ain't even goin' to have in you pocket for two, three years. An' the chick she gone an' spent it 'fore you ever seen it. An' she don't stop with furniture. No, man, she get herself them shiny new 'pliances an' dishes an' the like. An' you know, I ain't never seen one a them who won't be watchin' nothin' 'cept the color television.

"William," she say straight to me, "you're obliged to marry me."

"Woman," I tell her back, "I ain't 'bliged to do nothin'." Course, that when she start to cry an' that start to make me very uptight. So after a time I start tellin' her how everythin' it goin' to be all right an' she shouldn't go an' worry herself none. I s'pose I promise to marry her, dogs, but I don't know why I ever gone an' done it.

Course, soon as I say that to her she start to tell me how she an' her ma they already got everythin' 'ranged all proper like. She tell me her mother smooth out everythin' like with the blood business an' the license an' all the rest of the boo 'cause she close with some cat who work at the place. An' then, man, she tell me Friday it be the day. I shore don't know where I be Friday, dogs, but I shore hope it ain't in Newark gettin' married up.

Now I got to get together here, dogs, 'cause today I be scrubbin' with the heart doctor an' we be takin' on Number Forty-four over there. I like that, you know, 'cause I very upset 'bout this whole mess an' maybe if an' I can get to work I forget 'bout the whole thing for a while.

Oh, man, I in very bad shape, you know, an' I just mess up somethin' ter'ble in there, an' Number Forty-four he dead. An' it ain't nobody's fault but mine, an' how I done it was just dumb, man, dumb. The big white doctor he very angry with me now, an' I couldn't do nothin' but stand there an' take what he give me.

What happen was I take Forty-four outa here for his walk an' then I weighs him an' I knowed I gets the weight right. But where I mess up was in how much a the Nembutal I give him. What you s'posed to do is multiply the dog's weight by this here dec'mal, an' that it give you the number a the cc's you s'posed to stick in that little blood vein that run just on the outside a his ankle. What I done was multiplies wrong an' Forty-four he get two times what right for him. Well, he go down fast, but I don't take no notice a what wrong with him till I get him down on the table an' he all prepped like. That when I feel his legs an' they very cold, an' I looks to his tongue an' they ain't no natural color there. I switch off the breathin' machine an' I feel for his heart beatin'. But they ain't nothin' there. That when I know he dead, an' I ask the big white doctor if an' he think maybe there somethin' wrong with Forty-four. He check him out quick like, an' then he look angry at me. "How much Nembutal did you give this animal?" he ask, an' when I tell him he lay into me an' I don't do nothin' but stand there an' take it. He go on for a long time 'bout all the time we put into the dog an' 'bout all the bread each dog is worth, an' 'bout how the dogs they gettin' more valuable with each 'speriment we do. He yellin' at me 'bout how it ain't nothin' but stupid for me to go an' kill that there dog when he already have his splenectomy an' all his blood work an' all the rest. But I mess up Forty-four 'cause my mind it ain't here, you know, it on the Deeborah business an' not on what I be doin'.

That big white doctor he one mother, all right. He just told me that I got to come in here tomorrow, on the Thanksgivin' Day like, an' do a splenectomy so's we have 'nother dog to make up for Number Forty-four. Oh, man, things they startin' to press in on me, dogs. It gettin' so I can't see things so clear as when I came on the job. Things just don't seem like they workin' right, you know. The only thing that makin' any sense to me is fractions. All the rest a the school it just jive to me. An' who truly need to know 'bout fractions anyhow? No one, man, that who. An' this here job it ain't nothin', neither. I mean, I ain't even no Spec'men Supervisor yet. Pressin' in, that what things is doin', all right, pressin' in bad. Ain't nothin' in the world but this here mop an' the 'monia an' you dogs. An' what you care 'bout anyhow, dogs. *Nothin'*, you don't care 'bout nothin'. You all just like Deeborah, you all just out for youself. Well, I cuttin' outa this jive right now. Man, I finish with you.

THURSDAY

Oh, man, how long I sleep? I know it a long time now 'cause I down. An' I feelin' so bad, you know, so bad. My ma she goin' to be worryin' 'bout me 'cause all night I ain't home or nothin'. I s'pose she got herself the white priest out lookin' for me, an' when I gets home tonight she goin' to lay into me ter'ble 'cause she know the only thing that keep me out all night be junk.

Dogs, I done a ter'ble thing goin' back on the stuff, a ter'ble thing. I got to stay off it, if an' I goin' to be me some-body, you know. Now to get to work here an' whip out you spleen, Eighty-eight. But 'fore I does that I goin' to get me some dinner. I'm starvin'.

It only noontime, dogs, an' everythin' it seem to be gettin' back together. I guess I don't fly so long as like I thought, an' while I havin' my dinner I make me a promise like never to be on that jazz no more. Not me, man, this time I truly finish with it. Look here, now, I even got me some a the stuff left, an' I show it to you. It 'nough for a few hours if an' I wants it to be. But you watch this, man, there it go in the sink an' on go the water. That like twelve dollars' worth a stuff goin' down that drain, but that all right with me. I be straight from now on.

Hush up you barkin' there, dogs, I knows I don't have to be carryin' on like this an' fillin' you dishes on a holiday, but long as I here I gives you a bit extra.

You know, one thing it kinda funny 'bout me gettin' high last night. I never had no 'tention a gettin' high, it just seem to catch me when I thinkin' 'bout somethin' else, an' when the big urge it get holda you they ain't nothin' you can do 'bout it. What you should do, you know, is all the time be ready for when you goin' to have youself a urge, an' that way you stay off the stuff. Once the urge get inside you, like you finish. What happen last night 'xackly that. I be so miserable 'bout everythin' you know, an' it seem that when that happen to you it don't take you no more an' 'bout fi' seconds 'fore you runs into the man. He seem like he know when you needs it, an' sometimes he even know you need it 'fore you do. Like you could be walkin' down the street one mornin' when everythin' it fine with you, you know, an' you could walk right past the man an' nothin' happen. But some other mornin' you be goin' down the same street an' the man he see somethin' diff'rent in you face, an' he come right up to you an' 'fore you know it you flyin'. That the way the teacher he work the cats at NEW. Man, he got hisself a eye for the cat who need to be high, all right. He never once since I been there even look cross-eye at me, but last night I pass him in the hall outside the toilet an' he stop me. I tell you, dogs, it somethin' 'bout the way a cat look. "Hey, brother," he say soft an' cool like, "can I hold a cig'rette?" I gives him the cig'rette an' I see him lookin' 'bout like he uptight, an' after he light up the smoke he say, "How you feelin'?"

"What you want to know for?" I ask him.

"You low, man," he say. "You got troubles."

"I takin' care a things," I tell him an' I look 'way like ain't nothin' wrong.

"Sure, baby," he say, an' that when I look close at him an' get the urge inside me. I know then I finish 'fore I even open my mouth. "What you got in mind?" I ask him.

"I got what you need," he say, an' he know he don't have to be cool no more. He already read me just right. "How much you need?" he ask, an' I tells him I ain't had me none for like long time now. An' he give me just a bit an' I goes into the toilet an' my hands they shakin' an' I gettin' uptight 'bout gettin' the stuff in 'cause a all the trouble I used to have. But them blood veins they back now an' they right strong. Dogs, I 'member one time things they get so bad I couldn't get me no vein on my arm. I try an' try for like 'bout twenny, thirty minutes, an' the urge all the time it gettin' stronger. I sticks myself an' sticks myself but like no blood vein, man. Fin'ly I just take me a bit a glass an' cuts into the arm an' pours the stuff in there an' puts my hand over it till the high start. But it a no good high, an' after a time I pass out from losin' all the blood, you know.

So last night I gets just a bit in, man, 'cause if an' I shoot up much as I used to I fall over dead. Then I wait but what seem like couple a seconds an' then I start up, an' man it like startin' up the roller coaster 'cept at the top a that first hill the thing it don't go down. No, man, you just keeps right on goin' into the blue. You know, dogs, it a truly beautiful thing, truly beautiful.

Then when I loose I go out to the man an' he take like thirty dollars from me an' he give me the rest a the bag. I shoot part a that after the school finish, an' I make sure I lookin' straight when I in with the teachers. I don't want to be high for them, y'understand, an' so I sits there with my hands folded right on the desk, an' my eyes they lookin' straight 'head. Only George know somethin' goin' on.

"What you smilin' at?" he ask.

"Ain't smilin', man," I tell him.

"Oh, you ain't, huh?" he say. "Then why you mouth lookin' like that?"

"Like what?" I asks him, but course I ain't lookin' at him.

"Like if an' you don't close up you mouth you goin' to have bugs flyin' in there," he say. An' when I don't answer him he say, "Oh, no, man, why you go an' do it?"

"What you talkin' 'bout?" I say.

"You high, man," he say like he angry with me. "Now why you go an' get youself high?"

"Things they be all right," I tell him.

"You see the white priest?" he say to me.

"Jive cat," I tell him slow like.

"How come you don't tell me 'fore you mess with that business?" he ask.

"Look, man, Deeborah she goin' to have herself a baby," I tell him.

"So what that got to do with bein' high?" he say.

"She want to get married, man," I tell him.

"That the kinda crazy talk you gets from a woman," George say. "Havin' a baby ain't no call for a cat to be gettin' married."

"You know how she be," I tell him.

"That still ain't no call for you to be high," he say like he angry 'gain.

"Who care anyway?" I say, an' George he leave me 'lone after that.

So when the school it finish I goes to the toilet an' gets me a solid high, like three, four hour, you know, an' that 'bout the last thing I 'member 'fore I comes in here this mornin'. Man, it a good thing this here it a holiday 'cause if an' I come in high when I s'posed to be workin' that be it for me. Eighty-eight, come on now. We goin' for a walk 'fore I takes out you spleen. When you haves a good walk you don't crap on the table when I gives you the anesthetic. . . .

You know, dogs, this place here it really somethin' else when you sees it all. This here the first real time I haves to look 'round everywhere. All the other time the peoples they here an' you can't go bustin' into no room an' say you just lookin' 'bout. You start that business an' they let you go all right. But they ain't no cat in the whole place now, an' I just had me some kinda look 'round. Cuttin' up you dogs ain't but half a what goin' on here, you know.

When I carryin' back Eighty-eight here I stops in the hall 'cause I swore I hear me a cat meowin'. I think I wrong, you know, but just 'fore I opens the door there an' comes in I hears it 'gain. So I put Eighty-eight in his cage there an' I make sure he sleepin' good. Then I goes out an' looks for the cat. I find him all right. He in a room just like this one an' they a whole mess a cats in there just like you dogs here. Mosta the cats they quiet 'cept for this one who jumpin' 'round his little cage like he havin' a fit or somethin'. He do 'xackly the same thing over an' over 'gain. He jump hisself straight into the air off all his feet an' then he hiss an' cry out, an' when he come down he fall over an' start turnin' 'round an' 'round in the cage. An' I goes up to him, you know, like to see if he got somethin' wrong I be fixin', an' he like to tear that cage 'part when he lay his eyes on me. That when I see that most a his hair it fall out already an' he only got hisself like a very thin coat that cover his body. An' I look 'way from him an' I begin to see the other cats. They cut up in a lot a diff'rent ways, you know, not like you dogs in here who cut up all the same. There this one pretty little cat an' he got hisself a nice coat a brown an' white fur. 'Cept stickin' right out the middle a his forehead there a small piece a silver wire that got a bit a tape 'bout it. It just come right up out a the skin. An' that cat all the time he twitchin' his head side to side.

An' they sev'ral other little cats what all messed up in the head. One he just lyin' there with like half his brain on the bottom a the cage. I s'pose that from where his head coverin' it fall off, but I ain't goin' near no cat who have his head open up. Cats they ain't my line a work, y'understand, an' if I reach into that little cage that cat like to go crazy, an' who know, maybe he go for my eyes or somethin'. An' you can't bust a cat one, neither. You bust him one an' he take you number an' sometime he wait for you an' bust you back. He not like you dogs.

An' on other side a the room there I seen me this here complicated machine with a whole mess a lights poppin' on an' off, an' I goes over to it an' I see it got sev'ral tube-like things that come outa it an' go to the cages all 'long that wall. I see where they two switches on the machine an' one it on an' one it ain't. So I puts that switch on an' I like to tell you dogs that room it start to hum with what come buzzin' outa that machine. It start crackin' an' carryin' on like maybe it a machine gun or somethin'. That when I see the sign that sayin' all them cages 'long that wall there is radioactive. When I sees that I cut, you know, an' I do it fast 'cause I shore ain't one to be messin' with that jazz nohow.

But the cat room it ain't the end a what they doin' here, you know. It but one a the things that goin' on. I leave that place an' I goes down the hall a piece an' I comes to 'nother room with the same KEEP OUT sign they all's got, an' I opens up the door a crack an' peeks in. Well, they ain't nothin' in that old room but a mess a rabbits. They the cutest things, you know, an' I bet you dogs like to be out somewhere now chasin' you a few a them all right. But I tell you they ain't so awful cute like when you gets up close to them. They a mess like everythin' else in this here place. They all got 'bout the same thing wrong with them. They a big square on they back that been cut 'way, an' it look to me like some doctor he put hisself down some new skin there, you know. An' they sev'ral tags on the rabbits. One rabbit got a number on his left ear that the other rabbit he got on his right ear. I s'pose that mean who got whose skin. But they don't seem like they too messed up, like they ain't hurtin' bad from no operations an' such. 'Cept these two in one a them corner cages. They both just sittin' there with they heads hangin' so low, you know, an' it 'pear to me that maybe they very cold 'cause they both huddle up together an' they shakin' like crazy. I looks close to them an' I sees they gots the same numbers on they ears, an' what they done I s'pose is put the skin a one onto the other. They messed up, that for shore.

Next place I goes is the room I don't like the most. It like a ter'ble place, you know, an' anythin' them doctors want to be doin' with them animals it all right with me. Ain't one a them ever deserve hisself nothin' 'cept a cage an' some doctor to be cuttin' him up. That the rat room I in, man, an' let me tell you it make me uptight just to be standin' in there. When I turn on the light to see where I is, I like to jump through the roof, you know, an' like you ain't never seen no cat leave no room fast as I close up that door. Quick like I starts back for here, but I stops for a second outside a door an' I listens to some kinda rattlin' an' crazy-like chirpin'. I opens the door slow an' I like to tell you dogs they a pow'ful smell comin' from in there. It like to knock me over, it so strong. An' I switches on the light an' all sudden like them monkeys they start flyin' 'round an' 'round in they cages an' I thinkin' for shore some a the big cages they goin' to fall over. All diff'rent kinds a monkeys in there, you know. Big ones which is very fat, an' some real thin ones who got them long tails that like to reach to the floor, an' man the stuff in them cages there it ter'ble. Smell it get to me quick an' I cut.

So that pretty much the place here, dogs, an' I think what with the things that goin' on some a you's got life all right in here. I mean, you could be worse off, you know.

There, the cleanin' up all done in the lab, an' I set to get me outa here soon as I check me out on Eighty-eight here an' fix you up you water dishes. Eighty-eight he lookin' good now, you know, an' he 'bout to wake up. I goin' to give you like two dishes a water, Eighty-eight, 'cause when you wakes up you goin' to have youself a pow'ful thirst. But you ain't gettin' no food, not with you gut messed up.

You know, dogs, I done made up my mind 'bout somethin', an' that be the Deeborah business. Now we s'posed to be gettin' married up there like tomorrow evenin', but tonight when I sees her I goin' to tell her that she can forget 'bout Billy Peoples gettin' married up. Man, if an' I don't do that it be certain that I finish, an' I never have no chance to get to the college or nowhere. So far as I concern, man, she can kiss it all off. Now I knows it ain't goin' to be easy like, but I just goin' to tell her an' that be all they is to it. I goin' to say, "Kiss it off, Deeborah," an' then I goin' to have to wait while she tell me 'bout how I ain't no man an' the rest a the boo, an' when she finish I goin' to say, "Kiss it off, Deeborah, honey, just kiss it off." An' she buy the whole thing after a time, an' I knows that 'cause the womenfolk, man, they do 'xackly what you say if an' you say it mean 'nough.

FRIDAY

Man, the womenfolk they all outa shape. If an' you takes Deeborah for a starter like an' you ends up with my ma you know that once they opens they mouths an' starts complainin' 'bout a man it ain't goin' to stop, *never*. I just didn't catch it from Deeborah last evenin', I catch it from my ma too. She give me hell an' all the rest from like the first second I sets foot into the 'partment. What she do is just kinda soften me up for Deeborah 'cause after I finish with my ma I ain't in no kinda shape to be takin' that chick on. An' the white priest he there with my ma when I get home. They both sittin' on the couch there, an' my ma she got out her best linen hank'chief an' she holdin' it just under her nose like she 'bout to sneeze or somethin'. I knowed right 'way she been cryin' for the priest. But I tell you one thing, dogs, when she got out her best hank'chief she make sure she don't cry too hard, you know.

"Billy, Billy," my ma she yell when I come in the door. "You all right? Where you been? What you been doin'?" an' on an' on she go an' she never give me no chance to tell her what she askin'. An' she leap up from the couch an' she run at me an' she grab me an' she start huggin' me like to death.

"Be cool," I say to her an' I see the white priest over her shoulder, an' he smilin' so pretty like maybe he thought a somethin' sweet to tell me to save my old lost soul. 'Scuse me for laughin', dogs, but he just too much a jive cat to be believin'.

My ma she get through with the huggin' business, an' she pat her eyes with the hank'chief, an' then the priest he get up an' start over to me with his hand stuck out front a him. "How are you, Bill?" he say to me, an' he pick up my hand an' shake it in both a his. Then he put his hand on my shoulder like an' he say to me, "Do you want to tell me about it now?"

" 'Bout what?" I says, an' I can see he startin' to lead me to the couch where he goin' to sit me 'tween him an' my ma. If that happen I knows I be done for the night, so's I pull 'way from him an' sits at the table. "Tell us where you've been, Bill," he say so sweet like.

"I been on the job," I tell him.

"Come, come, Bill," he say, an' he got a smile on his face like to make a cat sick, "no one works on Thanksgiving."

"I do," I tell him.

"I called the Center," he say, "and there wasn't any answer."

"That too bad," I say to him, an' my ma all the time she sniffin' her head off.

"Where were you, Bill?" he say, an' his voice it sound to me like he know already.

"I told you," I say to him, but 'fore I can get 'nother word out he say, "Your mother and I want the truth, Bill." Then I say to him if an' he want the truth he best to button up an' let me get my story out. Then I tell him quick 'bout messin' up Forty-four an' havin' to come in on the holiday like an' do me 'nother splenectomy to make up for that. He say fine, but where was I all last night. "I don't know," I tell him.

"Bill," he say, an' his voice sound angry now, "the truth."

"I told you, man, I don't know," I say to him.

"Let me see your arm," he say sudden like, an' I knowed then I had it.

"All right," I say, an' I looks 'way from him like it don't make no diff'rence to me, "so I went an' got high." That when my ma she let herself out a wail I swear they hear it two blocks 'way. Man, she just belt it out, an' the white priest he put his arm 'round her, an' he start tellin' her he go to bat for me an' he straighten everythin' out. I 'bout set to say to him what kind jive you talkin' now, man, when he say, "Where did you get the stuff, Bill?"

"At the school," I tell him.

"Was it Sidney again?" he ask me.

"Course it wasn't no Sidney," I tell him.

"I've repeatedly warned you about Sidney being bad company," he say.

"I told you it ain't Sidney. He a all right cat," I say.

"Who was it then, Bill?" he say, an' his voice it soundin' so sincere like I think maybe the cat he tryin' to sell me a hot watch or somethin'.

"One a the teachers," I say, an' my ma she hear that an' she blow herself off 'nother long wail, you know, the kind that end itself up in like three, four sobs. It one a her worst yells.

"Which teacher?" the priest say.

"I don't know," I tell him, "I only seen him 'round like couple times."

"Oh, sweet Jesus baby," my ma belt out, "the devil he back in my Billy now," an' then she start rockin' back an' forth on the couch.

"Ain't no devil in me," I tell her. "I clean now."

"Oh, sweet Jesus baby," she say, an' I knowed she don't hear nothin' I sayin'.

"Do you have any of the stuff with you now?" the white priest he ask.

"I told you I'm clean," I tell him, an' then I goes on to tell him that I come down from the high at work an' how when I wake up I pour it all down the sink an' I swear off. "Now who was the teacher?" he ask 'gain.

"Look, I ain't jivin' you when I tells you I don't know," I say. "An' I can't see it be his fault nohow. I'm the cat who want the stuff," I tell him.

"Pushers," he say, "the devil's handymen." Now I want to tell you, dogs, he truly say that, an' he say it just like it the most 'portant thing he ever say in his whole life. "The devil's handymen." Now can you believe it? But I don't think he sayin' it so much to me as to my ma. She the one who all the time need the talk like that, you know.

So after a time when they fin'ly get theyselves together they start talkin' how I ain't never goin' to touch the junk 'gain, an' the priest he say to me that if I promise him I truly pour the junk down the sink at work he not goin' to turn me in, an' I thinkin' to myself that if an' you be soundin' like the *po*-lice one more time I goin' to be finish with you. But course I don't say nothin' like that. I just all fulla smiles like an' I yes-fatherin' him right on out the door.

That when my ma she grab me an' she go on an' on 'bout havin' herself a dream a me bein' all rolled up in some doorway dead as can be, an' them angels come down an' take me on up to heaven like an' she say she so grateful to the Jesus baby for deliverin' me back to her. Then she make me get right down with her on my knees in front a that tiny shrine she got in the livin' room, an' she say a quick ten Hail Marys like to the Jesus baby in thanksgivin'. Then she get up an' she hug me 'gain hard like, an' then she wipe her eyes an' she blow her nose an' she move off to the stove.

"I didn't buy us no big turkey, Billy, honey," she say, " 'cause I don't know if you be comin' home. But I got us this here now an' I been keepin' them warm for you," an', man, she open up that oven door an' she take herself out two a them T.V. turkey dinners. Now can you be believin' that, dogs, a T.V. dinner on Thanksgivin'? But it ain't so bad, you know, not once she let me get to it. That s'posed to come after the grace, you know, an' she start prayin' an' her eyes they tight close an' her nose it pointin' straight up to the ceilin'. By the time she finish up with the grace business I halfway through the peas.

I got to get me on the hustle here 'cause the big white doctor he say we goin' to do Forty-fi' early s'afternoon so we can have us a little party like in the lab. He say that the Friday after the Thanksgivin' it ain't s'posed to be worked, but since the big doctor told him that we got to come in today he say we goin' to get the work outa the way fast an' have us some grape. I don't s'pose these cats here they be too partial to the grape, you know, 'cause mosta them they the Scotch whisky kind. That be fine with me, man.

Forty-fi', what you lookin' so sad 'bout? I s'pose you know what we goin' to do to you, all right. Come outa you cage like so's I can take you for you walk. Les see, now, I ask the big white doctor what kind of dog you is an' he say you some kinda Doberman pinschers or somethin'. You a sleek-lookin' dog, all right. Hey, man, what you doin' showin' you teeth at me like that? You soundin' like you 'bout set to take my head off, an' from the size a you I 'spect you could do it without no trouble. But I goin' to fix you good, dog, so's you ain't goin' to be bitin' nobody an' that include me. I take me a bit a this here 'hesive tape an' I goin' to wrap it 'bout you mouth four, fi' times so you ain't got no chance. An' if you tries to take it off with you paws you be in trouble 'cause you pull off all you whiskers right 'long with it. You know, dogs, first time we take you to the lab they ain't never no problem with you. The trouble it come the second time we go. 'Pear to me that you know we goin' to be doin' somethin' ter'ble to you. I 'member Twenny-one dog, an' the second time I take him in there he get so uptight when he see the lab door that he lose control a hisself an' he dump everythin' right there in the hall an' then I had to pick him up an' carry him into the lab. An', man, his heart it poundin' so fast I couldn't even count me the beats. Then all sudden like his heart it just stop while he be in my arms, an' his head it fall over limp like an' he just die from bein' scared. Now you ain't goin' to be like that, Forty-fi' Doberman dog, that I can tell. You goin' to be fightin' all the way. You easy when we takes out you spleen, but you 'members what happen last time an' I 'spect you wants to go down fightin'. But you ain't no problem now with you mouth all taped up like, an' if you mess 'round with the tape I goin' to bust you one good. That ease you up a bit, all right.

Last night with Deeborah I do just like I say I goin' to. Man, right 'way when I walk in the place I can tell she got a feelin' things goin' to be diff'rent from when I tell her I marry up with her. But she start in just the same, you know, with all that boo 'bout me bein' her man an' 'bout how we goin' right 'head an' get us married up. Fin'ly I turns to her an' I says, "Deeborah, this here it as far as I go."

"What you mean, mister?" she say, an' quick like her voice start to get angry.

"Just what I tellin' you," I say. "They ain't goin' to be none a this gettin' married business for me. An' that be all they is to it."

"You just like all the rest of the men," she say, "you got no care for nobody but youself."

"That the way it got to be," I tell her.

"My mother she goin' to throw me out," Deeborah say, an' she start to cry like before, you know. Only this time it don't get to me. I just wait for her to try all the tricks, an' when she done I still sayin' they ain't no way I be gettin' married up. So fin'ly what happen was that Deeborah she come a bit' part an' she get herself more an' more uptight when I tell her that it truly finish for me. That when she stand up next to me an' she slap my face for me. "There," she say very mean like, "that's what you deserves, nigger," an' she slap my face 'gain. Now I tell you one thing, dogs. I gives most any chick one slap at me, but two it seem to do somethin' to me inside, an' 'fore I knowed what happen I busts Deeborah back. What she do is sit down hard like in the chair, an' she put both her hands to her face an' she start to cry. Then I see a bit a blood comin' from her nose an' all sudden I starts to feel sorry for what I done, but then she look up to me an' she say, "You still a nigger," an' I just turns 'round an' I cuts outa that place like quick as I can. I knowed that if an' I stay there a minute more I goin' to let her have 'nother shot, an' that be no good for me.

Forty-fi', man, we done you quick like all right. That heart doctor he don't mess 'round none when he get goin'. Them doctors they in there now doin' theyselves a bit a drinkin', an' they told me to come back when I done puttin' Forty-fi' 'way an' gives him his shot a pen'cillin.

You know, dogs, when that heart doctor he get through messin' up Forty-fi's valves he lay down them instruments an' he tell me to go 'head an' close that dog up an' he watch me for a while an' he make sure it goin' all right. Then when I start to loosen up them *re*-tractors he tell me I doin' fine an' he step back an' he take off his mask. Then he say, "Your ball first and ten, Mr. Peoples," an' I look up to him to ask him what kind a jive talk that is, but he look 'way an' say to the big white doctor if an' he has a cig'rette for him. Big white doctor give him one an' they move off to the corner a the lab an' start talkin'.

So I workin' 'way easy like on Forty-fi' there, an' after a time some a the other doctors who workin' on the project start to come in. They look at what I doin' an' they 'pear to me to be checkin' it all out, an' they all nod like to each other an' to me, an' then they goes an' gets hold a some beakers like an' they starts to pour out the Scotch whisky. Some a them doctors, man, they gots no style. Like the chink doctor who come in right at the beginnin', an' who don't do nothin' but smile all time like he crazy or somethin', an' the other cat who come in with him who sound to me like he a P.R. Neither one a them cats speakin' no kinda way I ever understands, but it 'pear to me from the way things goin' that they all get 'long very nice, you know.

After 'bout a half hour like, just when I pullin' Forty-fi's skin together smooth as you please, the big white doctor he come over to me an' he look down at the job I doin'. I looks 'cross the table to him an' I see his head it outa shape already. "Mr. Peoples," he say to me, an' I dig from the way he sayin' it that if an' he try he make hisself a wino like in no time, "you're doing a splendid job on that animal." I tell him they ain't no real diff'rence 'tween sewin' up a gut an' a chest. "For someone untrained," he go on, "you've got some real good hands. You're even better than some I've seen who've been trained."

"Like you told me," I say to him, "you either has the hands or you don't."

"You know," he say, an' he sway a bit towards the table an' he have to steady hisself on it, "one time I really wanted cardiovascular surgery."

"That right?" I say, but I don't look at him, not when he start talkin' like that. When a cat he start to tell you 'bout somethin' he want an' can't get for hisself you just got to sit back an' be cool 'cause he goin' to be talkin' to you at some length, you know.

"Ever since I was about your age," he say, "surgery was the only thing for me. I really loved it, you know what I mean?" I tell him I shore do. "Being a cardiologist is all right," he say, an' he take hisself a long drink from the glass, "but it's not very exciting. Cardiovascular surgery," he say, an' he roll them words outa his mouth like he in love with them. "That's what I wanted."

"You don't take youself out a bad spleen," I tell him.

"I'm competent," he say, "but a splenectomy's no major procedure. The heart," he start to go on, "that's where . . . " an' he stop hisself an' he take 'nother drink. "What the hell," he fin'ly say, "what the hell," an' he finish off the glass an' he say to me, "Better hurry up with that animal, the hooch is going fast." That when I bring you back in here, dog, an' now I goin' to get me back in there an' have me some free Scotch whisky.

Yeah, dogs, dig it. I cruisin' very nice now. It ain't no high like some junk or somethin', but it all right. An' it diff'rent from a grape high, you know. Grape high it leave you mouth feelin' like you passed an evenin' suckin' on lead pencils, but the Scotch whisky it leave you all cool like an' it last long time too. So what happen it be that I tries to talk with the chink doctor an' the P.R. doctor an' I thinkin' they's all right, you know. That until all sudden I knows they don't hardly speak no English. But the P.R. he speak better than the chink. When I asks him where he from he tell me Brazil. Then I asks him what he doin' here he can't be doin' at home.

"Tecnologia," he say, an' he smile at me just like the chink. "You so *a*-vance here," he say. "I am just learning for just three years, and then I am just going back to my own countree." He smile 'gain an' I smile an' I 'bout set to call him a jive cat when the big white doctor he come up to me with 'nother drink. Well, dogs, my head it buzzin' already but I ain't never said me a no to Scotch whisky. Then very proper like the P.R. cat he cut. First he shake hands with the big white doctor an' he say he got to be gettin' 'long 'cause he got hisself like a lotta work to be doin' 'fore he can go home. An' when he walk 'way from us the big white doctor he say to me, "Poor goddamn bastard, he works his ass off."

"Why he do that?" I asks.

"Dunno," he say, an' his eyes they gettin' a bit slow, you know. "Dedication, I suppose. The bastard spends about fifteen hours in this place every single day."

"That be good overtime," I tell him.

"The doctors don't get any overtime," he say.

"Then he light in the head to be workin' all them crazy hours," I tell him.

"Well," he say, an' he look at me an' he raise his glass, "here's to peace," an' he drink most of it off while I standin' there thinkin' what this cat talkin' 'bout all sudden with the peace boo. "Our history is nothing but a series of lousy racial conflicts," he say. "It's nothing but the white man against the yellow, the white against the black," he go on, an' his mouth curl up funny like he just eat somethin' sour, you know. Then he drink 'gain from the glass, an' I start to wonderin' how come he want to talk 'bout all that business. Only other cat who run off his mouth 'bout it be Millard. So he look down into his glass, an' then his head it pop up an' he say, "The inner city versus the affluent suburbs, that's where the next great war will be." Well, the cat he so far gone that I think I slip him some jive, you know, an' so I say to him, "When you think things they be gettin' goin'?"

"Soon now," he say, "the strings of racial tension are being stretched beyond their limits." An' on an' on he goin' with his boo. But you know, dogs, that jazz it don't get to me like nohow. If an' it did, I spend every minute like Millard figurin' me a way to get whitey. Or I be perm'nent on the junk. But one thing it bother me, an' that when he say, "It's true that the blacks hate the white man for his oppression, isn't it?"

"Ain't nobody oppressin' me," I tell him. "I gettin' 'long all right."

"One-to-one relationships work adequately," he say, "but I know that deep down in every black man there's a hate for the white man. I can feel it." Then he look to me an' he say, "Somewhere deep down you really hate me."

"No," I say to him, "that ain't true," an' you know, dogs, I think from the 'spression on his face I tell him the wrong thing. I truly think he want me to tell him I hate him an' all the rest a the white folk. Maybe what I shoulda done is pull a blade on the cat an' tell him that he best not to walk home 'lone s'evenin' 'cause if an' he do I be there to cut him up. But now I get to thinkin' 'bout it I don't know a nobody I ever truly hate. 'Cept for one time when George he beat me for eight dollars, an' I hate him so bad then I like to cut him up good.

MONDAY

It 'pear to me, dogs, that they just too much goin' on in the world for me to be keepin' track of. Like my weekend it have so much goin' on in it I don't know like where to start. First place I s'pose it be with Forty-fi' right here. He lookin' perfect for the rest a the 'speriments, all right. He just like Forty-three dog there, they both hangin' they heads an' they pantin' like crazy. Lemme just check you out on you 'cision here, dog. First I got to put the tape 'round you mouth or you be tryin' to take off my hand or somethin'. There, now you a fine Doberman pinschers dog like. Hey, man, don't you be jumpin' 'round like that an' turnin' 'way from me so quick. It just goin' to make you 'cision hurt more. Yeah, you lookin' all right now. I thought maybe on Friday I mess up under you armpit there, but it healin' up good on its own. An' I s'pose you be wantin' some water like after the weekend, but you got to go easy on the food, you know.

This weekend my ma she got herself a man. Well, he ain't no real man, y'understand, just some cat who come home with her from the church. Every now an' 'gain my ma she do somethin' like that, you know, an' the cats she bring home they all the time wig out on somethin' or other. It ain't never no junk or nothin' like that, my ma she never touch no cat who mess with his body. But if an' it just be his head that messed up, my ma she take him in in a minute. The cat she bring home this time he all strung out on visions an' the like. He carryin' 'round with him this here old piece a bark like from a tree he see one time he go to Staten Island. He say it got a vision in it, an' if you looks close at it you can see where there this funny outline a somethin' on it. But it ain't no vision, I knowed that. But this cat an' my ma they diggin' it all the way, all the time callin' it a special message from the Jesus baby. An' they puts it down front a the shrine there an' they pray mosta the weekend. Now that fine with me, you know, 'cause then my ma she don't know what I be doin' on the weekend. An' one thing I gots to tell you is what that cat he wear 'bout his neck. He wearin' four, fi' rosaries, a mess a medals, an' two pair a somethin' that look to me like dog tags, an' when he an' my ma they kneel down there an' he undo his shirt an' he take them out I like to bust out laughin'. An' when the cat pray his mouth it goin' crazy an' his eyes they tight close an' he get his whole face all twisted up. Look to me like he get hisself high just prayin'.

I don't know how long the cat he be 'round, but if it like the last one, he be stayin' 'bout a week. It be then my ma she get tired a his boo 'bout the visions an' she bounce him out.

An' just so none a you dogs be gettin' no wrong ideas 'bout my ma let me tell you she got herself three locks on her bedroom door, an' she make sure they all done up tight when she have a cat stayin' over.

Now I gots to stop jivin' you here an' get me to work. Forty-six dog there, you start to get youself together. We goin' to do you today, an' if an' we haves the time we goin' to do Forty-seven, too. . . .

Now what in hell goin' on in here, anyhow? I just out in the hall next to the lab an' I begins to hear you cats start to bark like maybe you goin' crazy. Now what you barkin' 'bout? Hush you up, there! I can't do nothin' with none a yous. You carryin' on like maybe somebody he goin' to cut you up without no anesthetic or somethin'. You there, Number Ninety-three boxer dog, what goin' on with you? All the other cats they look like they all barkin' at you, an' all you doin' is cryin' somethin' ter'ble. Lemme open you cage. *Man,* all them other dogs they like to be tearin' the front a they cages out just to get to you.

Now you sit down here an' give me a look at you. Oh, man, it look to me like we haves us some trouble with you. Boxer dog, honey, you in heat. Stop lickin' my face an' listen to me, dog. I say you in heat an' that ain't no good for you 'cause them doctors they ain't goin' to let you stay in the animal room here 'cause you mess up all the other dogs. See what you doin' to Forty-three an' Forty-fi' there? They haves the bad hearts an' if an' we keeps you 'round they go crazy smellin' you when they can't get to you. I best to check you out with the big white doctor 'cause this business can't be goin' on. Forty-three an' Forty-fi' there they be dead 'fore they s'pose to be if an' this keep up.

Oh, man, for a minute in there with that doctor it look to me like I be quittin' my job on the spot. Big white doctor he a mean mother, all right. I go to the lab where he settin' up things for the heart doctor, an' he hardly don't look at me when I tell him 'bout you bein' in heat. All he do is say to me like over his shoulder, "Dispose of the animal, Mr. Peoples." Now you cats know it don't get to me too much if an' a animal die from the 'speriments 'cause leastways maybe they learn theyselves somethin' from that. But I ain't goin' out an' kill no dog just 'cause it her time for a man. An' I say to that doctor, "You want me to kill that dog for no good reason?"

"Correct, Mr. Peoples," he say, but he ain't looked at me yet.

"But that dog she a healthy dog," I tell him. "They ain't no reason to be killin' her off."

"Get rid of the animal," he say hard like.

"No," I tell him, "I ain't goin' to kill me no good animal." That when he turn 'round an' he ask me how large a dog you is, Ninety-three. "She a very big dog," I tell him. "She like close to forty pounds an' she just right for the 'speriments."

"You're certain as to the size?" he say.

"All the way," I tell him, an' then he ease up a bit on you boxer dog 'cause he know you valu'ble 'cause a how big you is. Then he tell me to take you down to the monkey room an' see if we can borrow us some cage space in there so you can wait it out. An' when you all back together 'gain we get you back for the 'speriments. I be straight with you, boxer dog. If an' that big white doctor had told me that I got to kill you I wouldn't a done it. I woulda walked me outa here an' I never be comin' back. An' that the truth.

George he tole me Deeborah she all right now. On Friday night he cut from the school right 'fore the Self-Wareness boo, an' he go to see Violet. He tell me Deeborah she there, an' it don't 'pear to him that she got no busted nose or nothin'. That good, all right, that make me feel a bit better 'bout the whole thing. But what take off the heat for good is that George say that she got Herbert there with her an' they bein' very close for the whole evenin'. You know, dogs, maybe she jazz with Herbert an' he buy her line that he got to marry up with her. But it don't make no diff'rence to me no more. I done with that boo, an' next chick I mess with she ain't even goin' to know my name.

Now Forty-six he down on the table just fine, an' we waitin' on the heart doctor from the hospital to get hisself over here an' get goin'. But 'fore he get here I got a moment or two to sit me down an' rest up like. I tell you one thing, man, an' that be if an' them cats at the school they ever stops payin' us trainees for goin' they shore ain't goin' to have theyselves no program in like 'bout two minutes. 'Cause that the length a time it take a cat to get hisself down four flights a stairs when he in a hurry. You talks 'bout *jive.* Man, sometimes that school it so full a jive that I don't think I can take it no more an' I got to cut out. Only thing that truly keepin' me there it be that digit.

Like you take what they throw at us on Friday night. Right after George he cut from the classroom, the Self-Wareness cat he come struttin' in sayin', "All right, now, be with it." Then he start to tell us we goin' to have us a *im*-provement session this evenin', an' all us cats we goin' down to the library, which used to be the poolroom, you know, an' there we goin' to hear 'bout what it take to get into the Fire Department. Course he don't ask none a us if we *want* to be in no Fire Department. He just march us all down there all the time thinkin' to hisself it be a good thing for us to know what it take to get in the Fire Department. An' on the way down the stairs I walkin' side a him an' I say to him, "You mind if an' I cut out?" He ask me why an' I tell him I can't get into no Fire Department 'cause a my leg. An' he say to me, no, I got to stay 'cause it be a good thing for me to know. Millard turn 'round on the stairs an' he say, "Yeah, man, it be a good thing for everybody to know once we start torchin' whitey."

"Be with it," Self-Wareness cat say to Millard.

"It's comin'," Millard say back to him cool like. "You wake up one mornin' an' you looks out you window an' you goin' to see nothin' but where the city *was.*"

"Be with it now," Self-Wareness cat say 'gain, an' Millard he turn 'way from him as we gettin' to the bottom of the stairs.

Well, dogs, it right then that I see me the head man a NEW for like the first time. He standin' right outside the library door with the cat from the Fire Department. That there fireman he look so cool in his uniform all pressed an' the metal it shined up good, you know, an' for a minute he look to me like maybe he a marine or somethin'. But the head director cat he somethin' else altogether. He look just like one a them cats I work for when I a messenger down on the Wall Street. His suit it look cool on him, you know, an' it all nipped in just where it s'posed to be, an' I dig a cat who dress cool, no matter what he wear. Course if an' I puts me on one a them gray suits with one a them back flaps hangin' over my ass I be tryin' to jive somebody.

Forty-six dog he dead. But this time it ain't no fault a mine, that for shore. The heart doctor he mess up Forty-six all by hisself. What he do when he get in there on Forty-six's valves was to take hisself a bit too much of a cut with them long curve scissors. Man, the blood it spurt outa Forty-six's heart an' it spray that there heart doctor all over his gown an' some a it even get up on his glasses. I 'bout to bust out laughin' when the heart doctor he throw down them instruments an' he start cursin'. An Forty-six he dead quick like, an the big white doctor he tell me come in here an' get Forty-seven ready quick as I can. I ain't even got no time to take you for a walk, dog, an' that mean that I goin' to have to clean up you mess while the heart doctor workin' on you valves. But I learnin', all right. 'Fore you gets a chance to mess up the table like I goin' to have me the paper towels right under you so when you let go it be easy for me to clean up. Let's go, dog, they waitin' for you.

I sorry for laughin', but the cat who stayin' with my ma he somethin' else. When I come outa my room Sat'day mornin' the two a them they sittin at the table, an' that cat he sayin' like how he goin' to put hisself into a trance for like the whole day an' he want my ma to be prayin' like right 'long with him. Course she like that just fine, an' she tell me I got to be out the 'partment for the whole day. So I look to the cat an' I say to him, "Like what time you figurin' on bein' done with you trance?" He tell me it be in time for some supper an' I tell my ma I be back at like six sharp. She say fine an' I grabs me a Pepsi an' a bag a potato chips an' I cut from the place.

I go over to see George an' that when he tell me 'bout Deeborah an' Herbert. But he tell me he ain't goin' out with me then 'cause he an' Violet they goin' to the Statue Liberty. I hear that an' I thinkin' George he goin' to be in a mess a trouble if an' he keep on with the Violet boo.

So when George he cut out on me I goes over to Sidney an' see if he want to go down to the bar like an' shoot some pool, you know. But Sidney's sister she come to the door an' she stand there blockin' it an' she won't even let me talk to the cat. She say Sidney he workin' on the books an' he goin' to be at it like for the whole day. I tell her I just want to be speakin' with him for like a minute or two an' she say he workin' too hard even for that. You know what I thinkin', dogs, I thinkin' Sidney he jivin' everybody an' he prob'ly sittin' back in some small room high as you please. Then that woman she put her hand on her hip like an' she say to me that Sidney he goin' to be hisself a fireman an' so what I goin' to make a myself. So I say to her, "If an' Sidney he make it all the way to bein' a fireman I go 'round an' I make his first fire for him." An' then I cuts quick like. Sidney's sister she just like Deeborah.

So I ends up goin' down to the bar like 'lone, an' they only a few cats in there. Half a them is still sailin' 'long from the night 'fore, an' half is just startin' to get goin' for the rest a the weekend. I gets me a beer an' goes to the back where two cats shootin' pool, an' right 'way I see that one a the cats is the man I used to work the jewelry stores with. He see me an' he put up his cue an' he come over to me. "Baby," he say, "where you been?"

"Around," I tell him.

"You still in business?" he say.

"No," I tell him, "I got me a job," an' that when he start to laugh at me, an' when he get together he ask me what kinda job I got, an' when I tell him I Spec'men Supervisor he say it sound to him like I a cat who goin' places, all right. I tell him he got the idea, an' then he put his arm 'round my shoulder an' he walk me to the bar an' he buy me a few shots, you know, an' we get to talkin'. "Billy, baby," he say to me, "you the best cat I ever work with, you know."

"How many others you work with?" I ask.

"Six, seven," he say, "but we only made it once. It ain't like it was when you didn't have you no straight job, you know." But I don't take his lead, man, an' I tell him 'gain that I outa the business. "Sure, baby," he say "a cat is smart to get out when he can't do it no more."

"What you mean with can't do it no more?" I say to him. "I could walk into a store an' talk a cat into a corner so fast, man, he never know what hit him." That when he tell me that what he like to hear, you know, an' then he say he know just the place over on Lennox Avenue. He say they a cat over there who got hisself a whole mess a watches in a open case, an' all he need me to do is talk the man outside a the store. I tell him 'gain that I ain't in the business, you know, but he ain't takin' no for a answer, an' after he buy me a few more shots we take off for the store.

Now workin' a store it a very simple thing, you know. I goes in an' starts to look 'round for a few minutes, an' then I takes out my roll an' counts it so the man can get hisself a eyeful. An' then I goes to the front window an' starts to look over what he got there. Then I counts my money an' starts for the door. That when the cat he bite, all right. He say somethin' like, "Need some help?" an' course he seen my bread so he know I want to buy somethin' an' I ain't goin' to rob him or nothin'. "Yeah," I say to the man, "there some kinda ring way over in the corner there an' I can't make it out from here," an' when I opens the door an' goes outside to have a look he follow me like maybe he on a string I pullin'. Well, it my job to keep the cat out there for like a minute or two while my man he slip hisself in there an' put as much in his pockets as he can carry. When he cut out an' I see he clear I just says to the cat, thanks, man, but I got to be gettin' 'long. The whole thing it work only if I good at keepin' the man to myself. An' I very good at that, all right.

Well, I meet him back at the bar an' he countin' over the

watches an' I see that he hit the man for 'bout twenny good watches an' like six, eight a the ones that don't bring nothin'. He count out 'bout ten a the good ones for me, an' he tell me they maybe bring me like a couple hundred dollars. But I tell him I don't want them, an' he say to me like I makin' a big mistake, you know, not bein' in the business no more. So he take them watches an' he put them back in his jacket an' he cut out. So what I goin' to do with ten watches anyway?

Now the lab it all clean up, an' I was just thinkin' in there what I done on Sat'day night. I don't think I could tell no one what I done Sat'day night. If an' I did, an' if an' they be thinkin' I dig that kinda boo they like to laugh me right off the street.

Sat'day it a fine warm day for November, you know, an' the sky it all clear an' the air it feel good to me. An' 'long 'bout fi' or fi'-thirty I gets me a couple a six packs an' I goes up to the roof a the buildin' an' sits me down in a corner like, an' I don't do nothin' for a long time 'cept watch the sky get dark an' I sees the stars come out an' then the moon it come up over the buildin's an' it just hang there for a while all yellow, an' it a pretty sight, dogs, a pretty sight.

Every now an' 'gain I goes up there an' nobody he know 'bout it. An' I don't do nothin' 'portant up there like maybe think big things is goin' to happen to me. That a lotta boo. I just watches things get theyselves set for the night, an' when the sky ain't got nothin' left in it to watch I looks over the edge an' I watch what the peoples in the street they doin' with they evenin'. I seen me lots a things from up there, dogs, everythin' from couple a stickups in the street to a time where in one 'partment 'cross the way I see two cats kissin' each other. But when I up there it don't matter to me what the peoples be doin'. Seem to me that they can be doin' whatever it is that they feels like doin' an' it ain't no business a mine.

Sometimes when I up there I get to thinkin' 'bout you cats in here an' 'bout the school, an' I make sure a one thing when I up there. I don't never decide nothin' for myself when I up there. I try that a couple a times, an' I think I got everythin' figure out, an' when I come down from the roof things they ain't the way I 'magined them when I up there. After that happen couple a times I cut out decidin' things for myself when I on the roof. All I do now is just sit 'round an' watch the peoples doin' what they feels like. I tell you things they work theyselves out that way.

WINTER

MONDAY

Oh, *no,* man, how dumb *can* a cat get? Here I is the Spec'men Supervisor an' I forget what the big white doctor he told me on Friday I got to do this mornin'. An' I went an' give you you food already an' I forgets all 'bout it. Now I gots to collect all you dishes an' get that business started 'fore he come in here an' ask me how it all goin'. This whole thing it goin' to take me like couple a hours, but after I sets it up an' measures out everythin' it be runnin' smooth for like some time to come. An' I sorry to tell you dogs but it goin' to be somethin' you shore ain't goin' to like. Most a you the only fun you haves is when it come time for eatin', but from now on even that it goin' to be like the worst thing ever happen to you. The big white doctor he tell me that like most a you is in good heart failure, but some a you ain't. He say you can tell easy who in heart failure 'cause when you is you got all kinds a fluids collectin' in you belly. He tell me on Friday that one a the best foods we can give you to make you heart work worse it be salt. So I go an' forget to give you the salt this mornin', but I goin' to mix it all up now an' yous can eat 'gain. If an' you able to eat food what mixed half an' half with salt.

So like come on now, Forty-three dog, it time for you to be goin' to the lab to be gettin' you heart 'tack. I don't know how they goin' to be doin' this with but one little cut in you neck, but they say it like a easy thing. An' maybe you just best say so long to the rest a the cats here 'cause it don't 'pear to me you goin' to be comin' back no more.

Now you listen up, dogs, an' take you a good look at Forty-three in his cage there. I don't knows why they want me to bring him back in here when far as everybody know he dead already. He not truly dead, you know, but he might as well be 'cause what that big white doctor he done to him it a dumb thing like all the way. I s'pose they knows what they doin', but from what I just seen in there it don't 'pear to me that they goin' to be gettin' no results from the 'speriments if an' they keep on this way. Oh, yeah, I know they got fine instruments an' all, an' they got this cool deevice an' that there shiny doodad, but some time they just think that's all it take to make youself a great 'speriment. An' when I get Forty-three dog in there all them doctors they thinkin' they goin' to be like a big deal or somethin' 'cause they say what they goin' to do ain't never been done 'xackly this way 'fore. So if an' that be the case why don't they do theyselves some thinkin' 'fore they start messin' 'round.

What happen was that I get Forty-three down all cool like, an' I make the cut in his neck right 'long side his carotid artery. Then the big white doctor he take this here long shiny 'luminum doodad thing what got two openin's in one enda it. One opening it for the balloon an' the other it for injectin' the tiny plastic beads into that there dog's heart. The balloon it for closin' off the aorta while the beads they go to the coronary artery an' give Forty-three dog there his heart 'tack. Everythin' it go cool like, 'cept the big white doctor he don't leave the balloon thing blown up long 'nough, an' them little plastic beads they get outa Forty-three's left ventricle an' they go with the blood all over his body. An' you know what happen, man? Some a them beads they go right up that dog's other carotid artery right into Forty-three's brain. So what happen is that 'steada givin' Forty-three dog a heart 'tack right there on the table, they think what they done was give him a stroke.

TUESDAY

Forty-three dog there, it don't seem to me that you got youself much of a chance. I know you 'live, but you shore ain't doin' no movin'. You eyes they all right, they goin' back an' forth, an' you ears they prickin' up now an' 'gain, but the resta you ain't movin' like nohow. Lemme into this here cage an' have a look at you. Oh, man, you in bad shape, all right. Them doctors they shore 'nough done theyselves a job on you. Look to me like you paralyzed. I don't know what we goin' to do with you now. You ain't no good for the 'speriments no more, leastways I can't see where you be any good, but you still ain't dead an' I can't go puttin' you in the incinerator while you still 'live. What I goin' to do is like just let you lie there till some doctor he come in an' tell me that you can be given some kinda medicine or somethin' that take you right outa the picture. Maybe you like a little water first, huh, Forty-three dog? Here, I bring you dish up under you mouth an' I hold you head. You tongue there it ain't workin' so good, you know, but if an' I holds you head just right you get a bit. That's a good dog, all right. Now don't you go worryin' none, 'cause Mr. Peoples here he goin' to take care a you till you time come.

Now I got to get these here cages in shape quick like 'cause the cat room it got a big delivery comin' in early an' I got to be finish with this an' out on the platform in 'bout a half a hour.

Just one thing you got to know, Forty-fi' Doberman pinschers dog over there, an' that be the fact that s'afternoon you goin' to be gettin' you heart 'tack, an' I shore hopes for you sake that they don't mess up like they done with Forty-three dog here.

Self-Wareness cat he say that they a chance the state it goin' to be closin' down NEW. But they ain't goin' to be doin' that 'fore I get me my G.E.D., which is what you s'posed to call the 'xamination diploma if you wants to be official like. G it stand for graduate, an' the E an' the D stand for 'quiv'lancy diploma. Me an' George an' Sidney an' Millard we all goin' down tomorrow to N.Y.U. to take us that there 'xamination. Then when we gets it we maybe cut all that NEW business short an' move right on to the City University.

But anyway, what they say is that NEW it goin' to have itself a inspection like top to bottom, an' the Self-Wareness cat say they goin' to be some shakeups, all right. An' I s'pose they should be, you know, 'cause they a mess a things wrong at NEW. Cats gettin' paid every week an' they don't even come, just some friend he sign for them, an' other cats who be there all the time they don't get nothin'. An' you know what that do, man, it send a lotta the cats back into the street 'cause they don't collect no digit. You have a man in an' you don't give him no digit you in trouble. Like already half the cats they cut from the place, an' where we have us like fifteen, sixteen in the class when we all sign up they only like six now. An' I knowed all 'long that the teachers they s'posed to be takin' 'tendance in each class, but they never done it regular. Miss Beverley, the readin' lady, she do it regular, but the math'matics man he say he don't care who there, an' the Self-Wareness cat he say the director man he don't know how to run the place from the beginnin'. I tell you one thing that for shore, an' that be if an' I be runnin' this here animal room the way they runnin' NEW everybody he be in trouble.

Forty-three dog, I just got the word on you. You paralyzed all right, an' you time it ain't goin' to be long now. I hopes you done them doctors some good so Forty-fi' Doberman pinschers dog over there he have hisself a heart 'tack an' not no stroke. Now I got to put you to sleep, Forty-three dog, an' I shore don't like doin' that. But it best for you, you know. Now you takes it easy here while I slips you the needle an' lets you have this bottle a Nembutal. You ain't goin' to be feelin' nothin', Forty-three shepherd dog, it be just like you goin' to sleep real fast an' they ain't goin' to be no pain to it or nothin'. There, the needle it in you arm vein here, an' now I just take off the rubber strap an' lets the Nembutal run in slow like. It shore ain't goin' to take much to send you on you way, dog, 'cause I see you eyes they glassin' up already, an' you tongue it stickin' out just a bit 'tween you teeth, an' you beginnin' to lose control a everythin'. Now I takes the needle out an' I press down a bit on you arm so you don't go bleedin' all over the cage. But you ain't bleedin' at all, dog, 'cause you dead now from just the first bit a Nembutal.

Forty-fi' Doberman pinschers dog, what you growlin' at?

Now I got just two things to do here 'fore we takes Forty-fi' in for his heart 'tack. I got to take old Mother here an' separate her from her pups an' get them on down to the diet 'speriment room, an' then I got to get Mother started up on her salt food. Everyone a you dogs count, you know, an' I sorry for takin' them 'way from you but they valu'ble 'cause they free.

Forty-fi' Doberman pinschers dog, you make them doctors in there like very happy, you know, an' you lookin' to me like you hurtin' in the chest more 'an just a bit. Man, do you have youself a bad heart now. You know you have like 'bout six, seven heart 'tacks while you on the table. Yeah, I spect you knowed it 'cause a the way you look now. You 'wake already an' you lyin' there so still 'cause a the way you hurtin', but you should know one thing an' that be the way you please up them doctors. When the whole thing it over an' you still lyin' there on the table them doctors they smackin' one 'nother on the back an' they sayin' it work just like it s'posed to, an' the big white doctor he tell the big man that his whole idea it work perfect. The big man he tell the big white doctor that the procedure it goin' to run like clockwork all the way now an' they goin' to have 'xackly the results they started out for. An' you know what I thinkin' dog? I thinkin' who care? Lookit you here at the end a you time, dog, just lyin' an' waitin', an' I tell you one thing, man, you best die now 'cause if an' you don't tomorrow you goin' right back in there for like all them big deal drugs an' whatever else it seem to them they want to put in you body. Only one good thing 'bout tomorrow, dog, an' that be they don't put no long 'luminum tube down you carotid artery. That business it all over an' done with an' they ain't no way them doctors they goin' to cut you up no more. But they shore goin' to put a mess a stuff in you body.

One thing you got to know an' that be they takin' bets on whether or not you be 'live tomorrow, an' even though they want you 'live bad, they bettin' 'gainst it like two to one. Now if an' I had me but a little a that action I clean up them mothers good, man, 'cause I know you dog, an' I know you tough, heart 'tacks or not. But they one thing I don't like 'bout this business here, an' that be you the only dog who ever give me a hard time. But even with that, what I don't like is to see you with all you fight gone.

Like I told you, dogs, I ain't goin' to be comin' in tomorrow 'cause me an' George an' Sidney an' Millard we goin' down to N.Y.U. to take us that there G.E.D. 'xamination, an' they say it take a few hours, you know, so I told the big white doctor I goin' an' I ain't comin' in tomorrow. He say it okay for me to be goin' to take the 'xamination an' he say he wish me luck. He ask me when I know my score an' I tell him they be sendin' it over to NEW an' I find out there. Then he say to me, "You know, if you pass the exam and get your high school diploma they'll raise your pay." An' I tell him I be needin' a raise 'cause when I gets me my G.E.D. I goin' to cut from the NEW business like fast, man, 'cause I gots a whole lotta things I can be doin' with my evenin's, you know. Like I ain't had me no jazzin' in like four, fi' weeks now, an' my head it startin' to feel like it put on backwards or somethin'. Every evenin' Miss Beverley she lookin' better an' better, an' if I don't get me a piece a some action soon I goin' to jump her for shore.

Now lemme just have a last look here at you, Forty-fi' dog, an' see how you is. I think maybe you make it through tomorrow, you know, an' I goin' to put you water here so's you can have you a drink in the night without standin' up an puttin' you sore neck through the hole in the cage. Now all you gots to do is raise up you head a bit an' lap from the side.

WEDNESDAY

I know I ain't s'posed to be here, man, an' I almost took me the day off anyhow. You know what you got to do to take you that there G.E.D. 'xamination? You gots to make a '*point*ment with the lady down at N.Y.U. A '*point*ment, man, like maybe you goin' to the doctor's or somethin', an' it s'posed to be at least a day ahead a time. So we all goin' tomorrow for shore.

An' I tell you NEW it in trouble all right. They ain't even no classes last night 'cept in the beginnin' when we s'posed to have Miss Beverley, an' like I told you I could use me a hour a just lookin' at her. So I in my seat gettin' all set to watch her come walkin' in the door an' swing her ass so nice 'cross the front a the room, you know, when 'round the corner a the door come the Self-Wareness cat, an' he walkin' fast an' his head it so low it look like he followin' some kinda bug 'cross the floor. When he get to the front a the table he smack his fist in his hand an' he say, "Be with it, now, be with it. I got to speak with you men." So we all shut up quick like an' the Self-Wareness cat he look 'round to all a us. "Be with it," he say 'gain, but you know he ain't thinkin' 'bout what comin' outa his mouth. "Classes are going to be suspended," he fin'ly say.

"I goin' to get paid same as usual?" Sidney ask.

"Same as usual," the Self-Wareness cat say, an' Sidney he ease back in his chair so cool like an' he tune the cat out.

"What's up, brother?" Millard ask from the back.

"NEW was audited today by the state," Self-Wareness cat say, "and there's some difficulty with the attendance records."

"They closin' us down," George say, an' the Self-Wareness cat he turn on George like he 'bout to take his head off. He curl up his mouth like he very angry an' he say to George, "They wouldn't dare. This is the only program of its kind in Harlem, and the state people know that if they close us down they're going to have us in the street in like ten minutes. They do that we're going to torch us a few shops, all right."

"Hey, baby," Millard say with a big old smile, "you startin' to see how it got to be done."

"I say *if* they close us down," Self-Wareness cat say, an' you can see he gettin' uptight 'bout bein' so angry. So he get hisself together quick like, an' he tell us not to go startin' no rumors or nothin' 'bout NEW gettin' closed down.

"So why ain't we havin' no class s'evenin'?" I asks.

"Because the teachers have got to revise six months of attendance records and get them all in order so we can be refunded by the state."

"When you know if you be gettin' refunded?" George ask.

"We'll get it, all right," Self-Wareness cat say.

"You goin' to fix you up some nice lookin' books?" George say, an' the Self-Wareness cat he look down to George an' he start to let out a big old smile, but then he cut it short.

So then after a bit the cat take 'tendance an' while he doin' that George say to him, "Me an' my friends here, we goin' down to take us that there G.E.D. tomorrow."

"You made an appointment already?" Self-Wareness cat ask.

"What kinda jive you talkin'?" Sidney say, an' that when the Self-Wareness cat he tell us that you got to make youself a 'pointment like a day ahead a time.

"We make it tomorrow an' we go on Thursday," George say.

"That's all right for you," Self-Wareness cat say, "but who's going with you?" That when we all puts up our hands, you know, an' the Self-Wareness cat he tell George an' Millard that he think it be all right for them to try for the G.E.D., he think they haves a chance, but when he get to Sidney an' me he say he don't think it a good idea for us to be takin' the thing. "Why you say that, man?" Sidney ask.

"Because it costs ten dollars every time you take it," Self-Wareness cat say, "and I don't think you're ready to pass it yet."

"What make you think so?" I ask him, an' I tell you I gettin' angry with the man.

"I've talked with the other teachers and they don't think you're quite ready yet," he say.

"Well, it be my ten dollars," I tell him.

"I didn't say you couldn't take it," Self-Wareness cat say, "but when you do don't expect to pass it the first time."

"Jive cat," Sidney say to me as the Self-Wareness cat pick up the paper an' cut from the room.

"Don't you be worryin' none," I tell Sidney, "we goin' to be passin' us that there 'xamination," an' he give me some palm an' we leave the classroom.

It right then that Millard he turn 'round to Sidney an' he say, "Could you be usin' youself some dust for the G.E.D.?" Sidney's face it light up fast an' he tell Millard he shore could. "You want to work for it?" Millard say.

"I ain't goin' to steal it," Sidney say, an' he say it proud like he a fireman already, you know.

"Don't you worry none," Millard say, "you be workin' for it, all right." Then Millard he turn to me an' George, an' he ask if we want the same. George tell him he in whatever Millard got in mind, an' I tell Millard that I don't need no bread 'cause like I got me a job, an' Millard tell me I can take it or leave it an' I tell him I take it.

Seem that at night Millard have hisself a job, you know, an' he work at night 'cause the kinda job he got you don't go workin' at in the daytime. Millard he in the movin' business.

Big white doctor he a mean mother, all right. When we take Forty-fi' outa here an' back to the lab that dog he still got some fight left after all, an' when he make a little growlin' noise at the big white doctor that man just turn 'round on him quick like an' he kick him right on the point a his chin. Doberman pinschers dog he fall over an' he whinin' like crazy an' his paws they both come up an' they start to rub his eyes like maybe he can't see nothin'. But then after a while the dog he just lie there an' he don't move or do nothin' while I puttin' the needle into him, an' he go down easy as you please.

Now for you, Mother. You been havin' youself a fine vacation like with you pups, but they all gone now to the diet 'speriment room, an' you gots to get ready for you first heart operation s' afternoon. Heart doctor he comin' over special from the hospital just to do you, an' I gots to get you prepped an' opened up so the heart doctor he can just walk in an' mess up you valves an' walk out.

Millard he really a all right cat, you know, an' he doin' hisself a good business movin' cats 'round the city like.

What happen was that we all cut from NEW easy like an' we follow Millard down the street. None a us ever get close with Millard 'cause he like four, fi' years older an' he seen hisself a lot a what goin' on. But he cool an' he don't talk lest he got somethin' he want to say, an' when he say somethin' mosta the time he know what he talkin' 'bout. So we go 'bout eight blocks, you know, an' Millard he turn 'round to us an' he say we got to wait for him where we is while he go an' get hisself a truck. Then he turn 'way from us an' he go 'bout a half block more an' then we see him look 'round while he standin' under a street light an' when he see they ain't nobody comin' he quick like hop a fence an' dis'pear. "I shore hopes Millard ain't goin' to steal no truck," Sidney say.

"He just goin' to borrow one," George say. "He always just borrow one an' bring it back when he finish for the night."

"I ain't goin' to get caught on no stolen truck," I tell George.

"Be cool," he say to me, "that ain't the way it is," an' then he go on to tell us that one a Millard's sergeants from the army he get out 'long with Millard an' he work in the truck rental lot an' he always leave a set a keys in the office for Millard for when he got some cat to move. But the sergeant he cover hisself an' he tell Millard that if an' he get caught goin' over the fence or when he in the office the sergeant he ain't even goin' to know him. But when Millard in the truck everythin' all right 'cause he got the papers he need an' everythin' if he get stop by a cop.

So like after a few minutes here come Millard, sweet as you please, drivin' his truck outa the lot an' he blink the lights a couple a times an' we go down to where he is an' George he get in the front an' me an' Sidney get in the back. I tell you, man, it cold in the back a that truck, all right. Millard he drive very slow down to Hundred Twenny-fifth Street an' then he cut over to the river an' we starts headin' for the East Side. Me an' Sidney we start to see them cool buildin's where the rich white folk live an' I tell you I start to get uptight, an' I thinkin' to myself like whatever is Millard doin' down here. A colored cat he can't even show hisself down here at night or he be picked up by the *po*-lice inside a two minutes. But I figurin' Millard he know that, an' he got to know what he doin'. He take a turn onto Sevenny-second Street an' he go over 'bout two blocks an' he stop the truck in front a one a them new 'partment houses they got down there. It one fine place to live, all right. It got one a them awning things that come from the front door all the way out to the street, an' Millard say that they got a doorman an' everythin' who work 'round the clock.

So when we get outa the truck Millard he say that we got to wait right where we is while he go in an' check out the job. An' he say that we ain't to be messin' 'round with nothin' or nobody 'cause whitey he blow a whistle if an' he just *see* a black brother 'round his house at night. He say if we stay by the truck we got us a place we s'posed to be an' no pig he goin' to run us off from a good job when we ain't done nothin'. Then he go into the buildin' an' he talk with the doorman for a few seconds an' then he dis'pear. But soon as Millard he outa sight Sidney he light up a cig'rette an' he lean back 'gainst the truck cool like an' he say, "See them two white chicks comin'?"

"Oh, yeah," George say, "that all right stuff."

"Come on, man," I say to Sidney, "you start messin' 'round you goin' to blow the whole thing."

"Be cool," Sidney say, an' he start to walk 'cross the sidewalk to the two white chicks. "Evenin'," Sidney say nice like, an' quick he snatch off his beret an' he roll it up in his hands like he meek or somethin', an' he bend his body over a bit like he old. Them chicks they slow up but they don't stop an' Sidney he got to keep walkin' with them while he reachin' inside his coat pocket. Then he say, "I just a poor boy from the slums a Harlem, ma'am, an' I wonderin' if an' I could gives you a dime for a cup a coffee," an' he reach out his hand like he want to give them somethin', an' they turn 'way from him fast an' start on up the street. Sidney he almost bust up, you know, an' when they a few feet past him he call out, "So how you like it, honey? If you ever needs youself a good time I the man to see. Ain't no white boy ever treat you to what I packin'." But I don't 'spect the chicks they hear the last part, 'cause Sidney he too busted up laughin' to yell it after them. Sidney he stagger back to the truck, an' George he laughin' too an' he give Sidney the palm all the way. "Now you done it," I say to Sidney, "here come the *po*-lice." An' Sidney he look 'round to see this here prowl car pullin' up right 'long side a the truck. "Be cool," George say, "we ain't done nothin'." When the cop he roll down the window I see right 'way he a big mother, all right, an' when he open the door a the car to get out I see he got his stick all set like he goin' to be usin' it. "What's the trouble here, boys?" he say, but his voice it somethin' else, man. He got a voice that sound like some canary or somethin' it so high an' squeaky. An' Sidney he look from George to me an' then back to the cop, an' he say, "Nothin', *sir,*" but Sidney he say it in the same high voice that the *po*-liceman got. That start the trouble right there. The cop he put the end a his stick in Sidney's belly an' he say, "Don't mock me, boy."

"No, sir," Sidney say in his real voice, an' I tell you he say it fast, all right.

"Now what are you doing all the way down here?" the *po*-liceman he say, an' he keep the club right in Sidney's belly.

"We waitin' for to be movin' some man in there," I tell the cop, an' I pointin' to the truck.

"And what was the altercation with those young women?" he ask Sidney.

"Nothin,' sir," Sidney say, an' then he look down to the stick, "just *nothin'*. They white ladies an' I don't go messin' 'round with no white ladies."

"That's a good idea," the *po*-liceman he say, an' he ease up a bit on the end a the stick. It right then Millard he come outa the buildin' an' he walk right up behind the cop an' he tap him on the shoulder. The *po*-liceman he turn 'round slow like, an' Millard say, "What you doin' there with my man?" Millard he angry. "State your business here," the cop say.

"I got a right to be here," Millard say.

"Only if you've got a reason," the man say.

"Now you listen up, officer pig," Millard say, "I don't got to give you no reason for nothin'."

"You call me pig once more and I'm going to split your skull for you," the *po*-liceman say, an' he take his stick an' he pull it up so he holdin' it with both his hands 'cross his chest. Right then the cop who drivin' the car he get out an' stand by the car. "The rest of the boys here are just out for some fun," the *po*-liceman say to Millard, "but it looks to me like you could use some trouble."

"I ain't lookin' for trouble from nobody," Millard say, "but if it come my way I take care a it."

"Don't you try to provoke me, *boy*," the cop say, an' I see Millard lose control a hisself for like a second or two. But then he cool down very quick like an' he say to the cop, "Number one, I'm not a boy, an' number two is I'm not goin' to swing on you first. You want to lay open my head, you go 'head an' do it, but it goin' to be with my hands right here at my side."

Well, it right there that the cat we s'posed to be movin' he come out the buildin' an' he ask what the trouble is, an' soon as the cop check us out with him he say everythin' all right an' we ain't done nothin' wrong. Then the white cat he go back into the buildin' an' the cop he turn to walk back to the patrol car. But 'fore he leave he swing his stick what only like 'bout two, three inches an' he catch Millard right on the upper part a his arm where the muscle it go over the bone there. I see Millard he in some kinda pain, all right, but he don't show the cop how much he hurtin'. All he do is slow like he say to the cop, "When I start the war, pig man, I goin' to start it with you," an' then he turn an' we follow him into the buildin'.

Mother, you have youself a bad time in there, but I think you be pullin' through all right now. When that heart doctor he come over from the hospital he in a awful mess, an' he swearin' an' cursin' his head off 'bout some nurse who mess up one a his patients. Then he seen how I open up you chest, an' he start treatin' me like I the nurse or somethin'. What I done was like go into you chest one rib too high, you know, an' that make it diff'cult for the heart doctor to get to the valves he want to mess up. An' course he in a big hurry like always an' you have you heart stop like three times on the table. Last time it stop it take like maybe a few minutes to get it goin' 'gain. They say you in some danger a not havin' no kinda brain left, but they say that if you makes it through the night you be okay for the resta the 'speriments.

Now I want the resta you dogs to know like one thing, an' that be I gettin' worried 'bout you 'cause only Ninety-three she eatin' her food. Ain't none a you cats touch nothin' for near three days now. That salt it ain't that bad, you know. Oh, man, how I goin' to get you to eat? Maybe if I puts a little layer a the good food over the top you take youself a big old mouthful an' be into it 'fore you know what's happenin'. Here, I try that now. Sevenny-nine dog, you be the first. I puts me down a little layer a the good chow an' see if it cover up the smell a the salt. Now I puts you dish back here an' les see. Dig, man, it workin', all right. Sevenny-nine dog, there, you take youself a big old mouthful an' then you back for a second 'fore the salt taste it get to you. Now you coughin' a bit an you gaggin', but you eatin' an' that what count. Now that ain't so bad, Sevenny-nine dog. Here, I gives you a bit more 'cause the big white doctor he say you can haves all the food with the salt an' all the water you want. Now I just move me down the line an' I do the same with the resta you, an' you be eatin' good soon. But I goin' to have to keep me on the hustle here with you water dishes 'cause you all time goin' to be thirsty with all the salt you gettin'.

So we move the white cat into a slick little place, an' when we done he give Millard the money an' he divide it up an' give us like fifteen dollars apiece. Sidney get the bread in his hot little hand an' he say right 'way he goin' lookin' for some grass, an' when I tell him that he be in trouble if an' he get outa shape for the 'xamination he say for me not to worry 'cause he nail that down easy like. Then he ask George if an' he want to go with him an' George say he s'posed to see Violet, but then he say he been doing everythin' she say for like too long a time now an' it do her some good to sit up all night waitin' for him. He goin' with Sidney. Well, man, I tell them I shore ain't goin' to be messin' 'round now when I 'bout set to get my G.E.D., but then Sidney an' George they get on me like how I gettin' uptight with the school business, an' 'fore you know it, man, all three a us is cruisin' 'long one them streets down there an' we all set for some cool action, all right.

George say he been down to the Village like a few times 'fore, an' he say he know a bar that be just right for us. George he right 'bout that all the way an' we ain't standin' at the bar for more an' 'bout two minutes 'fore these two white chicks come in. They start to pass us an' Sidney he lift his beret an' he say, "Evenin'," an' the two chicks right 'way they stop an' we all start talkin'. Well, that ain't 'xackly true, y'understand, 'cause like I don't say nothin'. George an' Sidney they do all the cool talkin' 'cause they out to have theyselves a white chick. I tell you one thing, man, an' that be white chicks they ain't for me. When I looks at a white chick, man, like nothin' happens to me inside. Yeah, I sees where they pretty an' where they set to go for a cat, but for some reason or 'nother I gets turned off. But if you gives me a dark-colored chick, man, I set to let her have the business in like 'bout a minute. That what speed up my motor. But George an' Sidney they sometimes go for the pale stuff, an' when they do they go big. Sidney he go for anythin' that a girl, an' one time I see him try to make it with a chink, an' that really turn me off. But Sidney he be the kind what stick his 'quipment in anythin' so long as it be warm.

So we all standin' there talkin', an' after a couple a minutes the two chicks they kinda lean into the bar an' begin to get close with George an' Sidney. George he buy some shots an' beer, you know, an' the chicks they help theyselves. "Like you hip to this place?" one a the chicks she say to George. She a cute little blond thing, you know, but she a bit heavy. Somehow George he like the heavy chicks. "Yeah," George he say cool like, "this a all right place." Then he throw off a shot, an' he say, "I comes in 'bout every week."

"You from 'round here?" I asks her.

"We got a pad about three blocks from here," she say. "We've been there ever since we split from N.Y.U."

"Why you do that?" George say.

"It's all a drag, baby," she say, "squares and everything. Come on, man, you know what I mean."

"No," George tell her, "but I s'pose I be findin' it out when I goes."

"Man," she say, "college is nothing but the biggest deadline anybody's ever had." She take a sip a the beer an' she say, "Like rules, man, all the time the squares hit you with rules. So when we couldn't take it anymore Pax and me we split."

"Pax you friend here?" George ask. Little blond chick nod an' she say that ain't really her name but when they split from N.Y.U. she start to call herself that. "What you call youself?" George ask.

"Speed Queen," she say.

"You fly on that junk?" George say.

"Forever," she tell him.

"Speed it ain't no good," George say.

"I love it," she say to George, an' she reach in her pocket an' she take out three pills an' she pop them quick like.

"You crazy to be on the speed," George say, "it better to be on the junk."

"Ain't no good to be on the junk, neither," I tell her.

"Who cares?" she say, an' she take 'nother drink a the beer.

That when I look over to see Sidney gettin' 'long very nice with Pax. Sidney he got his arm 'round her waist, an' she pulled in close to him, an' Sidney he got his hand all the way down the back a her jeans right up to the thumb. Sidney he don't waste no time. Speed Queen she see this an' then she start to lean on George, an' she ask him if an' we all want to come up to their pad. George he say that sound good to him, an' Speed Queen she lean over an' whisper somethin' to Pax, an' then all sudden we headin' for the door an' I ain't even got me no time to throw down the last shot.

Well, man, they pad is 'xackly that. Ain't nothin' but this here big old room above a drug store, you know, an' they six, seven mattresses in there an' a little stove to cook you up somethin' on. An' all over the walls they got these here big poster things a all the cats they think is cool. The toilet it in the hall. But the place it got plenty a heat, an' when we gets inside we all takes off our coats an' sits down on the mattresses 'gainst the wall. Pax she break out some grass, an' it 'bout the best grass I ever had me, you know, an' Pax she get high like right off. Only I thinkin' she puttin' on a act 'cause no grass it get to you like that. She sit down with Sidney an' they start to go at it very easy like. Speed Queen she take herself some pills an' she offer George an' me some. We tell her we don't mess with nothin' like that, an' then she sit herself down in front a George an' she take this little box out a her jeans an' she put it down right in front a George. It a box fulla pills an' she start poppin' one right after 'nother. When George ask her what she takin', she say she don't know, it a kick not to know what goin' to hit you. Speed Queen she be dead soon.

After a bit Sidney an' Pax they get up an' they go to a corner a the room an' they turns out the light over there an' it dark 'nough so's a cat can't see what they doin', but after a while I hear Sidney laughin' an Pax she let herself out a giggle or two an' then they awful quiet for a long time. An' George he lyin' on top a Speed Queen right in front a me. But Speed Queen she don't know nothin' 'bout what goin' on. She not 'xactly out cold, you know, but she flyin' so high she don't know what happenin' to her. An' when George he see that he ain't goin' to get nothin' offa her that he goin' to like, he just roll off her. "Lookit this, man," he say to me, "she so fulla pills she don't know what her body doin'. That ain't no fun, man," he say. Me an' George we the same way 'bout that business. A chick she ain't worth jazzin' les she have her mind on what she doin'.

So George he startin' to get hisself agitated 'bout not gettin' nothin' from the chick, an' when Sidney come outa the corner George ask him if maybe Pax she take him on too. Sidney say he don't know, but he shore finish for the night. Right then George he dis'pear into the corner an' Sidney he look down at Speed Queen an' he shake his head an' he sit down. "From the way she carryin' on over there," Sidney say to me, "you be next, man."

"Not me, baby," I tell him, an' that be the truth. When I haves me a chick I the only one who does. Leastways I the first one who does. I ain't never had me no seconds offa no chick an' I shore ain't goin' to start with thirds. But you know, now I get to thinkin' 'bout it I mighta had me a piece a that stuff if an' my mind it a been on what goin' on. But after 'bout a hour there even the grass don't give me no real good high. An' that 'cause the whole time my head it ain't with the action. All the time I really thinkin' 'bout the G.E.D. an' how good it goin' to be to nail that down. I figure I put in my time, you know, an' now I set for that there 'xamination.

That when I cut out. I have 'nough, y'understand, an' the whole business it ain't makin' no sense to me. My head it on the G.E.D. like I said, an' when I cut from that place right 'way I glad to be outside. That 'cause all sudden like it very pretty in the street, you know, an' that 'cause it snowin'. An' man, didn't it snow. I walk me a whole mess a blocks in it just 'cause it look so nice just comin down 'round the street lights an' everythin'. But s'mornin' it just a mess in the street, an' the buses an' cars they splashin' everybody. But when it comin' down, man, snow it a all right thing.

FRIDAY

Man, but the big white doctor he crazy. He just 'nother crazy white cat, far as I concern. Just 'cause I ain't in yesterday he think he goin' to do everythin' by hisself. Man, I don't 'spect that cat can pee by hisself from the way he mess up yesterday. Just lookit that there, fi' empty cages. Sixty-two right up through Sevenny dog, an' they all dead. Fi' good dogs an' that mother went an' killed them all just 'cause he one stupid cat. An', man, he in trouble with the big doctor, all right. When I come in s'mornin' I hear the big doctor yellin' his head off at him, an' the only thing I thinkin' is that he don't yell loud 'nough. I listenin' in the hall outside the big doctor's office, you know, an' I find out that the big white doctor he mess up on Sixty-two when he give him the Nembutal 'cause he try to do it by hisself. Man, only cat 'round here that can give a dog his Nembutal all by hisself is me, an' the big white doctor he shoulda knowed that. Then when he give Sixty-two dog the first bit a Nembutal an' the dog he go down, the big white doctor he keep on givin' him more an' more just to make sure he stay down. Sixty-two dog he dead 'fore he ever get on the table. Then the dumb mother he take Sixty-four dog an' he don't give 'nough Nembutal to him an' the dog he wake up on the table an' the big white doctor he have to fight with him to give him 'nother few cc's. Only while he holdin' Sixty-four down his elbow it hit the switch on the breathin' machine an' turn it off. Big white doctor don't realize what he done till the ECG it ain't showin' no more heartbeat. An' Sixty-eight dog he bleed to death 'cause the big white doctor he cut right through the carotid artery. That all I heard, man, an' that 'nough. Big doctor he say if an' the big white doctor he try that business 'gain he goin' to make sure personally that he never get no money for researchin' on his own. Big white doctor he hear that he all sudden one meek mother, all right. We gots us 'nough you dogs to get done with what we tryin' to prove, but we ain't got 'nough so we can be messin' 'round with you. Each one a you got to count.

Oh, man, that lab is like the biggest mess I ever seen. They blood all over, an' it look to me like it ain't never goin' to get cleaned up. Man, they even dog hair an' blood on the walls. Look like the big white doctor he run all over the lab chasin' them dogs just tryin' to get a needle into them. I don't 'spect we goin' to be doin' any 'speriments today. It goin' to take me like three, four hours just to get that place lookin' like a lab 'gain. But 'fore I get to that I got to take me some time here to clean out you cages nice like, an' from the mess you make in there it goin' to take me some time to do that, all right. This place it got to start lookin' like a animal room 'gain.

So, with the hose an' the 'monia business an' I be tellin' you 'bout how I nail me down that there G.E.D. 'xamination yesterday. Wednesday night, man, I go to the school, an' Sidney an' George an' Millard they all there an' we haves us a talk with Miss Beverley 'bout what to 'spect on the readin' part a the 'xamination. She tell us to look for just what they give us. They a part where you got to match up a mess a words an' after that you got to do the opposite with them. An' then they a readin' part just like some a the stuff Miss Beverley give us in them readin' books. Only they harder, man, an' some a them they like to turn a cat's head 'round. This here one I 'member it a long mother an' you s'posed to answer like six, seven questions when you done readin' it. Reason I 'members it 'cause I have to read it like a few times, you know, an' it a whole lotta boo 'bout how a television set is s'posed to work. I don't mean 'bout how you turn it on an' what kinda dials make the picture do this an' that. They write theyselves a big old essay 'bout how the mother s'posed to be workin' *in*side it where all them tubes an' wires is. An' they go on at some length 'bout this here transistor jazz an' I don't s'pose I done too well on that question, but mosta the others I knowed I nail down.

An' we seen the math'matics man on Wednesday night, too, an' he say he think Millard he be the only one who pass. Just like that, man, right outa his mouth come them words. He tell George that he think he got a outside chance, an' he tell me an' Sidney that we pass if an' we very lucky. I ask him why he say that, you know, 'cause he makin' me very angry sayin' me an' Sidney ain't got no chance, an' he tell me they's too many a them word problems for me to get the number right I need to pass. An' I tell him that maybe I have some difficulty with some a them word problems, but I shore goin' to get all them problems that has to do with the dec'mals an' fractions. He say that all right, but he don't think I make it 'cause after them word problems on the 'xamination they start throwin' the algebra an' geometry at you. Well, I tell him that I still goin' to make it an' he say he hope I do. But I tell you one thing, man, an' it be that the math'matics man he know what he talkin' 'bout when it come to that 'xamination. They a few problems in the beginnin' on the addition an' subtraction boo, an' then it move off quick like an' you gets hit with like three, four problems on the dec'mals an' fractions. Then the whole 'xamination it get diff'rent from what I ever seen. All sudden it like I readin a book 'steada takin' me a math'-matics test. But the first few a them word problems they gives you they easy like. They the ones 'bout buyin' so many apples or pencils for like so much an' they wants to know how many like can you gets for a dollar or how much is a dozen goin' to cost you. That easy, man. All you got to do with that business is take the numbers they gives you an' multiply them an' if you sees the answer in the multiple-choice column, then you got it. If an' you don't see the answer there you divides the numbers they give you till you gets one a them answers. I get all a them, man.

But then they starts throwin' a whole mess a stuff at us like two, three sentences long, an', man, I can't follow that nohow. They this one I 'members an' I knowed it by heart 'cause like I have to read it so many times. It say, "Given the formula, $I = P \times R \times T$, calculate how much interest you will have to pay to a bank if you borrow $200 for six months." Then it say at the end: "Let I=Interest, P=Principal, R=Rate at 7% per annum, and T=Time in years." Shoot, man, what they tryin' to pull on me, anyway? How I s'posed to know 'bout all that boo, anyway? I ain't never even been inside no bank 'cept one time with George when we go in to get us a whole mess a matches.

You know, I goin' to have to go over to the hospital dispens'ry an' get me some a that there special stuff what take blood off a floor. I been in there tryin' to scrape that stuff up offa them tiles an' my thumbnail here it broke itself off. An' when it done that I thinkin' to myself why you workin' so hard when they a chemical goin' to take this mess up for you. Sometimes I a dumb cat, you know, an' I don't see what right in front a my face. Like I think maybe that's what I done on the part a the 'xamination what called the Social Sciences. Some a them things, man, they too far out for me ever to be understandin'. Like this here one question 'bout that there Roosevelt cat, who was a President some time back, an' they give us a whole long bit 'bout him an' what he done. So like 'bout this time on the 'xamination I gettin' smart, you know, an' 'fore I read the bit 'bout Roosevelt, I read me the questions so I know what to be lookin' for. An' the thing it goin' all right, you know, an' then I gets to the last question an' it say, "What was the T.V.A.?" I looks back to the paragraph an' I thinkin' what they askin' a question like this for when they ain't nothin' writ 'bout it. So I raise up my hand an' I call the lady over to where I sittin' an' I say to her, "I don't know what they be wantin' me to answer this question for when they ain't nothin' here 'bout it." She tell me each paragraph it have one question at the end a it that ain't got nothin' to do with what I been readin'. So I say fine to her an' then I ask her what she mean. An', man, she say to me that it a gen'ral knowledge question an' you just s'posed to *know* the answer. You ain't s'posed to get it outa nowhere 'cept you head. I 'bout set to tell her this here it all a bunch a jive, man, when I look up to her to see her smilin' down on me like maybe I her long-lost kid, you know, an' she's so happy to have me there takin' the 'xamination. Then she say,

"You just do the best you can," an' she pat me on the shoulder. What I like to know, man, is who make up that there 'xamination. I tell you one thing, an' that be they a few things I keepin' in my head that I don't 'spect he know for a gen'ral knowledge question, an' I like to sit his ass down an' watch him make hisself up some answers just right outa his head.

But I figure I make out all right, you know, an' I nails down that there G.E.D. without no problem. An' from the way the other cats they talkin' it don't look like Millard an' George they do so good. Sidney he like me, man, an' he know he pass. Millard an' George they ain't sure they pass, you know, but I 'spect they done okay.

There now, the lab it all clean, an' the big white doctor he in there lookin' things over so he can get set for like Monday. Big white doctor maybe he not so bad a cat, you know. He just told me he sorry for messin' up the place, an' for a while in there he even help me get the room lookin' right 'gain. But course he don't do none a the heavy cleanin', he just mess 'round at the sink with a few a them instruments. But I think he just there to be keepin' outa the way a the big doctor. I seen him just 'fore I come back in here an' I tell you he lookin' mean an' angry, all right. Big white doctor he know when to stay out the way, all right.

But there one thing 'bout the big white doctor that it good to see, an' that be the fact that he a bit uptight 'bout how many dogs he kill. He say he didn't like mean to do no harm to none a them, but somethin' it just get inside him an' he don't care how many dogs he use up yesterday. He say he somehow just got to feelin' that he *had* to do the 'speriments all by hisself. He say to me that he feel somethin' inside a him kinda let itself go an' he don't care 'bout nothin' but gettin' the results for the big doctor. Then he say he think maybe he should never be hisself no research doctor. He say he ain't got the temp'ment for it. As of now, man, he ain't got the dogs for it, neither.

MONDAY

Ninety-three dog, I tell you I goin' to take you outa you cage an' I goin' to beat you till you begs me to take you into the lab an' do some 'speriment on you. You best to cut out you barkin', dog, 'cause like I have me 'nough a it. I know I been in here like couple a hours now an' I ain't said nothin'. But they ain't nothin' I could be sayin' to you that you care 'bout. You all is just a mess a dogs, you know, an' that ain't nothin' special. Now I *told* you to shut up you mouth, Ninety-three, or I goin' to kick you right under your chin stickin' outa that hole in you cage. You askin' for it dog, I tell you that. Shut up you mouth, damn you, dog. *Shut up.*

I sorry, Ninety-three, I meant to hit you cage an' just scare you like. I didn't mean to really bust you one an' hurt you like that. Oh, man, but didn't I catch you one right on the chin. Here, now, lemme get this cage door open an' have me a look at what I done to you. Now I sit down here an' hold you head up an' rubs you ears till the hurt it go 'way. That a good dog, all right. Now you hush up you cryin' like, dog, or the big white doctor he be in here wonderin' what all the noise it be 'bout. There, now, that be better. Les see, Ninety-three dog, I shore gave you a belt, all right. Lemme open up you mouth an' have me a look. Oh, my, you bleedin' from you mouth *an'* you nose. But don't look like nothin' serious, you just done cut up you tongue a bit. Now dog, you stop that. You beginnin' to make me feel small, you know. I said stop you lickin'. Dog, what wrong with you, anyway? Here I goes an' gives you a kick hard as I knows how right on you button, an' now you lyin' there with a bit a blood runnin' out you nose an' you lickin' my hand. Dog, what the matter with you, anyhow? Here, lemme get some a them paper towels an' a bit a water an' I fix up you face for you.

Truly, I sorry, Ninety-three, an' from the way you looks I 'spect you knows it. Lookit the way you whole rear end it waggin' back an' forth an' you little tiny boxer tail it goin' like a mile a minute. Here now, hold still while I wipes off you nose a bit an' see that you ain't bleedin' no more. Now, dog, don't you be lookin' up to me with you old ugly face an' carryin' on like I 'bout the best friend you ever have youself. You lookin' just like you know why I bust you one. I didn't get me no G.E.D. or nothin', man, an' I very low 'bout that, all right. But like I say, dog, I sorry for bustin' you one. I know that ain't no 'scuse, but when you was barkin' an' carryin' on that way it was like maybe you was askin' me how I make out on the 'xamination. Well, I tell you it ain't good.

I been carryin' these here two papers 'round with me for like the whole weekend an' every now an' 'gain I takes them out an' looks at them. Here, I show you what they is. This here one it got the scores on it you needs for you G.E.D. The math'matics man he write them down for me to show me what I need. The whole mother it tricky, all right. You gots these fi' sections that make up the whole 'xamination. Now what you gots to do is make you a 35 in each section, dig? Now that ain't diff'cult. But if an' you make *just* a 35 in each section when they adds up you score it only give like 175. An' that be right where they get you, man, 'cause for a cat to get his G.E.D. he got to make hisself a 225. An' they got theyselves 'nother way they tie up you ass. That be you can go an' make you a 225 but if an' one a the fi' sections it below a 35, then you don't get no G.E.D. So like what a cat got to do is make hisself at least a 35 in all them sections an' then in one or two a them you gots to make like 'round a 50 or so to get the whole score up to a 225. An' I found me out 'nother thing, too, an' that be a old 225 it don't get you into SEEK. They say you gots to have you at least a 250 for SEEK, an' the higher you do the more you got a chance to get in. Math'matics man he tell me that in his other class he have a cat who make the highest score they ever had at NEW, an' that was like a 311. I don't know who that cat be, man, but I tell you he smart 'nough to be gettin' hisself anythin' he be wantin'. An' I tell you 'nother thing, too. He a lot smarter than me.

Now I got to show you how I done, an' it ain't too good, like I told you before. My whole score it like a 161, which is a long way from a 225, you know. But in some a them sections I do all right. Like on the Social Studies I make me a 48, an' the readin' part it a 32, which mean I only needs me like three more to pass that. An' the vocabulary it okay, I make me a 36 there, an' the grammar part it in the bag too, 'cause I make me a 39 there. But where I in big trouble it be the math'matics. I only make me a six there, an' the math'matics man he tell me I in bad shape 'cause I could make me like a hundred in everythin' else an' if I don't get the math'matics part up to a 35 I ain't never goin' to see me no G.E.D. diploma. Man, from a six to a 35 it a long way to go.

So like I don't think I be cuttin' outa NEW for a while yet, 'cause I got to stay close with the math'matics man. He say I got me a chance if an' I goin' to do me some work on them there word problems. One thing good, man, an' that be Miss Beverley tell me she very surprised that I make it passed on the vocabulary an' the grammar. An' she surprised the readin' it a 32. She tell me that now the time for me to be gettin' goin' on the readin' so that when I takes it 'gain I makes me a whole lot better score. That way when I gets the math'-matics up to a 35 the readin' an' the other business it be very high. Then I get me like a 250 an', man, I breeze into SEEK.

Oh, yeah, like I 'most forgot what the other cats done. Millard he somethin' else, all right. He come out the 'xamina-tion an' he say he didn't do no good at all. Well, Millard he be gettin' into SEEK now for shore. Millard he make hisself a 293. That right, a 293. Now ain't that somethin' else. But Millard he been 'round a whole lot, an' he say that some a them things he just knowed, but he don't know where he ever learned them. All he say is that he know it ain't in no book. So when I find out that Millard he make a 293 I ask him if he be cuttin' from NEW. He tell me no, he goin' to stay 'round for a while 'cause he don't want to get no job or nothin' an' NEW it keep payin' him long as he keep comin'.

An' George he surprise me with what he make. He get hisself a 221, an' he very angry 'bout not makin' the 225. But the math'matics man tell him that he very lucky he not make a 225 'cause if an' once you make it you can't never take the 'xamination 'gain. Mathmatics man say that the best thing you can do is like make you what George did an' then study up real hard an' take it over 'gain. That way you make the 250. An' he tell George that if an' he had made hisself the 225 it be all over for SEEK 'cause that 225 it don't get you in. But George he still angry.

Now you tongue it 'pear to me that it ain't bleedin' no more, Ninety-three dog, an' what you done is go off to sleep with you head on my knee while I been shootin' off my mouth. You a all right dog, Ninety-three.

Now would you all please look at this here dog. I knowed we haves us a order in for one more dog with the place that supply us, just so we make sure we got 'nough a them statistics for the big doctor when he does his writin' up a all the 'speriments. But I don't know what they goin' to do with this here dog. He ain't fit for nothin'. This here little poodle dog he can't hardly even pull the chain 'cross the floor 'cause he don't weigh but two, three pounds. An' would you please look at the way they got him all shaved up. He look like he done have hisself 'bout six operations already, an' when the big white doctor he see this he goin' to pop off, all right. They ain't no way we ever goin' to be usin' a dog like this. I don't 'spect his spleen it be any bigger than a half dollar, an' his heart it so small that we couldn't do no operation on him if an' we had to.

Now we gots to get you cats in the Sevennies and Eighties shaped up here so we can be givin' you all you proper heart 'tacks. I just now talkin' to the big white doctor in the lab there an' he tell me we a bit behind in where we should be an' it goin' to take us a lotta work to be meetin' all the deadlines that the big doctor set. Big white doctor he tell me that we be gettin' 'nother operatin' table so we can be doin' us twice the work on you dogs. He say that he goin' to have the chink doctor an' the P.R. cat come down an' team up with us so we can run us off like four, fi' a you dogs every day. Big white doctor he crazy if an' he think he can do that business.

'Specially if he talkin' 'bout bringin' in those other two doctors. Man, they don't know nothin' 'bout it, an' from the way they speakin' English all the time it don't 'pear to me they ever learn.

An' when the big white doctor he see the little poodle dog there he ask me what we ever goin' to be doin' with a dog like that. He think that little dog he the funniest thing he ever seen. An' while he laughin' at the poodle dog the little cat he start his old high-pitch barkin' an' he never take his eyes off that doctor. So like after a few minutes a the big white doctor laughin' at the poodle dog the little thing he walk slow like over to the doctor an' he look up at him. The big white doctor he look down just in time to see poodle dog lift his leg an' pee right on his foot. An' the big white doctor he so surprised to see what happenin' he don't move his foot for like a second or two, an' then all a sudden like he mad as hell. Poodle dog he just big 'nough he able to pee on the doctor's sock, an' he get mad as hell 'cause it all run down into his shoe. Course I don't say nothin', but I tell you that little poodle dog he take care o' hisself, all right.

An' after a while, when the big white doctor he calm down, he say that he goin' to take that little poodle dog home with him for his wife, an' I thinkin' that a all right thing to do 'cause if an' he ain't got nowhere to go poodle dog he have to be put to sleep. Ain't no way we could be keepin' him here, not when he ain't goin' to be doin' us no good with the 'speriments. This ain't no hotel, you know.

So when we gets our G.E.D. score on Friday night, Sidney he come up to me an' tell me it time for us to be goin' to see his man an' get what we need. He ask George if an' he want to come 'long, but George he say he got to go see Violet an' tell her how he make out on the 'xamination. An' Millard he say he can't go with us 'cause he got to be movin' some cat over in Brooklyn. Sidney say it don't make no diff'rence to him, not with what he goin' to do, an' we cut from NEW so fast we didn't even stop to see if we got us a digit from the state for last week. We figure we got the bread we need, an' when you all set to go an' see you man, nothin' get in you way. An' when we cuttin' out the door, Sidney he turn to me an' he say, "You know, like I be clean for a long time now but it don't do a cat no good to get clean. Only time I right with the world it be when I fly."

"How long you been clean?" I ask.

"Two, three months now," he tell me, an' that be a long time for Sidney. I think he truly want to be a fireman.

"You gots to go easy s'evenin'," I tell him, "if an' you ain't had nothin' for 'long as you say."

"I go easy," he say to me, but I knowed from the way he say it that he goin' to shoot up a whole mess a stuff right off. That trouble for a cat who ain't had hisself nothin' in like a long time.

So what we done was to go to this lounge that Sidney know, an' soon as we walks in Sidney he see his man, an' he go right up to him. "Iceman," Sidney say to the cat, an' he a dude 'cause he wearin' hisself like one a them there three-piece suits. "How you doin'?"

"What you want, little man?" Iceman say to Sidney.

"Usual," Sidney say, an' he already got his hand in his pocket on his roll.

"Where you been in so long?" Iceman say, an' he take off his shades so cool like. Iceman's eyes they all mess up. He never look like he lookin' right at you. His eyes they go off in his head like east an' west, you know, an' Sidney he just stand there for a second or two an' then he tell Iceman he been straight. "One time you one a my best numbers, little man," Iceman say to Sidney, "an' one day when you go straight you just leaves me holdin' some stuff for you."

"I need a bag," Sidney say to him.

"It goin' to cost you double," Iceman say.

"Double?" Sidney say to him, an' he turn to look at me.

"Double 'cause you needs it," Iceman say. Sidney he just take his roll outa his pocket an' he count out most a it an' he give it to Iceman. Cool like, Iceman he reach out in front a him an' he take hisself two ice cubes from a big red bowl he got there an' he put them in his mouth. He look at Sidney for a second an' then he look to me. Then he crack them ice cubes up an' it make a ter'ble sound, like maybe all his teeth they breakin' off or somethin'. Then without ever reachin' into his pocket or nothin' he just hand Sidney a bag. It look to me like Iceman he doin' magic or somethin', but Sidney he tell me later that Iceman he got special sleeves in his dude suit an' all he got to do is like shrug or somethin' when he make a hit an' a bag come outa his sleeve into his hand. Iceman he cool.

So we take the bag an' we cut back to my ma's place, an' we go there 'cause Sidney say his sister she havin' in a gentleman friend from the army like, an' she don't want to have nobody there. An' my ma's place it be all right 'cause my ma she out at the church all the time now. It goin' to be a long time 'fore I sees her 'gain 'cause last Wednesday it the beginnin' a Lent, you know, an' nothin' it turn on my ma like Lent. She go herself a little crazy in Lent with how much time she spend messin' 'round at the church. She there for Mass all the time, an' for them Stations of the Cross, an' she always sayin' some kinda rosary or 'nother. One thing good 'bout Lent, man, an' that be I don't have to do me no worryin' 'bout what go on in the 'partment. She only eat a bit an' sleep a bit there.

Sidney an' me we go in, an' right 'way he start to get a funny look on his face. He take the bag an' he look at it, an' his face it start to glow, you know. He start breathin' a bit heavy, like maybe he think the bag it a chick he 'bout to jazz, an' then he say to me, "Oh, man, I got to have a lift or I goin' to go crazy."

"You gots to watch youself," I tell him, "or they be findin' you in some hallway with a needle stickin' out you arm." But Sidney he don't take no notice a what I sayin', an' when he get set to shoot up the only thing that truly save his life it be that he mess up on the blood vein. If an' Sidney he get that whole load in there he be dead now. But he don't like but get half a it in, an' it be just 'nough to make him fly good. But like I told you he ain't had hisself no stuff for like a long time, an' when that happen an' you shoots youself up a good-size load you gets high quick like, but you goes to sleep, too. An' Sidney he know that, an' while he on the way up he fixin' hisself 'nother batch so that when he wake up he can fly 'gain quick. Inside a ten minutes Sidney he asleep on the floor with his head 'gainst the radiator.

It right then, dogs, that I know I be in some trouble. When we come outa NEW an' we go to the lounge I want to shoot up bad, but when I see Sidney sleepin' 'gainst the radiator I don't want to shoot up. Now I tell you that never happen to me 'fore, but I a cat who always done what he feel like doin', an' if I don't feel like shootin' up then I ain't goin' to do it just 'cause the cat I with done it. All sudden, man, I sees me the book the math'matics man he give me, an' I thinkin' to myself it be best if an' I start to learn me up them first few pages, you know. So I sits down an' begins to read the stuff an' every now an' 'gain I looks over to see if Sidney he be all right. My ma she come in 'bout midnight, an I hear her go to her room an' I very relieved when I hear her turn all three a them locks. An' when I hear her hummin' I know she gettin' set to sleep on the floor. She tell me one time that the white priest he told her that the nuns they sleep on the floor durin' Lent. My ma she buy that boo, all right.

Sidney he wake up 'bout two o'clock an' he feel good. He say to me, "How long I out, man?" an' I tell him 'bout three hours. "Iceman he give me some good stuff, all right," Sidney say, an' he reach for the needle 'gain. While he light a match for the needle I look at him an' I start to laugh. "Sidney," I say to him, "you a dope fiend, you know."

"Dig it," Sidney say, an' he laugh back at me, "I a dope fiend all the way."

"An' you ain't never goin' to 'mount to nothin'," I say, an' we still laughin'.

"Oh, yeah?" Sidney say, "what you make on the G.E.D.?"

"You know what I make," I tell him. "A 161."

"That right?" he say.

"I got me the paper to prove it," I tell him.

"But what you make on the math'matics part?" he say.

"I told you already," I say to him.

"Yeah," he say, "but I want you to tell me 'gain."

"I make me a *six*," I tell him, an' I close my eyes halfway an' I look at him like it be the best grade a cat can get hisself.

"Six it ain't no good, you know," he say, an' he make his voice sound like he a teacher or somethin'.

"So what you make on the G.E.D.?" I ask him, an' all sudden like I 'ware that Sidney he don't tell me his whole score. All he tell me is that he make a 19 on the math'matics, an' he actin' like he some kinda big deal.

"I made a 19 on the math'matics," he say, an' he take his belt from the floor an' he tie it 'round his arm an' he pull it tight.

"I know you make a 19," I tell him, "but what you get on everythin'?"

Sidney he feel careful for the blood vein like. "I made a 101," he say, but he don't look at me.

"That ain't no good," I tell him, an' he start to laugh 'gain just a bit when he put the needle in.

"Yeah," he say when he done shootin' up, "I know it ain't no good." Then he lean back 'gainst the radiator an' he say, "I don't 'spect I goin' to be no fireman."

SPRING

MONDAY

Well, lookit that there, Ninety-three dog she wakin' up already. I don't guess they anyway to be keepin' you down, dog. Mosta the cats that make it through the heart-stoppin' business they ain't even waked up from the Nembutal when I comes in the next mornin'. But Ninety-three here she got her eyes open an' her little bit a tail it goin' back an' forth pretty good. I knows you 'wake, dog, an' I goin' to have me a look at you chest. Come on, now, lemme get the cage door open like an' have me a look. You burned up pretty good on you chest, dog, you know that. No, now you don'ts have to be gettin' up. Stay where you *is. Dog,* stay where you is. Stop lickin' me, man. There, that's a good dog, you sit there an' let me have a look. In some places here you burned up bad, you know, but in others it look like you ain't got nothin' to worry 'bout. But Ninety-three dog, why don't you look like you feel the pain? That what I don't understand. You eyes they all still glassed up from the Nembutal, an' you look like you been on one fine high, you know, but the resta you body ain't even takin' no notice 'bout havin' you heart stopped an' started or nothin'. Seem to me like all you want is for me to be pettin' you an' scratchin' you ears. Lookit that, now, all I gots to do is put a couple a fingers on you ear an' you bend you head over so meek like. You 'bout the best kinda dog a cat could have hisself. Maybe I be gettin' permission from them doctors to be takin' you outa here for like maybe a long old walk. It gettin' nice outside now, man, with all them trees an' flowers comin' up just like they s'posed to. You an' me we could go down 'long by the river an' have us a fine time. An' the sun, man, it fin'ly gettin' warm 'gain, an' I tell you I a cat who dig the sunshine all the way. Maybe I ask an' some afternoon when they ain't no business goin' on here we can go on out an' walk us up by the river a piece.

Now I gots the lab all cleaned up an' I all set to get on outa here an' over to the school. Tonight we all goin' to make us that there 'pointment for the G.E.D. I only got to sit here for like a few more minutes an' then it be time for me to go.

You know, man, the more I thinkin' 'bout it, the more I know things they goin' to work theyselves out all right. I know I act up bad when I miss the G.E.D. the first time, but this time I be set for it. I done that whole book that the math'matics man he give me, an' I tell you I set for anythin' they throw my way. An' I got me all kinds a time to be gettin' into SEEK. They take people right up through August, an' they ain't even got nobody in it yet. Millard he just been hangin' 'round waitin' for his letter, you know, an' last week he start to get uptight 'bout the whole business 'cause he ain't heard nothin' from them, an' he call them up an' they tell him that they ain't sent out no letters to nobody, but that they start this week. So Millard he just waitin'. Me an' George an' Sidney we got all kinds a time, man, an' we all get in if an' we gets what we s'posed to on the G.E.D.

Hey, Eighty-two dog, what you whimperin' at? You got to be gettin' youself ready for tomorrow, you know, 'cause tomorrow it be you day to have you heart stopped. But just lookit you, dog, they ain't no way you be makin' it through tomorrow. Everythin' them doctors do to you all year it work perfect. You can't even stand up no more by youself. They say you the best sample a the heart failure they have in the whole 'speriment. You all swoll up with the water in you body from like you valves not workin' an' too much a the salt food. An' you chest it just heave itself up an' down pantin' all the time for air, an' you in such bad shape you can't even raise youself up to do you business. That make for a mess, all right. Now damn you, dog, just while I be talkin' to you you mess up you whole behind an' lookit that, man, everythin' it coverin' up you backside an' you tail. Now how I s'posed to be gettin' outa here when I got to take time to wipe you up? Now I got to clean you up a bit an' then I got to go an' wash up 'gain. Now why you gone an' done that just now? Fi' minutes later, man, an' I be out free an' clear. Lemme open up you cage an' move you over. There, that right. Oh, man, lookit that. Seem like they ain't no way a cat can crap solid when all he do is lie 'round all day. Everythin' it just runnin' all over the place. You know what you needs, dog? You needs a bath an' you needs you cage cleaned. Well, you ain't goin' to be gettin' neither, I tell you that. Not when it after fi' o'clock. I goin' to clean it up best way I can, but you goin' to have to wait till the mornin' for me to be doin' a proper job. I ain't no nurse, you know.

TUESDAY

You cats think you in trouble, huh? Well, I tell you 'bout a cat who got hisself a whole lot more 'an you got this mornin'. Millard, man, Millard. He in a big old mess a trouble, all right. If an' they can be provin' 'gainst him all the stuff they say they goin' to, you know. But Millard he a smart cat, an' they goin' to be havin' theyselves some trouble pinnin' down Millard for what happen at NEW. Oh, they know he do it, but they ain't no way Millard just goin' to come right out an' tell them he done it an' he want to take his punishment. An' 'cause Millard he don't say nothin' they a lotta *po*-lice prowlin' 'round NEW askin' all kinds a questions. An' them *po*-lice they got they ain't just no cop offa no corner, you know. They all detectives an' special cats who s'posed to know 'bout these here things. One cat he told me that if an' NEW it was run by the federal gov'ment they be havin' in the F.B.I. Man, you don't mess with no F.B.I. But like I say, the *po*-lice they gots to prove everythin' 'gainst Millard 'fore they be puttin' him 'way, an' they ain't nobody at NEW who goin' to tell them *po*-lice that it was Millard for shore who done tell them other cats to do it. He even show them how to do it.

Like what happen last night, man, it somethin' else all the way. We all down in the lobby hangin' 'round loose like, you know, an' we all just jivin' 'fore the first class begin. Me an' George we talkin' 'bout takin' down that there G.E.D. tomorrow, an' Sidney he with us for like a few minutes. But Sidney he flyin' very high, an' after a few minutes a lookin' at George an' me, Sidney he say, "Jive, baby, jive," an' he hit up George for a cig'rette an' then he go over to the front door a the place. What Sidney do is he start greetin' every cat who come in the door. He rockin' back an' forth on his heels an' he wavin' his cig'rette 'round in his hand tryin' every now an' 'gain to put it in his mouth. He even drop it couple a times an' when he fin'ly pick it up he careful like rub the filter end with his shirt. An' most a the time his body it bent all outa shape. His ass it stickin' way out an' the top a his body it all bent over like he a old man. Every time a cat come in the door Sidney say to him, "How you doin', man?" an' he give the cat some palm. Then he turn 'round an' he give a little wave to me an' George. An' all the cats who come in they takin' it all very nice, you know, an' we all havin' a fine old time. Every cat 'cept Millard. When he come in Sidney try to give him some palm an' Millard he stop cold an' he turn to Sidney an' he say, "What you tryin' to do to me, little man?"

"Yeah, *baby*," Sidney say, an' he raise his hand all the way over his head like he goin' to give Millard some palm like he never got 'fore in his life. All sudden like somethin' seem to happen to Millard. He grab Sidney by the throat, you know, an' he shove him up 'gainst the wall like maybe Sidney he tryin' to knife Millard or somethin'. Then like a flash, man, Millard bring back his left hand an' all sudden he open up his fist an' his fingers they seem to spring out like maybe they s'posed to be a switchblade or somethin'. Then he hit Sidney in the belly with the side a his hand. Sidney he look up at Millard, an' it look to me like maybe Sidney's eyes they goin' to pop right outa his head. Then slow like Sidney's eyes they close up an' he start to sink down to the floor. Me an' George we get to Millard just when he set to put Sidney 'way for the whole evenin'. Millard he set to give Sidney a hit on the back a his neck when George stop him. Millard he got his right hand open an' he bringin' it back over his head. But George he get there just in time to grab hold a Millard's hand an' let Sidney hit the floor without no more punches.

But Millard he ain't through, man, he just beginnin', an' it be George who in trouble now. Sharp like, Millard he bring his elbow back an' he find George's chest. George right 'way let go a Millard's hand, an' when Millard swing 'round he catch George 'cross the side a the head with his other elbow, an' I tell you right there George he finish. He start for the floor an' Millard he give him a quick little chop to the side a his neck as he goin' down an' George he out like a light. Millard he whip 'round to me an' I see then that he all strung out on somethin'. He lookin' to me like he on a crazy wine high, but the *po*-lice say later that he ain't on no booze or no pills or nothin'. So he look to me an' he say, "You want some, baby? Come on, I takin' on everybody tonight."

"You the king," I tell Millard, an' I starts to back 'way easy like. Millard he crouched an' he got both his hands up like he teachin' somebody the karate, you know, an' the cats that there they in a big old circle 'round Millard an' they all starts to back off slow like. Ain't nobody goin' near Millard. Then all sudden Millard he make some very fast moves with his hands an' feet through the air an' he go after a cat. But like I told you, Millard he actin' like he flyin' on somethin' an' he miss the cat he after an' he cut one a them big lamps they got there clean in two. It right then when he turn 'round that he see the two security cats comin' down the stairs. That make his eyes bulge, you know, an' when he see one a them cats reachin' for his weapon, Millard he drop his hands an' his head fall limp like on his chest. "Break it up," one a the security guards yell an' mosta the cats they start to take off quick 'cause they thinkin' maybe they get taken in 'long with Millard. Security cat who got his weapon out he come up easy on Millard an' he say, "You crazy or somethin'?" Millard he just got his head hangin' low, an' his arms they down by his side. Slow like he shake his head an' I hear him say very soft, "No, I ain't crazy." Then with like the quickest motion I ever seen a cat make, Millard he shoot his hand up an' he catch that security cat right the middle a his face. All sudden blood it pourin' outa the cat's nose an' his weapon it on the floor. Security cat he sinkin' to his knees an' his face it in his hands. Security cat's nose it broken bad, you know, an' I know it broke 'cause a the sound Millard's hand make when he hit the cat. It sound like maybe some cat he find a way to crack all his knuckles at the same time. It right then when Millard squat down to go for the weapon that the other security guard he lay back an' he swing his stick at Millard's head. He hit Millard so hard that the sound a the stick 'gainst Millard's head it make a big old echo in that there hallway. Millard go straight down on his knees, an' blood it comin' out the back a his head an' it runnin' down over his collar an' his coat. Millard he don't seem to know where he is, but he still straight up on his knees when the security cat hit him 'gain. Millard he out cold then, man, an' he cut up his lips bad when his face it hit the floor hard. That when I thinkin' that the whole thing it over, you know, but then I see the security guard lift Millard up by the back a his coat an' I see he goin' to hit him 'gain. I jumps in an' grabs the guard's arm, an' I say "Come on, man, he all done now." Security cat he get hisself together fast then 'cause he know that if an' he hit Millard 'gain maybe he kill him. Right then couple a teachers I seen only maybe once or twice show up an' they shoutin' all kinds a things for people to be doin'. First thing they do is one teacher he help up the security cat, an' he give him his hank'chief to try to stop the bleedin', an' then he sits him down in a chair. Other cat he start to wake up Millard. It right then that the real *po*-lice shows up. Some cat musta called in when the whole thing start 'cause in the door come four *po*-lice an' they lookin' like they mean business. But when they see that everythin' it all right they puts they sticks up under they arms an' right 'way out come them notebooks. Two a the *po*-lice they go stand by the door so nobody he be leavin', you know, an' the other two they start askin' the security guard who hit Millard an' what's goin' on. It be then that I looks over an' sees that George he tryin' to get Sidney up off the floor an' get him outa there. If an' the *po*-lice find him high, they take him in an' lock him up. The way Sidney need the stuff, man, if an' you take him an' lock him up for a while I 'spect he go crazy. So I go over an' helps George an' we stand Sidney up an' when the *po*-lice man standin' by the door ask us if we all right we tell him we fine now an' we get Sidney up to the toilet on the second floor. After a few minutes up there Sidney he begin to come 'round an' when I see he all right I tell George I goin' back down an' see what they done to Millard. They got Millard sittin' in one a them little wooden chairs in one a them offices down there, an' his hands is cuffed to the back a the chair.

Now then I got to be gettin' Eighty-two dog here all set up for the heart-stoppin' 'speriment. Oh, man, I forgot all 'bout you, Eighty-two, an' you still lyin' there in half the mess I don't clean up last evenin'. Come on, dog, here I goes an' opens up you cage an' you ain't even tryin' to get up. Come on, Eighty-two, let me move you offa this here stuff an' get you cleaned up 'fore I takes you to the lab. Oh, my, you ain't goin' no place, is you, dog. Only place you be goin' now is to the incinerator, dog, 'cause you be dead as hell. You musta died last evenin' right after I took me off outa here, 'cause you already stiff an' cold. Well, you be just one more dog I don't got to clean up after no more. But they one thing I sorry 'bout, dog, an' that be that I don't clean you up last evenin' an' you got to go an' die in you mess. But none a that make no diff'rence now, man, 'cause I got to go an' get me a sack to put you in....

So now like all you cages is clean an' I haves me my dinner an' I ain't got nothin' to do s' afternoon but sit here an' make shore I got me these here word problems down. Tomorrow it be the day I be passin' my G.E.D.

Oh, *yeah,* like Millard. I clean forgot 'bout Millard what with all this business goin' on s' mornin'. When Millard he sittin' there in that chair an' the real *po*-lice talkin' to him an' everythin', the nurse they got at NEW she come in an' she take 'way the security guard with the busted up nose. Ain't nobody lookin' after Millard's head. You know, Millard he do some way out things, man, but what he do when the *po*-lice askin' him questions it be the craziest thing I ever seen Millard do. When the cop he ask Millard his name, Millard he answer the man in what sound like Chinese. Cop ask him 'gain an' Millard he give him the same treatment. An' when the man ask Millard all 'bout where he live an' stuff, Millard don't say nothin' to the man that ain't in the Chinese. *Po*-lice cat he don't like that an' fin'ly he take Millard's hair an' pull his head back. Millard he look up to the cop, an' his eyes all glassed up bad, you know, an' he like spit out some more Chinese at the cat.

It then that they see they ain't goin' to be gettin' nothin' outa Millard an' they starts to search him. They don't stand him up or nothin'. They just careful like reach into his pockets all time makin' sure that they don't step in front a Millard. If an' they do Millard he set to kick out at them. But they know that an' they empty all his pockets from behind the chair. Ain't much Millard got 'cept 'bout fifty dollars from some kinda movin' job, an' a little chain with all kinds a things on it I ain't never seen. An' outa his back pocket they take his wallet an' they open it up an' reads who he is an' where he live. Outa the other pocket they takes two pieces a paper, one it a envelope, other it this here kinda small poster for when they s'posed to be the next meetin' a some a the cats Millard travel with. When they done emptyin' Millard's pockets, they put the stuff down on a desk an' the one cop he come back an' he ask Millard 'gain who he is. Millard he look up to the man an' he nod his head to the desk an' he say, "Read it youself, pig." Cop, all he do is smile down at Millard, an' he keep smilin' an smilin' till Millard say 'gain, "Pig."

"Pig it is," the cop say, "but this pig here," an' he tap his badge with his finger cool like, "this pig here is going to take you to jail." Millard all sudden he look like he dis'pointed that the *po*-liceman don't haul off an' smash him up good.

It right then that the two detectives they come in the door, an' they all time travelin' just the way the cats in the prowl car do, one white cop, one colored cop. Colored detective he come straight up to Millard an' he start actin' like he very tough. He say he goin' to take Millard outside with him to the back a the buildin' an' he goin' to beat him 'bout the head till he say what been goin' on here. Millard just look at him long an' hard an' fin'ly he say, "Brother, why you still got a part in you hair?" Colored detective he very angry 'bout that an' he say to Millard, "You're in very serious trouble, boy. You'd better start explaining yourself." Millard answer the cat in Chinese. Now what happen then is that the colored detective he look like he give up, you know, an' he walk 'way like he disgusted. White detective he come up slow like to Millard. Detectives they work that way, y'understand, like they a team, an' one a them he always the tough cat an' the other he so nice it like he tryin' to be you long-lost father, you know. He squat down front a Millard an' easy like he put his hands on Millard's knees.

Very soft like he say, "How long were you in Vietnam?" an' Millard he look down to the cat like he been figured out. "Too long the way it looks to me," white detective say, an' give one a Millard's knees a pat like he understand everythin' that goin' on. Millard nod his head. Millard he ain't been speakin' Chinese, he been talkin' in a bit a Vietnamese he learn when he over there. But white cat he know that, an' he look down to the floor like he all sudden very sad 'bout somethin'.

"Wouldn't you like to tell me about what happened here tonight?" white cat say. Millard look down to him an' for a second his face it get soft, but then right 'way I see Millard tighten up his jaw muscles hard. Then he say slow an' like he mean it, "You too late now, man, them fires already been set." White detective all sudden he ain't nobody's father no more. "What the hell are you talking about?" he say to Millard, an' he jump up an' look 'bout him.

"This here place it gettin' set to *burn,* man," Millard say, an' he smile a big old smile like maybe he just roll a seven or somethin'.

"Come on, boy, you'd better talk now," white cat say, "or you're going in for a lot more than assault." Millard he never get to answer the cat. It then that somebody who smell smoke pull the fire alarm an' everybody start runnin' 'round like they clean outa they heads. Detectives they take Millard out in the main hall an' they'd a bit a smoke. The teachers an' the director man they look like they goin' every which way, an' the rest a the cats they takin' off out the buildin', an' Millard he stand there for a second or two an' he laugh. Then the detectives they drag him outa the buildin'.

So like what happen, man, it ain't no big deal. NEW it don't burn down like Millard say it goin' to, an' in like 'bout a hour we all back in the classrooms like nothin' happen. Only kinda fire they was it be in two garbage cans in the basement, an' then they put the cans by the ventilators. They some smoke, but it ain't nothin' much, you know. An' that be good thing for Millard 'cause the *po*-lice they can't hang nothin' on Millard for what two other cats done. An' 'nother good thing for Millard it be that the director man he don't want none a this business in the newspapers, 'cause if an' the state people they get wind a this they be some trouble with the refundin' that comin' up.

What the *po*-lice done with Millard was to take him in to ask him some questions like 'bout why he flip way he did. I don't 'spect they be findin' out from Millard what light up his fuse. An' I tell you I ain't goin' to be tellin' them, neither. When they have Millard outside in the car an' the fire business it all startin' to clear up, they tell me to go back inside an' get Millard's stuff they left on the desk. I do like they say, but I don't give them everythin'. What I do is look at that there envelope they took from him, an' when I see who it from I opens it up an' starts to read it. I don't read much, an' that 'cause it one a them letters that starts off, "Dear Applicant: I regret to inform you . . ." an' all the resta the boo that go with it. Millard he don't get into SEEK.

Man, it seem like bein' Spec'men Supervisor a cat ain't got no chance to like do nothin' on his own. All I wants to do is sit me down here an' get to work on these here word problems. An' when I makes sure I got them down good, I goin' to have me just one more look at how you mess 'round with findin' out 'bout circles an' the triangles. Math'matics man he tell me that he think that the word problems an' the geometry they be the toughest things for a man to get down. But you know, when I back in the tenth grade I don't never have me no problem with circles an' the like. Seem to me that stuff come easy for some reason or 'nother. Diff'rence 'tween a word problem an' one a them problems with a circle it be that I can *see* the circle an' I can see what they askin' me to do. Not with word problems, man. No chance.

So what I just come back from doin', man, it a weird thing, all right. Big doctor he come by the door like 'bout half hour ago, an' he got with him this here doctor I never seen 'fore. He tell me that this here doctor he goin' to be doin' some 'sperimentin', an' they gots a load a animals comin' in an' he want me to get out there to the platform an' take care a them. You know what that cat he doin'? He messin' 'round with sheep, man, an' they ain't even no big sheep, neither. Them's just lambs, an' he goin' to start cuttin' them up soon as he get his lab straight. Messin' with dogs it be all right, you know, 'cause at least a dog he mind what you say. But sheeps is dumb, man, an' you gots to shove them into they cages.

But all that boo it be over an' done with, an' I got to get me down to work. I goin' to spend all my time tonight with the math'matics man, an' he told me that anythin' I don't understand I got to ask him 'bout. Now you take this here word problem. "If ten years ago a certain ship were to cross the Atlantic Ocean in 5 days, 5 hours and 13 minutes, and if a ship were to cross today in 46 hours less, what is the total travel time of the latter?" Now right there it be 'xackly what I talkin' 'bout. I know what they askin' me but I ain't got no idea how to go 'bout findin' out the answer. I know I got to do somethin' with the hours an' the day business, but the whole thing longer I looks at it more I don't see how to do it. But I know one thing, man, an' that be what I goin' to do tomorrow when I comes to one like this here on the G.E.D. I goin' to guess at the answer, an' I goin' to be guessin' quick like so's not to be wastin' no time on them.

THURSDAY

I ain't goin' to dig deliverin' you cats to that there new sheep doctor, I tell you that. When I take over Sevenny-one dog just now the new doctor he take hisself one look at him an' then he start actin' like I the one who done everythin' to Sevenny-one to make him look like that. Sevenny-one he s'posed to be one a them Irish setter dogs, you know, an' he s'posed to have a sleek-lookin' body an' have shiny red hair an' everythin' that go with it. Well, what I bring to that there doctor it don't look like no Irish setter dog. Don't really look like no dog at all, it look like just a big old lump at the end a the leash. An' Sevenny-one's gut it all swoll up from the fluids his body been collectin' an' his hair it all been shaved off for the most part. New doctor he take hisself a look at Sevenny-one an' he drop down to his knees an' he begin to 'xamine him. While he doin' that I say to the new doctor, "Somebody tell me that you goin' to be transplantin'. That right?" New doctor he just grunt me a answer an' then I say, "Which way you goin' to be doin' it?"

"Doing what?" he say, an' he fin'ly look up to me.

"The hearts," I say, "which way you goin' to be transplantin' them?"

"Sheep to dog," he say. An' now I get to thinkin' 'bout it I can't see him doin' it no other way 'cause the sheep they got the good hearts an' you all got the bad ones. But I know 'nough 'bout the whole thing to know that you all is dead now for shore. Oh, I know they goin' to be givin' you a good new heart, but like it ain't you own, an' from what the big white doctor told me 'bout things gettin' *re*-jected, man, it not be the new heart that fin'ly kill you, it be you own body what don't understand what goin' on.

An' I tell you one thing, man. When I takes you outa here, you ain't never comin' back to the animal room. An' that be 'cause the new doctor he told me that after he done puttin' one a them there lamb hearts in you they got to keep you in a sterile place so you don't get you a mess a germs. The new doctor he say that the animal room it too dirty a place for a dog to be after his heart been replaced. I tell him I understand that all the way, the animal room not 'xackly the cleanest place goin', but then I looks down to Sevenny-one an' I asks the new doctor if an' I can come an' see Sevenny-one while he be recoverin'. He tell me I can come an' see him anytime they ain't doin' no big operation. So I glad 'bout that, you know, 'cause the way I see it we all been together for a long time now, an' they ain't no reason I goin' to leave you 'lone in no new place.

Shut up you mouth, Ninety-three dog, an' close up that evil eye you givin' me. You lookin' at me 'xackly like Miss Beverley done when I told her what I reads on the job when I got me some time. Well, I tell you what I want to tell her an' that be that I can read what I wants to read. She told me that it ain't no good for a cat who want to be passin' his G.E.D. to be readin' comic books. Shoot, man, I likes comic books, an' if I want to be readin' one a them I goin' to do just that. If Miss Beverley she have her way I all the time be readin' big old books from some library or somethin'. An' I don't know what she be carin' 'bout anyway 'cause I already nail me down the readin' part a the G.E.D. an' now I can just lay back an' read what I want. Trouble with Miss Beverley be she all time tryin' to make a cat improve on hisself. I all right the way I is.

All right, Ninety-three, if an' I puts up the comic book will you be stoppin' you barkin'? Here, I roll it up an' puts it over here. That make you lay off a me? All you ever want is to have some cat scratch you ears, an' that a sure sign you gettin' to think this here it the best home you ever have. So while I scratchin' you ears I tell you 'bout what happen Tuesday night an' on the G.E.D. business.

I go right to the school an' I looks up the math'matics man with the diff'culty I be havin' with them word problems an' that one mother 'bout the ships. He cool me just fine, you know, an' I knowed all a it when I went to take me my G.E.D. yesterday. That problem it easy, all right. But they be one thing that happen on the G.E.D. that I don't know if I done right 'bout. They's this here one problem they ask, "Of the following numbers, which one is the largest?"

$$2^4;\ 3^3;\ 4^2;\ 5^{-5}$$

Well, man, that just look like a crazy mess a numbers to me, an' when I read it I can't tell me nothin' 'bout it. Just seem to me that maybe they makin' some kind a stew outa numbers. But I do what I promise myself 'fore I takes the 'xamination, an' that be when I don't know me a problem I guess, an' I guess quick like. I sees the fi' there with the fi' 'bove it an' that be the one I guess. After the 'xamination I walk out with George an' Sidney an' I ask George 'bout that problem an' he tell me the answer it be the three thing. I ask him why he think so an' when he try to 'splain it to me I don't know what he talkin' 'bout. So I turns to Sidney an' I says, "Which one you put down?"

"I didn't get that far," Sidney say, an' he start to look 'round for a toilet so he can go an' shoot up.

I just come back from Sevenny-one dog, an' I tell you that what goin' to happen to you all it ain't goin' to be nice like. They got Sevenny-one in this here glass cage, an' they a big old sign on the door that say, "Sterile Conditions: Do Not Approach." An' inside they be Sevenny-one dog lyin' on his right side an' he got a tube comin' right out from his throat, an' he got two others runnin' one in his front leg an' the other in the back one. An' they's this big old cut 'cross his chest where they went in an' took out his old heart, an' it look to me like they done a all right job a cuttin' him. They cut him open 'xackly on the scar he have from where we mess up his valves. An' he just lyin' there with his eyes shut up tight, an' his chest it goin' up an' down easy like an' the cut it stretch itself out a bit every time Sevenny-one dog he take a breath. But he don't have to be takin' too many breaths, you know, an' that be 'cause they pumpin' oxygen into that there glass cage. He havin' everythin' done for him that it poss'ble to do. An' while I standin' there Sevenny-one he open up his eyes, an' I tell you they 'bout the glassiest eyes I even seen. It look to me like he can't see nothin' outa them, you know, but after a minute like I raise up one a my hands an' I kinda waves to him like, an' he move his head just a bit toward me an' I think I see his tail move a bit. Then he close up his eyes an' he go back for a nice long old nap. The new doctor he in there an' he watchin' everythin' I do 'round that cage just to make sure that I don't go touchin' nothin' I ain't s'posed to. An' when he see Sevenny-one dog go back to sleep he come over to me an' he say, "He's a very strong dog."

"He ain't no quitter, doctor," I tell him, an' then we stand there for a while just watchin' Sevenny-one dog. Fin'ly the doctor he say to me, "If the experiment works, from a surgical standpoint that is, we should see dramatic results on the dog in a very short time." I ask him why, an' he tell me that when you puts you in a new heart an' it ain't leakin' or nothin' it work a whole lot better than the old one. He tell me that be the first step, an' if an' he didn't mess up none when he doin' the cuttin' an' the tyin' then Sevenny-one he probably lose all that fluid he been collectin' in his gut, an' his breathin' it get a whole lot better. That doctor say that Sevenny-one he probably be able to stand up in a day or two. Now if an' you cats could be gettin' youself a look at Sevenny-one dog, ain't none a you buy one word a that doctor's boo. Sevenny-one dog I bet he be dead 'fore this time tomorrow.

'Fore I left the lab he ask me to pick out which one a you dogs is like the sickest an' he want you to be brought down to the lab right 'way. Now lemme look 'round here an' see what I got left. I ain't been payin' much 'tention to you cats who in real bad shape 'cause I been figurin' that every mornin' when I comes in here you all goin' to be dead. Seem to me that the one who be in the worst shape, leastways today in the worst shape, it be old Mother here. She done have everythin' done to her that it poss'ble to do, an' she lookin' to me like she on her last legs, all right. But I don't s'pose she really any worse off than a lotta you others. But today she just look to me like she the worst off. So I goin' to be takin' you down to see the new doctor, Mother. You Number Thirty-four, an' you been 'round here long 'nough, you know. You like the oldest dog I got by like maybe thirty, forty dogs. But I sees right 'way that I got me a problem, an' that be how I goin' to get you down to that other lab. You can't even stand up no more, not to be mentionin' strollin' down no hallway. An' I sure ain't goin' to carry you, not with all them fluids you got in you gut. If I picks you up that fluid it goin' to be hurtin' you belly an' skin somethin' ter'ble. I know what I goin' to do, an' that be I goin' to put this here leash on you an' then just drag you easy like into the hall an' put you into that there red wagon that they usin' to be bringin' in the food for the diet 'speriments. Ain't nothin' but a old kid's wagon, but that be the way I get you down to the new doctor. I goin' to pull you in the wagon.

Oh, man, you all seen me messin' with Mother to get her out a here an' on down to the new doctor an' the trouble I have. Well, I know I shouldn'ta done it, I feel from the start that somethin' bad goin' to happen to Mother. One thing that all right, man, an' that be what happen when I get Mother into the wagon. She shakin' a bit, you know, like she hurtin' all over an' she don't know what goin' to happen to her. But when I gives her a pat on the head an' starts to pull the wagon real slow like, she all sudden sit up an' start to bark at me. An' her tail start beatin' a bit 'gainst the side a the wagon. It ain't like no real waggin' that goin' on, but it sure a nice thing to see. An' Mother she can't get 'nough air into her lungs to be doin' no real barkin'. She just kinda go, "Woof, woof," an' her cheeks they fill up with air just a bit, but the sound a her barkin' it ain't goin' to win no medals.

So what happen when I get her to the new doctor an' takes her outa the wagon it be 'bout the worst thing that happen yet. I say to the new doctor, "This here dog is like the oldest one I got." He look down to the dog an' he shake his head. "We calls her Mother," I say to him, an' when he ask me why I tell him 'cause right after she done have her spleen out she have a mess a puppies right there in the cage. He give a little grunt an' he shrug up his shoulders an' then he reach over to the little counter he got there an' he pick up this here hyp'dermic needle. "Put the animal to sleep," he say to me. I looks at him for like a second or two, an' I don't take no needle outa his hand. Fin'ly I say to him, "What you mean sleep?"

"Just kill the dog, Mr. Peoples," he say.

"Why you want her dead?" I asks.

"I want her heart," the doctor say, an' he actin' like he gettin' tired a talkin' to me.

"You goin' to be puttin' in a new sheep heart?" I asks.

"No," he say, "I'm just going to be doing a path study of the progress your team has made in the destruction of the valves." He give a big sigh, you know, an' he try to hand me the needle 'gain. I ain't got me no choice but to be takin' it, you know, an' when I do the new doctor he turn 'way from me an' I kneel down front a Mother. I don't say nothin' out loud, you know, but inside I thinkin' that I sorry you time is come, Mother, but it got to come sometime. An' I say inside that I sorry I the one who got to do you in. Mother she sittin' there on the floor an' she lookin' at me like she know what I talkin' 'bout, an' I know 'cause a what she do next. She lie right down on her side easy like an' when I goes to slip her the needle all she do is pick up her head an' look back to watch what I doin'. She watch all the time while I puttin' a whole mess a Nembutal into her leg, an' when she see me pull out the needle she put her head back down on that floor an' she just close up her eyes an' she give her chest a big old heave an' then she just die. But they be one thing that bother me, man, an' that be how fast she die. I ain't never seen no 'mount a Nembutal kill nothin' that fast. What I think is that Mother she just go 'head an' beat the whole thing.

So that be it for today, an' I goin' straight from here to NEW an' have the math'matics man call up for me to N.Y.U. an' see what scores I make on the G.E.D. An' like this time tomorrow, man, I haves me that there diploma. Only thing I worried 'bout it be the math'matics part, but I think this time I make me at least a 35. When you get like a hundred questions you got to make you at least a 35. An' I deserves to be passin' that there 'xamination now 'cause I done all the work I s'posed to an' I stay off the stuff, an' I done all the things they say you got to do 'fore you can be you a high school graduate.

FRIDAY

Last night, man, it somethin' else. Outa sight. Leastways what I can be rememberin' of it. Only clear picture I got in my head is where we all end up last night. I can see George an' Sidney an' me an' we all in this here livin' room someplace, an' they a mess a chicks an' some other cats I ain't never seen 'fore. Some a the peoples there they lyin' 'round on the couches an' the chairs an' some others a them they dancin' slow an' cool like. An' they's some all right kinda music playin', but that be all I 'members 'bout it. An' I 'members doin' like 'bout the most drinkin' I ever done in my whole life. It shore I goin' to be stayin' off that stuff now, man. All the wine it ever do for you is put you head very far outa shape. I fly so high last night that when Sidney he try to lay his bag on me I can't even get the needle in my arm. But I 'spect I lucky where that concern 'cause if an' I did get that mother in I 'spect I be dead now 'cause I been clean for a long time. You shoot up a mess when you be high on somethin' else, an' when you ain't had you none in like a while, then you die. But the way I feelin' right now dyin' it don't sound like the worst thing in the world. When you stretch youself out on the wine, man, you askin' for trouble. Leastways when you on the junk you just wakes up easy like an' maybe you a little angry you ain't high no more, an' maybe you do somethin' 'bout it.

An' George, man, he gettin' to be somethin' else. All the time this here school business been goin' on George he take it all very serious like. He all time play straight with Violet an' he don't never mess 'round with no other chick. Well, he mess 'bout every now an' 'gain, but he don't never see the same chick twice. I 'members last night he tellin' me how Violet she talkin' 'bout gettin' married up an' how she say that after a while when he have hisself a good job they be movin' out to Long Island. George tell me that what she talkin' it just a lotta boo an' he make hisself a promise not to marry her. George say she still fat as ever an' he gettin' tired a massagin' her rubber. Right then while we talkin' George he turn 'round an' he put his arm 'bout some cute little thing that walkin' by. He pull her close to him an' he say to me, "Man, this here a all right lady," an' he grab her chin with his hands an' he turn her face up to his. Then he say, "She pretty, an' she love George. Don't you love George, honey?" Chick she look up to him an' she flyin' pretty high all right.

"Your name George?" she say.

"Since I one year old," George tell her.

"What you mean since you one?" chick say, an' she kinda try to ease 'way from George.

"My mama she didn't give me no name for like the whole first year I 'round," George say to her. I watch him try to give her a hug, you know, an' all George do is he spill his wine down the back a her sweater. Chick she don't feel nothin'.

"What you mama call you?" chick ask.

"A whole bunch a diff'rent names," he tell her, "an' fin'ly after a year she decide I lookin' more an' more every day like a George. So she call me that."

"You a funny man," chick say, an' she take George's hand an' she start to lead him to the bedroom. While I watchin' them go I all sudden findin' myself gettin' set to fall over. It seem like my knees they just all come unloosed an' I see from the way I standin' that my feet ain't takin' no more orders from my head. When I see I swayin' back an' forth pretty good I try to tell my feet to be together, but they ain't hearin' one word I sayin'. They just keeps on rockin' back an' forth an' back an' forth. That when I know it be time for me to go an' sit down. An' it be right when I get myself into a chair that I hear George's little chick let herself out a holler from the bedroom.

"Look what you gone an' done to my sweater," she yell, an' then she open up the bedroom door. She ain't got nothin' on an' she holdin' up the sweater for like everybody to see. I don't waste no time lookin' at no sweater, I tell you that. But the whole thing it happen so fast that nobody get a good look but me, an' the chick she just get the sweater up in front a her face an' George he slam the door an' they ain't no more sound come outa that room for a long time.

That be when I see Sidney sittin' 'gainst the door on the other side a the room, an' I goes over to him an' I asks him for a pull on his bottle. Sidney he look up an' he got a very funny look on his face an' his teeth they covered up with a whole mess a spit, an' his eyes they rollin' 'bout in his head like they ain't no real eyes. Fin'ly Sidney he see who I am an' he raise up his hand an' he open his mouth a bit more like he want to say somethin'. But when he try to speak all he do is like drool a mess a spit down his chin. He feel what he doin' an' he look down to his chest an' he just watch the spit pile up on his shirt for a minute or two. "Sidney," I say to him, "you in big trouble, you know. You ain't got no control a youself no more." He look back up to me an' he try to say somethin' else, but all that happen is that he open up his mouth wide an' his tongue it slide 'bout halfway out an' it hang to the side. Then he start to slip to the side an' he go right on down to the floor an' then I know Sidney he finish for the night.

George an' Sidney an' me we all meet at NEW like we say we goin' to, an' then we went us up to the math'matics man's office, an' he phone up the lady down at N.Y.U. for the scores we make us on the G.E.D. Lemme tell you we all very uptight when we get in that room. What the math'matics man he do is he write down each a our names on a separate piece a paper an' then under the names he write down the subjects we take the 'xaminations in. Then when he finish drawin' a line next to each subject, he make his call. First the lady she give the math'matics man Sidney's score.

SOC. STUD.	17
READING COMP.	12
ENG. GRM.	21
VOCAB.	17
MATH.	36
	103

Sidney he go up two points over what he get last time. Math'-matics man he hand the paper to Sidney without even lookin' at him. When Sidney he take hisself a look at them scores he bust out laughin'. He know he ain't never goin' to pass no G.E.D., an' he say the way he goin' up like two points every time he pay ten dollars for the 'xamination it goin' to cost him 'bout a grand to get the diploma. Sidney he also be 'bout a hundred years old.

Then the math'matics man he take hold a George's paper an' he write down his scores.

SOC. STUD.	54
READING COMP.	51
ENG. GRM.	57
VOCAB.	49
MATH.	40
	251

An' when I see the math'matics man put down that there total, an' I see that George he got hisself a 251, I turn 'round an' I look to him an' I see he got his palms out. Me an' Sidney we just start hittin' him we so happy for him. George he have his high school diploma. Dig it.

Then the math'matics man he come to me an' he write down how I done.

SOC. STUD.	52
READING COMP.	40
ENG. GRM.	42
VOCAB.	51
MATH.	9
	194

When the math'matics man he have to write down a nine for what he been tryin' to teach me, he break his pencil in his hand an' he throw it clean 'cross the room. He thank the lady for givin' him them scores an' then he hang up the phone. He look right down to my paper an' he curse, an' I see that he cursin' the paper an' he cursin' me an' he cursin' hisself too. George he turn to me an' he say, "Oh, man, no. Not a nine."

"Somethin' very wrong with me an' the math'matics," I say to George. Math'matics man he fin'ly look up an' he angry. "What the hell happened?" he shoot at me.

"I don't know," I tell him. "When I come outa that 'xamination I sure I done me all right."

"A *nine*," he say, an' he look back to the paper on his desk, an' he shake his head back an' forth for a minute. Then he angry, all right. He say, "Your goddamn mother could get more than a nine."

"Yeah," I tell him, "but overall she never make herself no 194." An' George an' Sidney they bust up on the spot, an' the math'matics man he see that maybe a nine it ain't the end a the world. After he stop laughin' he ask me what I goin' to do. I looks to Sidney an' George an' back to the man, an' then I say, "Fly." That when we cut from NEW an' go find the party.

I tell you one thing, dogs, an' that be I finish with NEW. They ain't no way I be makin' it now. I mean, like I could keep workin' an' keep takin' that there 'xamination an' I be makin' higher an' higher scores. Fin'ly I could make me like a 400 or somethin' without no math'matics an' that ain't goin' to do nothin' 'cept make me angry. If an' you don't make you a 35 like in every part a the test you ain't never goin' to see you no diploma. An' they's one thing I know, man, an' that be no matter what happen I ain't never goin' to make me no 35 in the math'matics. So all I goin' to do tonight is go by NEW an' get me my digit an' get it cashed somewhere an' fly 'gain. From now on, man, all I goin' to do when I leaves here at night is fly. I don't care what it be on or nothin'. One thing it sure, an' that be I ain't goin' back to no NEW. Just ain't no reason for it.

Well, now, I tell you somethin' that make you all feel good. I just come back from checkin' on Sevenny-one Irish setter dog, an' he lookin' very good, you know. I go down to the new doctor's lab an' I see that the door it open just a bit, an' when I sees they ain't no big operation goin' on I go in. I 'spectin' to see Sevenny-one dog lyin' just like he was yesterday, only I 'spect to see him dead this time. No chance, man. That some other kinda dog the way I sees it. That little sheep's heart they put in him it look like it doin' the trick, all right. Would you be believin' it if I told you that Sevenny-one he standin' up in that there glass cage they got? He ain't standin' like too straight, you know, but he standin'. An' his belly it look like it gettin' rid a all the fluids that been collectin' there when he have his old bad heart. His eyes they still all glassed up, an' his mouth it hangin' open a bit, but he look to me like he in a lot better shape with that there new heart. So it be right then while I standin' there that the new doctor he come in an' he walk right over to me. "What do you think, Mr. Peoples?" he say to me.

"You some other kinda doctor," I tell him. "That dog he ain't looked so good in like three, four months."

"His progress will be more dramatic for the next several days," he say.

"He lookin' almost brand new now," I tell him.

"Well," he say, an' he turn 'way from the cage, "of course the animal's condition is illusory." I say fine to him, what that mean, an' he turn back to me an' he say, "Physically, the dog's improving, but chemically his body is already beginning to produce massive quantities of the substance that will attack the new heart and eventually kill it."

"So how long Sevenny-one he got?" I asks.

"It's impossible to say with any certainty," the doctor say, "but if we had transplanted another dog's heart he would, of course, have had a longer time. But with a sheep's heart the rejection mechanism is more dramatic." Right then I feel myself startin' to get angry, you know, an' that be 'cause I can't see no reason for not givin' Sevenny-one a new dog's heart. I 'bout to say that to the doctor when he go over to his table there an' take down some kinda bottle. He take hisself a hyp'dermic an' he stick it into the top a that bottle an' he draw a whole mess a fluid into his syringe. Then he turn back an' he move to open up the cage door. "What you goin' to give him?" I asks. He answer me with one a the biggest, longest words I ever hear come out a doctor's mouth. An' when I ask him what that word it s'posed to mean he say, "It is a drug that reduces the body's ability to kill a foreign organ." Course I don't make me too much sense outa that, neither. But he go on. "But the irony of it is that this substance which will eventually attack the heart also protects the body from germs. Hence the sterile condition of the cage and the isolation of the dog." Now that 'xackly what the cat say, an' what I like to know is who he think he talkin' to. I ain't no doctor, you know. But who I am that don't seem to bother him, man, an' he go on an' on with his boo 'bout all the doctorin' business an' all the time I just standin there goin', "Hmmm, hmmm, I sees what you mean." An' the man he don't even know that I the one who puttin' him on, an' he don't see nothin' in me rubbin' my chin an' screwin' up my face like I so serious 'bout the whole thing. If that cat he care to take the time he see right 'way that they ain't no way for me to be understandin' one word a what he sayin'. He just talkin' 'cause what he say he think it soundin' good. Me an' Sevenny-one there we don't care what he sayin'.

After a bit he give the dog what he want to give him, an' then Sevenny-one dog he just lie back down on his right side an' he have hisself a nap. Then the doctor he turn to me an' he say, "How many dogs do you have left in your animal room?"

"Not countin' Sevenny-one there," I tells him, "I got me twelve, thirteen."

"In what condition?" he ask.

"Bad," I tell him. "Mosta them they can't even walk no more." Then he ask me if I have like one or two what 'pear to be in good shape, an' I catchin' on to what the man doin'. He want to take the best a what I got in here an' use them first, but I too smart for the man. "No," I tell the doctor, "I ain't got me no dogs that goin' to be any better than Sevenny-one there." Right 'way the cat he look dis'pointed, an' then he ask me if he can come down here an' have hisself a look. Ain't nothin' I can be sayin' to him, but if an' he wants to it be all right with me. Only thing I told him was that it be better for him if he come down here when the room it all cleaned up an' the smell it ain't so bad. He look at me like maybe he went an' made a mistake askin' if he could be comin' into the animal room. I know he don't want to smell this here place. Course that what I countin' on 'cause I don't want the man in here lookin' all a you over for like the best dog he can find. If I do that he goin' to take Ninety-three outa here for shore. Come here, dog, lemme give you ears a scratch. You know, dog, what I doin' here with you it ain't no good. I gettin' close with you, man, an' I tell you that ain't a good thing. You a good lookin' boxer dog an' you 'bout the happiest dog I ever seen. Ain't nothin' we ever done to you that make you mad or nothin'. Oh, man, I confused, all right. I don't want that new doctor to come in here an' take you out, but I know that 'xackly what goin' to happen. An' when you gone, Ninety-three, I don't know what I goin' to be doin' 'cause the rest a these dogs here they ain't in no shape to be sayin' even a good mornin' to a cat. Ninety-three, you 'bout the only one in here worth talkin' to. Hey, man, I know what I do. I hide you under one a these here cages so when the doctor he come in he don't find you. But I can't be doin' that 'cause soon as you smells you 'nother cat you come out from under the cage an' you jump up on him, barkin' an' tryin' to lick him to death. That ain't like the best thing that you could be doin' you know. But the way I sees it I in trouble no matter what I do. I already told the doctor that they ain't no good dogs in here, an' if he find you, Ninety-three, it be my skin he take off for lyin' to him. I know what I goin' to do, man, an' that be I goin' to take you outa the animal room 'fore the man comes. I take you an' put you in the diet room for a while, an' that way the man he don't take you outa here, an' he don't catch me lyin'.

Now you sit there an' mind you business, Ninety-three dog, 'cause I got to make this here whole thing look good. First thing I do is take 'way you water dish an' you food dish an' put them in the sink, an' then I take off the 'hesive tape from the cage here with you name on it. Now all I got to do is wipe out you cage a bit an' it lookin' like they ain't never been no dog in here. There, now you all set, dog, an' now we goin' to the diet 'speriment room for a while.

Oh, yeah, *dig*, man, it work so cool, you know. New doctor he fooled all the way, an' Ninety-three there she goin' back in her cage an' she safe as can be now. An' I know that new doctor he never come back in here. Like never. He come 'bout as close to losin' his dinner as any cat I ever seen. An' when I see him start to get uptight from the smell I say to him nice like, "Is somethin' wrong, doctor?" an' he shake his head while he goin' from cage to cage. But then when he stop an' he take out his hank'chief an' put it over his nose I ask him 'gain, "Is they anythin' wrong, doctor?" an' this time he turn 'round an' he look at me like he know I puttin' him on. But they ain't no way he can be sayin' anythin' to me 'bout it. Through the hank'chief he ask me if you cats be all I got, an' I say, "They ain't the prettiest things in the world, is they?" an' then he turn 'way from me an' that when he start to 'xamine a few a you, but he don't take but a minute or two to check how big you guts is from the fluids. It right then that I see the cat he in trouble if he stay 'round for like 'nother minute. An' he look at me an' he know it, too. All sudden he stand straight up from one a you dogs over there an' he say, "Thank you, Mr. Peoples," an' then he move to the door 'bout as fast as a cat can.

Okay, Ninety-three dog, back in you cage, man. I put you water dish an' you food dish back, an' I make you out a new piece a 'hesive tape that say "Ninety-three," an' I put it right back here on you cage door.

MONDAY

I don't know what the math'matics man he doin' teachin' math'matics. He make out a whole lot better if an' he be sellin' cars or somethin'. When I go to NEW Friday night to pick up my digit he waitin' for me right there in the little room where we gets them. He say to me soon as I walk in, "Could I talk with you for a minute?"

"What you want?" I ask him.

"From the way it looks to me, you're leaving the program," he say.

"This be the last digit I takin' outa this place," I tell him.

"I want to talk to you about it before you quit," he say.

"Yeah?" I say to him, "what we got to talk 'bout?" I don't want to speak with that man nohow. All I want is my digit an' to cut outa there, an' I don't want no teacher tryin' to mess me up when I know what I goin' to do.

"In a way," he say nice like, "we haven't got anything to talk about. At least there's nothing I can say to you that'll keep you here."

"You right 'bout that," I tells him, an' I turns 'way an' signs the paper in front a the lady who in charge a the digits.

"All I want to do is make you a proposition," he say.

"That right?" I say to him, an' I ain't lookin' at him. "What kind?"

"You've passed four out of the five parts of the G.E.D. and all you've got to do is pass the mathematics part."

"I ain't never goin' to do that," I tell him. All sudden like, his eyes they get like slits, an' he look like he blushin', 'cause his skin get a bit pink. "Look," he say, "you can pass that examination. I know you can."

"If you be so sure," I say to him, "then why don't I make me more than a nine last time? An' after all the work I done."

"That's what I want to talk to you about," he say, an' he look down to the floor like he gettin' sad 'bout somethin'. "It's my fault," he say. "I've been going at the whole thing wrong. There's more than one way to teach you mathematics."

"That right?" I say to him, an' I got to be straight with you, dogs, all sudden like I int'rested. I don't know why, man, but right there that math'matics cat he coulda sold me any old used car he have on his lot. It not be what the cat say, it be the way he sayin' it, an' 'fore I know it I thinkin' that maybe they be 'nother way I can be passin' that there 'xamination. So easy like I opens up my digit an' I checks the amount, an' I know all the time what it goin' to say. Why I do it be 'cause I needs the time to think. Then the math'matics man he say to me, "Come on, let's go upstairs and talk it over." I tell him okay, an' I put my digit in my pocket an' go with him.

When we get to his office he say to me, "If you're willing to stay at NEW I can arrange it so that you'll spend the whole evening on mathematics. After all, you only have to retake that part of the G.E.D."

"Yeah, I know," I tell him, but right then I can't see me spendin' like no two, three hours every evenin' just on math'-matics. That mess up my head bad. But then I say to him, "You really think I can be takin' that 'xamination an' pass it?"

"I guarantee it," he say, an' he smile easy like.

"How you guarantee somethin' like that," I asks.

"You leave that to me," he say. "You see, where I've gone wrong was to try to teach you everything about high school math. What I should have done was teach you about the examination."

"That make some sense," I tell him.

"There are about thirty different types of problems on the G.E.D.," he say, "and once you've got down what kind of types they are, recognizing them will be simple. Once you know which kind of problem it is, solving it will be easy."

"But what 'bout them word problems?" I ask.

"You let me worry about that," he say, an' then he take this here pad outa his desk an' he say, "You willing to try?"

"Yeah," I say, "I give it 'nother chance."

"What have you got to lose?" he say, an' he smile easy like at me.

"Ain't never had nothin' to lose," I tell him.

Sorry to have to cut out on you like so fast then, but I just 'members that it be time for me to go see Sevenny-one dog. He in bad shape. Ain't from his heart, the new doctor say that workin' pretty good. Trouble with Sevenny-one it be that he got hisself some pneumonia, an' the reason for that it be that he ain't got nothin' in his body for fightin' off no germs. An' the new doctor he tell me that they mess up a bit over the weekend 'bout who s'posed to be comin' in to take care a Sevenny-one. He say he think I goin' to do it or some other cat, an' what happen is that Sevenny-one's cage it get too cold durin' the weekend an' the doctor say the dog he get sick from that. He say Sevenny-one he goin' to die soon. "Ain't you got somethin' that keep him goin'?" I asks.

"Not when the pneumonia becomes this advanced so rapidly," he say. I think that right then if I have a blade in my hand I stick that mother. If he ask me to come in over the weekend I do it, but nobody ever ask me an' 'cause a that Sevenny-one he be dead soon.

Then while I standin' there lookin' in at Sevenny-one the new doctor he say to me that I s'posed to bring one a you dogs to him for like 'nother operation s' afternoon. "Which one you want, doctor?" I ask him.

"Any dog will do," he say. "The dogs you've got in the animal room are miserable specimens anyway."

"Yeah," I say, lookin' at Sevenny-one.

"Any dog will do," he say 'gain.

All right, so listen up, now. Which one a you wants to go down to see the man an' get you heart changed? Shut up, Ninety-three dog, you ain't goin' nowhere. Why you always jumpin' 'round like maybe you think you goin' to a party or somethin'? Back up in you cage, man, or maybe I take you down there right now. That's better, dog. None a the rest a you can even stand up, but some a you is lookin' 'bout to see who be goin'. How 'bout you, Eighty dog? You don't look like you in too bad shape today, an' you ain't been doin' nothin' for a long time 'cept lie 'bout havin' you heart get worse an' worse. You a very funny-lookin' dog, you know. Some a the dogs we have in here they been very fine-bred dogs, you know. But with you, man, they ain't no way a tellin' nothin' 'bout what you mother an' father look like. You body it so mixed up with other dogs ain't no way a tellin' nothin' 'bout where you come from.

Here, now, I lift you outa you cage an' see if you can stand up. No chance. You legs they all stiff an' curled up under you body. Look to me like they dead, you know, 'cause they cold an' they ain't no hair grown back on them from where I shaved them up for all the needles. Now you stay where you is on the floor, dog, an' I get me the little red wagon to be takin' you down to the new doctor.

Some other kinda things happen on Friday night an' Sat'day. Some things good, some others ain't. Like what happen is that when I get done down at NEW I cut outa there an' went me over to Sidney's house. Sidney he finish now, man. I knocks on the door an' when Sidney's sister she answer I don't make no nice talk with her or nothin'. She a mean chick, an' I don't make me no nice talk with no mean chicks. "Where Sidney?" I say to her.

"You just like all the rest, Billy Peoples," she say, an' she standin' in the doorway lookin' me up an' down.

"What you talkin' 'bout?" I ask her.

"If my brother he be your friend," she say, an' she point a finger at me, "you never leave him like you done last night."

"What you talkin' *leave* him?" I say an' I try to get me a look 'round the door to see if Sidney there.

"I know you was there," she say.

"So I was there," I tell her. "So what that mean?"

"You be the one who give my little brother them drugs all the time," she say.

"Who told you that?" I say to her an' all sudden like I very angry.

"My brother is a good boy," she say, "an' he never get into no trouble 'less someone like you give him them drugs."

"What you talkin' 'bout *me* givin' Sidney stuff?" I asks.

"They always got to be one like you," she say, an' her face it look like she gettin' set to cry.

"Is Sidney here or ain't Sidney here?" I say.

"Sidney in the hospital," she say. An' just when I 'bout set to ask her what he sick with she say, "An' he in trouble with the *po*-lice 'gain. All 'cause a you." An' she point her finger at me 'gain.

"You talkin' jive," I tell her.

"I was in the hospital with my brother the whole day," she say, "an' all he able to do is ask where you are. An' I just come me from the *po*-lice an' they tell me only way my little brother he stay outa jail it be if he go to Lexington. An' I lost a whole day's pay," she say. It be right then that I hear this big low voice from the other side a the door say, "Hey, baby, write the man a letter."

"A minute," Sidney's sister say, an' then she say to me, "You goin' to be 'scusin' me now. I gots me some more 'portant things to be doin' with my evenin' than standin' 'round talkin' with a dope fiend." An' she close up the door right in my face.

Well, man, what happen to Sidney it was goin' to happen sooner or later. I guess that what happen it be that Sidney he fin'ly take too much a everythin' an' when everybody wake up Friday mornin' they get all uptight 'cause they can't wake up Sidney. I knew they be havin' some trouble with that when I move him outa the way from the door. An' I guess that when they can't wake him up they call the *po*-lice an' they come an' took him to the hospital. Well, I got to go 'round an' see Sidney an' find out if that be what happen. If that ain't what happen, I 'spect it be close 'nough.

An' somethin' happen on Sat'day you should be knowin' 'bout. I layin' in my bed like real late, you know, an' my head it buzzin' a bit 'cause after I seen Sidney's sister I went down to the bar an' I had me some wine all right. An' I just layin' there listenin' to the trucks goin' up an' down when they comes this here knockin' on my door.

"Billy," my ma she yell out, "you friend George he be here to see you," an' I thinkin' it very strange that George he comin' to see me on a Sat'day mornin'. So I get up an' I go right out to see him, an' lemme tell you George he dressed out like no time I ever seen him. He sportin' hisself some fine duds, all right, but the trouble with them they be the kinda duds I have to wear when I workin' as a messenger on Wall Street. "What up with you?" I say to him.

"I have been accepted by SEEK," he say. But the fact he get in it ain't nothin' to the way George say it. All sudden he like maybe some kinda king, you know, an' he can be talkin' down to everybody.

"How you get in so fast?" I say to him.

"I delivered the scores to the SEEK office myself," he say, "an' they sent the letter yesterday afternoon."

"Hey, man, that's all right," I tell him. You know, I happy for George, but right then they's somethin' 'bout him that don't jive. It like he gettin' a bad smell 'bout him, an' all sudden I a bit 'fraid a him. I turns to my ma an' I say, "You dig that? George he get into SEEK."

"George can do word problems," she say, an' then she turn 'way from me an' she go an' pick herself up a rosary. "But you make it someday. I still prayin' for it to Saint Jude."

"You tell Violet?" I say.

"I just come from her," he say, an' he start to fix his tie, "an' we ain't together no more. Violet she a ugly like always."

"So which school you goin' to?" I asks.

"Hunter College," he say, only he say it like it s'posed to be some kinda club that only he belong to. "On Park Avenue," he say, an' I feel myself gettin' set to let him have 'bout the best punch I got when he say, "I'm goin' down there this afternoon to have me a look at the place."

"That why you dressed out like a dude?" I say.

"You got to look respectable if an' you goin' down to Park

Avenue," he say. Then he ask me if an' I want to be goin' with him, an' I say, "Why me? It don't mean nothin' to me."

"Why don't you go 'long with your friend, Billy?" my ma she say. "It do you some good to see what a college look like." Right then I sees I gots me a choice a goin' with George or stayin' home the whole day an' bein' talked to. So I go with George.

You know, dogs, I tell you Hunter College it ain't so bad a place. From the outside it look just like a big old buildin', not like no college s'posed to look like, an' on the inside they's a whole mess a rooms just like they have at my high school. George he walk 'round the place like he own it, an' he makin' me feel very uptight. He say to me, "Dig this," an' he walk up to a cute little white chick an' he say to her, "Hey, baby, where the office a the man who runnin' the show here?"

"Who do you want?" the chick say.

"I just been accepted by the SEEK program an' I'm goin' to be a student here," he tell her.

"What's SEEK?" she say, an' George he turn to me like maybe I s'posed to answer the question for him.

"Ain't nothin' to be all worked up 'bout," I tell her. George he whip 'round on me an' he start preachin' to me 'bout how jealous I am a him an' everythin', an' the chick she just shrug her shoulders an' walk off. "Man, what you mean sayin' somethin' like that to the chick?"

"George," I say to him straight, "you a jive cat all the way with this here college boo."

"Well you ain't never goin' to make it," he say to me.

"If gettin' into the SEEK thing make me out the way you carryin' on," I tell him, "then I don't never want to go to no college." An' then I cut from him an' went home.

SUMMER

MONDAY

Hey, man, dig what just happen. I just seen Millard on the subway comin' down here. An' he lookin' very cool, I tell you that. Millard he back in the army an' he say he goin' to be in them special forces. Now ain't that all right? When Millard he was at NEW I sometimes seen him lookin' good, but I never seen him lookin' so strong an' lean. He tell me that what happen to him it be that the *po*-lice they have to let him go 'cause they ain't no way they prove nothin' 'gainst him. An' what he done was to go right back down to the recruitin' office an' sign hisself up. He tell the sergeant there that he sign up only if an' they guarantee him they send him someplace where they be some fightin'. I ask Millard why he want that an' he tell me, "Shoot, man, you kiddin'? I got to learn me up a whole mess a things, you know."

"Ain't you 'fraid a gettin' you ass shot up?" I ask.

"They ain't nobody been made yet who goin' to shoot my ass up," he tell me. Millard he leaner an' tougher now, but he still 'bout the same, you know. So we ridin' 'long for a spell, an' then he ask me how things they be at NEW. I tell him things they ain't so good 'cause the State it fin'ly goin' to cut off all the bread. "What the brothers goin' to do 'bout that?" he ask, an' his eyes kinda narrow up.

"We goin' to picket the City," I tell him.

"That right?" he say, an' he laugh 'gain.

"The director man he say if we do us some picketin' we goin' to get the dust," I tell him. "The director man he told us that he got hisself a friend down at City Hall who said all we got to do to get us the bread it be to go down an' make us a fuss. The cat who yell the loudest, he the one who goin' to get it."

"That sound right," Millard say.

Then he ask me 'bout Sidney an' George, an' when I tell him what happen to Sidney he say he could see that comin' for like 'long time, but when he find out that George he get into SEEK an' he only make hisself a 251 on the G.E.D. Millard he get very angry. He holdin' on to one a them silver poles on the subway, you know, an' I see him give it a squeeze like maybe he goin' to break it in half right there. He curse quiet like an' then he ask me how I been doin' an' I tell him I still be at NEW an' I pass everythin' on the G.E.D. but the math'matics part. "I been workin' on that for a long time now," I tell him.

"You make it, little man," he say to me.

"Yeah, I make it," I say, but just 'tween you an' me, dog, I ain't so sure.

Millard he get off at Times Square, an' just when I goin' to tell him goodbye he say to me, "Little man, if they don't start treatin' you right soon you be in touch with me, hear?"

"What you goin' to be doin' 'bout it?" I ask.

"Man, why you think I in the army?" he say.

"You learnin' all you can 'bout war," I say to him 'cause all sudden like I see what he talkin' 'bout. He smile at me an' he nod, an' then when he go to leave he hold up his fist an' he give me the power sign an' all the rest a the stuff that go with it. Then he just ease hisself out the door a the car. I glad Millard he goin' back in the army, man, 'cause that where he belong.

But you know, one thing that I tell Millard it be the truth, an' that be the business 'bout the State closin' down NEW. Last Friday night we find out from the director man that they ain't goin' to be no more digits or nothin' from the State come this here Friday. He say he been tryin' for like weeks to speak some sense with them, but when the State it make up its mind on somethin' that be it. But he tell us that he very close with his friend down at City Hall an' he got it all set for us to be goin' down there tonight. Director man he tell us that he been told by his friend just how we got to do it an' he lay out all the plans for us on Friday night. He say that what we got to do is we got to make the dem'stration big 'nough so we get on the television an' in the *NEWS.* But he say we can't go gettin' violent 'cause if that happen his friend at City Hall he ain't goin' to know nobody an' they send in the *po*-lice to break us up fast. He make us all promise that we ain't goin' to do nothin' but walk 'round an' carry our signs. Then he tell us that we got to show up early tonight to like make up them signs. After he say that he tell the Self-Wareness cat to get what he need for the signs an' charge it all up to NEW. Self-Wareness cat he tell the director man that he need like so much cardboard an' wood an' like 'bout twenny bottles a black liquid shoe polish. Director man say to get plenty a stuff 'cause we goin' to make a whole mess a signs. Self-Wareness cat tell him he take care a everythin'.

All 'long now, I been thinkin' that the big doctor he a all right cat, but I tell you I don't think that no more. You know what that mean mother he done to me? He just fire me. That's right, he just get up on his high old horse an' he fire me. Bang, man, just like that he fire me. Shoot, man, he ain't no kinda human bein', I tell you that. All time I be here he treat me fine, you know, but when he call me in his office a few minutes ago he ain't no longer the kinda man I thinkin' he is. He say to me, "Sit down, Mr. Peoples," an' he point to a nice-lookin' chair. "I'm afraid I've got some bad news for you," he say. "I'm going to have to let you go."

"What you mean lemme go?" I ask him.

"As of the end of the week," he say, "your position here is terminated."

"You tellin' me I bein' fired?" I asks. Cat he ain't bein' straight with me.

"I'd rather not couch it in those terms," he say.

"What be the matter?" I ask, "ain't I doin' my job the way I s'posed to?"

"You've done an excellent job," he say. "You're the best animal man we've ever had."

"If I be doin' my job all right, why you firin' me?" I asks.

"It has to do with our budget," he say.

"You want me to work for less?" I ask him.

"No, that has nothing to do with it," he tell me.

"Then I don't understand nothin' that goin' on," I tell him, an' he sees that I gettin' angry, all right.

"You see," he say to me, "the entire project we've all been working on has been government-sponsored, and the funds we had available were limited to a year. We assumed that we would have sufficient funds to continue for, say, another six months to a year. But our application for extension has been delayed to the point where I'm having to disband the program."

"Why the gov'ment it all the time be so slow?" I ask.

"I don't know," he say an' he shake his head like all sudden he very sad.

"So I got just this here week?" I asks.

"Yes," he tell me, "but I wish I could have given you a longer period of notice. However, five working days is the Center's policy."

So I sit there for a while an' I don't do nothin 'cept scratch my head an' look at the man. Fin'ly I say to him, "They any other jobs 'round that I can be doin'?"

"None that I know of," he say, "but if I hear of anything promising I'll keep you in mind." Now that a bunch a jive, man, 'cause the cat he done his hatchet job, an' after he done with that all he want from me is to get up an' leave as soon as I can. He don't want to talk to me no more now that he done firin' me.

The way it look to me, dog, is that I goin' to have to be gettin' me a job. But the way things be I goin' to have to get me my G.E.D. 'fore I can get me a job that goin' to be all right with me. If I can do that then things maybe they work theyselves out all right. But if an' I don't then I ain't goin' to be fit for nothin' 'cept all the things I done 'fore like bein' a messenger an' checkin' pockets at the cleaners like my ma. Seem to me that if a cat he put hisself in a good year workin' for somebody then he ought not to get hisself fired. Seem to me he ought to be gettin' hisself better an' better jobs. I tell you one thing, Ninety-three, an' that be I ain't goin' to be no messenger or no pocket checker. I go on the Unemployment 'fore I do that business 'gain. An' if they won't take me on the Unemployment then I set myself up so I get on the Welfare. Or I get myself close with some chick who on it.

Damn, man, you know what I like to be doin' right now? I like to maybe be rippin' this here place to pieces all by myself. I'd like to be kickin' down all them cages an' go into them labs an' just start breakin' up everythin' I lay my eyes on. That be the way I take care a that big doctor for kickin' me outa my job. Yeah, dog, I know what you thinkin' the way you lookin' at me. You thinkin' it ain't the big doctor's fault, an' maybe you be right. But if an' it ain't the big doctor's fault then it be the gov'ment's fault. An' if it truly be the gov'ment who lettin' me go they ain't too much that I can be doin' 'bout that. Ain't no way you can bust the gov'ment in the nose.

Now I got to get me together here an' be takin' Fifty dog down to the doctor who goin' to be doin' his last transplant a the sheep heart. Leastways it be the last transplant he goin' to be doin' on any dogs I been keepin' in my animal room. Fifty dog he the last one I got besides you, Ninety-three.

Come on outa you cage, Fifty dog. Come on, I say. Look, you goin' to lie there all day like maybe you some kinda sick dog or is you goin' to come on outa there like a man? You ain't goin' to jive me, dog, I knows you can stand up all right. I see you do it last Friday when I takin' out that cute little white dog next to you. An' I know why you stand up, an' that be 'cause little white dog she a girl dog an' you thinkin' maybe you get youself some action offa her. Well, if you can be standin' up on Friday then you can be standin' up today. Come on, man, I tired a gettin' that old red wagon an' pullin' you all down to the doctor. Here, I put the rope 'round you neck an' I pull you out. See, you can stand up all right. *Hey*, dog, what you doin' relievin' youself all over the place? Oh, my, but you goin' an' goin' an' it don't look to me like you got no control a what you doin'. You standin' there an' you whole body it shakin' so bad an' you just lettin' everythin' go. An' you don't even know you doin' it, neither. What's the matter with you, dog? You 'fraid a what goin' to happen to you? I s'pose you is. You seen all them other dogs go outa here with me, an' you know ain't one a them ever come back. I can't go blamin' you for havin' no control a youself. But just 'cause you think you know what goin' to happen to you don't mean I goin' to let you off. You got to come 'long with me, Fifty dog, an' when I come back from the lab I clean up you mess.

So it just be you an' me now, Ninety-three, an' they ain't goin' to be no more dogs comin' into the animal room no more.

Now I got to clean up Fifty dog's mess. You know that dog he a strange dog all the way. When I take him outa here just a few minutes ago he shakin' an' shakin' an' he still doin' a bit a piddlin' in the hall. But after we go 'bout twenny, thirty feet he all sudden seem to get together. He stop for a minute an' he give hisself like the hardest shake I ever seen a dog give. An' when he done with that he sits down in the hall an' he start like maybe to give hisself a little bath, you know, an' I figurin' that this be his last chance for that so I don't do nothin' but let him do what he want. First thing he do it be his privates, an' when he done with that he go to work on his face. He rub out his eyes, an' when he done with that he gives his paws a few licks an' then he go inside his ears. Then when he start to feelin' like he in better shape than when he in here he give hisself 'nother little shake an' then he look up at me. I don't do nothin' 'cept look back down at him. It be right then that he turn 'round an' he start to walk off to the lab like maybe he leadin' me. An' he ain't so strong, you know, not after all we done to him an' all the time he spend in his cage there, but he give me a surprise with how hard he pull on the rope. An' he have his back straight as a board an' his head it up like he tryin' to see over somethin', you know, an' his ears is like stickin' straight up like maybe he listenin' for somethin'. An' when we get to the lab door he sit down an' wait for me to open it up for him. An' when I do that he go in without no pushin' or shovin' from me, an' when he see the doctor he just sit right down on the floor an' look up at him. Doctor he hand me the Nembutal an' I put Fifty dog out fast.

There now, all that mess it cleaned up, an' you can come outa you cage now, Ninety-three. There, the whole animal room it be yours from now on, an' I ain't goin' to do nothin' but let you run 'round in here by youself. Ninety-three dog, what you doin'? You actin' like I ain't never seen you act 'fore. You pacin' from one cage to 'nother an' you givin' each one a them a smell. *Hey*, dog, get outa there, you ain't got no business in Fifty's cage. Come on, man, I lettin' you run on you own an' all you do is go an' jump in 'nother dog's cage. Come on, I pull you outa there. Now you stay out here on the floor where I want you to. Ninety-three, dog, get 'way from that cage over there. Stop pawin' it like all you want is to get inside. All right, you askin' for it, back in you own cage, dog. If an' you don't want to be out here with me then that be you business. Come on, get in, man. There, I close up the cage door, but I leave it open a bit case you change you mind an' want to come out.

Dig, Ninety-three, this here must be my day for seein' people. When I go for my dinner at the cafeteria just now, you know who I see? I see the big white doctor. He still a jive cat all the way, but just the same it nice to see him, you know. I goin' through the line with my tray, an' all sudden from behind me I hear this cat say, "Mr. Peoples, I presume?" See, he still a jive cat, all right. I turn 'round an' I ask him how he been doin' an' he tell me that he gettin' 'long just fine so long as he don't have to be doin' no research. Then the man ask me if I eatin' with anybody, an' when I tell him no he point to a table an' we sits down. "The best thing in the world for me was to get back and start finishing up my residency," he tell me.

"You smart to get out when you did," I tell him.

"I heard the program was closing down," he say.

"Yeah? How you hear so fast?" I ask.

"There've been rumors now for a couple of weeks," he say.

"That right?" I say to him. "I only heard me this mornin' that I be outa my job."

"What are you going to do?" he ask me nice like.

"Shoot, man, I ain't goin' to do *nothin'*," I tell him.

"Why?" he ask me.

"Why should I?" I say.

"Well, you've had some good experience in the Center," he say. Dig, Ninety-three, he call cleanin' up mess day after day good 'sperience. Then he say, "Did you get your Equivalency Diploma?"

"No," I tell him, "I took me that 'xamination like two times, an' I almost get it the second time but I ain't got no chance a ever gettin' it 'cause a the math'matics." He ask me why an' when I tell him that I make me a six an' a nine on the mathmatics part he shake his head like he very sorry 'bout somethin'. Then he ask me if I already give up on the whole thing, an' I tell him I goin' to try it one more time. "If you could get the diploma," he say, "there are several jobs here in the hospital you might qualify for. But you can't be considered without the diploma."

"It don't look like I goin' to be gettin' no diploma," I tell him.

"Well," he say, "I know of one job you'd be suited for, but of course it does require a high school diploma. The doctor in charge demands it." You know, Ninety-three, I didn't even ask him what that job be, an' that a good thing, you know, 'cause if an' it sound like a good job an' I get me all worked up 'bout it an' then I mess up the G.E.D. 'gain I goin' to be like very dis'pointed. All I tell him it be that I goin' to try it 'gain, but I figurin' that what goin' to happen is that when I get outa here I goin' to go on the Unemployment or the Welfare.

Now it be time for me to get me on down to the lab an' get rid a that dead sheep.

Fifty dog he lookin' to be in good shape, you know. He come through his operation like the best one a the whole mess that transplant doctor done. He say he ain't never seen a blood pressure that be as good as what Fifty dog got. He say that mosta the time them blood pressures they been so low it like maybe them sheep hearts they don't want to beat the way they s'pose to. But he say the little sheep heart he put in Fifty dog it must be like somethin' else, 'cause that dog he make his blood pressure give a nice high readin' for the doctor. While the transplant doctor he takin' Fifty dog's pressure I standin' there watchin'. When he satisfied with his readin', he turn to me an' he say, "It's a pity that the Center is having trouble with its refunding."

"No lie," I say to him. "What you goin' to do when we close up?"

"The staff is only being cut back at the unskilled level," he tell me.

"That right?" I say to him.

"But if we're not refunded soon," he say, "I suppose that a few of the less key technicians will also be let go."

"Oh, yeah?" I say easy like, like I truly care, you know, but I don't care if an' they be lettin' Christ hisself go. All that count with me it be that I goin'. But after a second or two I say to him, "So who goin' to be doin' the work in the animal room?"

"I suppose the doctors will have to fend for themselves," he tell me, an' I can see on his face he don't like that idea nohow.

"It ain't no nice kinda work," I tell him.

"I'm aware of that," he say.

"Soon as the Center it get itself some bread you hire youself a animal man. That a important job," I tell him.

"Frankly," he say to me, "a competent animal man is indispensable to the functioning of the Center." I tell him that he be right 'bout that, an' then he say he sorry I gettin' let go 'cause I been doin' me a all right job. I tell him I sorry I bein' let go 'cause I likes the work. That a nice old lie, ain't it, Ninety-three? Then he say to me, "Where are you going from here?"

"Don't know," I say. "Only got let go this mornin'."

"You'll make out all right," he say, but he don't say it like he sure 'bout it.

"What you goin' to be doin' for spec'mens, doctor?" I ask him, 'cause I know he ain't got no more dogs left.

"I shall have to get as much mileage as possible out of this one," he say, an' he point to Fifty dog lyin' out cold in his glass cage. "But if he doesn't work out I shall just have to move on to other animals."

"Like what kind you be usin'?" I ask.

"Most likely cats," he say. "But I'd much rather work on dogs. Cats are very troublesome, very hostile." I tell you I glad I ain't taken' care a no cats, man, 'cause a cat he don't stand for nobody cuttin' him up. You mess 'round with a cat sooner or later he come an 'tack you. I ask him why he goin' to work on cats an' he say, "There's a surplus at the moment." Man, I tell you if an' the big doctor he come to me an' he say, all right, Mr. Peoples, you ain't bein' let go if an' you take charge a the cat room I tell him no chance, man, I cuttin' out. Cats they ain't my line a work.

Man, I tell you Ninety-three dog, they somethin' wrong with my head. I ain't never payin' no 'tention to what I s'posed to be doin'. Seem like my mind it always be somewhere else when I got to do somethin' important. I be havin' a bit a trouble with my gut, see, like I told you last week, an' my ma she say that it from eatin' too much sodas an' chips an' garbage like that in the mornin'. She keep tellin' me I got to have a lotta real wholesome food 'fore I starts the day. I just takes what handy, you know. So what I done that mess me up it be that just now when I go to sit on the toilet I forget to put down the seat, an' I fall into the bowl. An' when that happen I just sits there an' I thinkin' to myself that if an' I can't be 'memberin' to put down no toilet seat how I goin' to 'member which problems is which when the G.E.D. it come up 'gain. A cat he can do a lotta dumb things, man, but not 'memberin' to put down a toilet seat it got to be the dumbest.

Now I got to get me outa here an' over to NEW an help with makin' up them signs. Tonight we goin' to picket City Hall.

TUESDAY

Dig it, Ninety-three dog, you know what I got right here in my hand? It be a letter from Sidney. Sidney he must be gettin' straightened 'round if an' he can be writin' me a letter an' have it get all the way here to me. Sidney he pass the math part a the G.E.D. just fine, you know, but he ain't no good nohow with no English. Even the readin' lady, Miss Beverley, she can't teach no English to Sidney. So lemme read this here thing an' see what the man he has to say for hisself. Would you please have youself a look at the writin' a this here thing? Look like some old man done push the pencil 'cross the page with like both hands.

Der Bily

How are you. Things here are o k now. Im strait. It took me along time to be strait but I strait now. In the begining I have a bad time you know. Cause they give me stuf that mess me up. Now I doing voc train. an when I o k they going to let me come home. I want to come home bad and see my freinds.
What have you been doing did you make the ged. I hope you did. Someday I going to make my ged to. I got to go now cause they want me to do something. Write me a letter.

Your freind
Sidney

Sound to me, Ninety-three, like Sidney he have hisself a bad time down there. I know a couple other cats who had to go there, an' when they come out they say they goin' to be straight an' they swear up an' down on they mothers' graves they goin' to be straight. An' when they gets on the train to come back home a couple porters on the train they make them fly all the way back. Sidney he ain't never got no chance, man, not 'less he be a whole lot stronger than I ever seen him be.

Now lemme get you some food an' water, dog, an' fix you up for the day. You sure is a all right dog, Ninety-three, an' I tell you it be the best thing in the world to be takin' care of a dog what like to be taken care of. There, now, you all set, an' while you eatin' up a storm I gots to tell you somethin' cool that happen last night at NEW.

While we all in the little library they got there an' we waitin' for the buses to come to take us down to City Hall the math'matics man he come up to where I be sittin'. He say to me, "How would you like to take the G.E.D. on Wednesday?"

"I take it whenever you say I be ready," I tell him.

"You're as ready as you're ever going to get," he say. Last Friday I fin'ly got me down the last a them thirty problems he been givin' me an' when he see I can sit me down an' run through all a them by heart I guess he figure I set to go. Then he tell me he make me a 'pointment with the lady down at N.Y.U. for tomorrow. That lady she see me once more she goin' to start thinkin' I there so much maybe I dig takin' 'xaminations. So I tell him I goin' to go an' he ask me if an' I got the bread for it an' I tell him not to go worryin' 'bout me 'cause I doin' all right. He tell me fine, an' then he see that I sittin' right next to a checkerboard what some cat already set up. He put his hand on it an' he ask me if I want to play. Now that a bad old question to be askin' me, man, 'cause checkers it be my game. "Sure," I tell him, an' all he do is move the board in front a me an' he say, "Your move." I takes out my dollar bill an' lays it on the table next to the board, an' when he see me do that he match it without sayin' nothin'.

Right then a couple a cats they see what goin' on an' they come over to have theyselves a look. Now I gots to tell you, Ninety-three, that I 'bout the best checker player at NEW. Nobody ever beat me at checkers. An' if an' they was like some kinda big checkers championship I 'spect I be right up there, you know. But I tell you, I worried 'bout playin' the math'matics man 'cause thinkin' the way you got to in checkers it be the way he make his livin'. But from the way things go I don't s'pose he be too happy 'bout tellin' a whole mess a people that he a math'matics teacher. He may be hisself a good math'matics teacher, man, but he sure ain't no checker player, I tell you that. He ain't got no kinda moves at all. He just know how to play the thing straight, you know, like takin' man for man. I play like that when I in the second grade, man, an' I learn me fast how to play like every one a my men they belong to a army or somethin'. I take the first four men he put out front a me, but I don't take them so he able pin down one a my men. An' after I gets me number fi' he start to get a bit uptight, you know, an' that be 'cause they's a whole bunch a cats standin' 'round the table watchin.' "You've got some good moves," he say to me, an' I can see him studyin' up that board for like all he be worth. But he finish then, you know, 'cause if an' I get the first three men without losin' none a mine then I know they ain't no way I ever lose. I don't know why it be, but when I playin' checkers I can see me like, six, seven moves I gonna make without havin' to look real hard at what goin' on. Seem to me that everybody he ought to be able to do that, it come so easy to me, but the math'matics man he don't see but maybe one, two moves, an' when I see that I start thinkin' that maybe I can take him without losin' none a my men. I done that couple a times 'fore, but it be when I playin' Sidney an' he only thinkin' 'bout gettin' the game over so he can go fly or somethin'. So when I take like three more a his men without losin' none a mine the math'matics man he see what I tryin' to do. He look up to me an' he know he been whipped good, but he dead set 'gainst me winnin' without him takin' at least one a my men. So I got to play it careful for a while, an' one time

I nearly slip into a trap he set up, but I don't, an' when he down to 'bout two men left an' he see I 'bout ready to set them up for the kill he look up to me an' he say, "A six and a nine on the G.E.D., huh?" an' then he shake his head an' he make the move that I been waitin' for an' I knock off his last two men. He pick up the two dollars an' he give them to me. Some cat standin' behind the math'matics man he say to him, "Brother, you just been beat by the best they is." Math'-matics man he get up from the table an' he turn to the cat who say that an' he tell him he a believer, all right. Then he turn back to me an' he say, "If you don't pass that examination on Wednesday I'm personally going to break your neck."

"I be in there tryin'," I tell him, but the math'matics man he don't dig that takin' the G.E.D. it ain't like playin' no checkers. Checkers it just fun.

So what happen after the buses they fin'ly get there it be somethin' else, all right. First thing it be that the buses is all late 'cause they mess up on where NEW it be an' they can't find no address for it. Anyway, man, when they do get there all a us trainees we get on. Now I 'spect they 'bout two hundred a the trainees in all, you know, when we come to school, but only 'bout a hundred shows up to go down to City Hall. But the director man he ain't dumb, you know. He know he messin' with his job an' everythin' an' he know he got to make hisself a good showin' in the dem'stration if an' he want to keep NEW goin'. An' I 'spect he know that like a hundred cats it ain't no real dem'stration, an' so what we do after we all on the buses is that we start goin' 'round some a the other neighb'hoods an' we picks us up a whole mess a cats I never seen 'fore. Some a them is from other places like NEW an' some a them is just off the street. I 'spect we make us like 'bout six, seven stops an' it ain't till all fi' them buses is filled up that we starts for City Hall.

It be then that we start to make us our signs. Each bus it have a leader who one a the Self-Wareness teachers, an' they start handin' out the shoe polish an' the big old cardboard. Some a the cats I never seen 'fore they all get in the back a the bus an' they have they radios there an' they jivin' 'round an' singin' 'long with the sounds so cool like. One cat he have the highest voice I ever hear an' he singin' so cool like a bird. But none them is makin' out no signs, I tell you that. That up to us real trainees.

So we all there, an' George, who be one a the trainee leaders like I told you, he handin' out a whole mess a blue paper with all these here slogans on them that we s'posed to put on the signs. George he gettin' to be somethin' else with all his boo. He make up all them slogans by hisself an' they some pretty mean ones, I tell you that. First one on the list it be:

REFUND *NEW* OR I'LL BURN DOWN YOUR HOUSE

Now that what you call gettin' to the point right off. But that be George's way, you know, 'cause he goin' to college an' he goin' Afro an' natural an' he got all them words down just so 'bout how you s'posed to talk to whitey. George he a jive cat now, man, an' I don't go spendin' much time no more speakin' with him. Next sign on the paper he give us it read:

GIVE US THE BREAD OR YOU'LL BE DEAD

Some a the cats they start right in an' makes up a whole mess a signs with that stuff on them. George he go 'round to each cat an' he make sure they got the spellin' down just so. Then George he come to me an' he give me a slogan to write down. It say:

CLOSE UP *NEW* AND I'M COMING AFTER *YOU*

"George," I say to him, "why you want us to go writin' down all this business?"

"That's the only thing whitey understands," George say, an' he tap the cardboard just like I s'posed to be goin' 'head an' writin' it just 'cause he tell me to. It be right then that the Self-Wareness cat he come to the back a the bus an' he take one look an' sees what we writin' on the signs an' man his head it like to go through the roof a the bus. "Man," he say to George, "you want the dust from the city or you just out to have yourself a good time?"

"You want me to beg for the money from the city?" George throw at the Self-Wareness cat.

"Course I don't want you to go begging," the Self-Wareness

cat say to George, "but if you go and start threatening people they aren't going to give you anything, whether you deserve it or not." George he think that over for a second or two an' fin'ly he say, "So what you want on these here signs?" But George he say it angry like, an' the Self-Wareness cat he read it, all right.

"You just say it like it is," the man tell George. "The City hasn't turned us down yet, you know. If they do, then we go after them," he say.

"All the same," George say, "you still askin' me to beg." Then he turn 'round an' he say to the rest a the cats, "You listen to the man here an' you write you some nice signs." Then he take his paper with all the slogans he writ on it an' he shove it in his pocket an' he go up an' sit in the front a the bus. Then a cat look to the Self-Wareness man an' he hold up a sign. "How 'bout this one?" he ask the Self-Wareness cat. The sign it read:

NOT THE FIRE *NEXT* TIME—THE FIRE *THIS* TIME

An' the cat next to him he hold up one he been makin' an' it say:

KILL WHITEY

Self-Wareness cat's eyes they all sudden start to get very big in his head an' he take them two signs an' he rip them up an' shove them under a seat. "Now be with it," he say. Then he tell us to start makin' up signs that is like nice signs. We make up a whole mess a signs that say:

REFUND *NEW*

NEW IS ALL I'VE GOT

KEEP MY SCHOOL OPEN

Jazz like that, you know.

All the time we makin' out the signs the cats in the back a the bus they still just swingin' with the radio an' carryin' on like they only there to be diggin' a bus ride. Every now an' 'gain when we at a red light one a the cats he lean his head out the window an' he yell at some nice lookin' chick. One chick she even wave back.

So we make up like a sign for everybody an' when we done with that the Self-Wareness cat he come back an' he got the boards an' the stapler thing to be puttin' the signs up with. An' while we all staplin' he give us a little talk 'bout what we s'posed to be doin' when we get down to City Hall. He say the first thing we got to be is like very cool an' orderly, 'cause if an' we get outa line we blow the whole thing. "And if anybody gives some trouble to the police he's going to answer to me," the Self-Wareness cat say. Out the back a the bus come, "Don't you worry none, man, I got no reason to be speakin' with the pigs." Self-Wareness cat he don't say nothin' an' I 'spect that a good thing 'cause he look to me like he all set to go outa control. "Just remember," he fin'ly say, "you're getting forty-five dollars every week from the government. It's your pay you're messing with." That seem to cool mosta the cats down a bit.

So when we get there all the buses they park together an' the director man he go from one to the next havin' a little talk with each Self-Wareness cat makin' sure they done they jobs right, you know, an' that none a us trainees is goin' to be gettin' outa line. Then they let out each a the buses one by one an' the cats they all get in single file an' they carryin' they signs up so high anybody can read them. An' they start walkin' 'round this big old square down there near City Hall an' fin'ly they forms up a circle that maybe half a block long an' 'bout twice as wide. It be just when I get offa the bus that I sees the *po*-lice. Seem like they come from nowhere, an' each a them got his stick out like he gettin' set to use it. When all the buses is empty an' the cats is all formed up into the circle George he start to chant. "*Refund NEW, refund NEW, refund NEW,*" he yell, an' right quick the other cats they start to pick it up. The *po*-lice they start to get uptight a bit when the shoutin' start an' fin'ly one a them come up to George an' he ask him to step outa the line. He tell George that yellin' an' shoutin' it ain't part a the deal that been made. George he look to the man square, you know, an' then he shout in his face, "Article one, section one, of the Constitution of the United States of America guarantees my rights to freedom of speech." He stop an' look to the man to see what he goin' to do. Man, the *po*-lice cat you can see he just half a inch 'way from boppin' George on the head just for the fun a watchin' him sink to the ground. But the *po*-lice cat he control hisself an' he tell George he can *speech* anythin' he want but if he shout any more he goin' to jail for disturbin' the peace. George he get back in the line an' he shut up.

You know, Ninety-three, I got to tell you that picketin' an' protestin' it ain't never goin' to be my thing to do. It one big drag, baby. All you does is walk an' walk an' you keeps goin' 'round in a big old circle. Nothin' happen 'cept you get hotter an' hotter an' after a bit you only walkin' so's to keep from fallin' down. After a bit the Self-Wareness cat he see that everybody gettin' tired an' he tell George to start singin' some songs, an' that pick us up a bit, but after a while the whole thing it just die out. An' we just keep goin' 'round an' 'round. I 'spect last night I walk me maybe four, fi' miles, you know, an' just when it gettin' dark, things they start to slow up. Soon as it just a bit diff'cult to see some a the cats they start slippin' off the line an' gettin' outa there. Only a couple go in the beginnin' an' all they done was just to ease 'way from the circle an' put they signs 'gainst the subway entrance an' then easy like slip right down to get a train. Then some more cut out an' 'fore you know it they's only a handful a us left in the circle. An' soon as the *po*-lice see the cats slippin' off they start to pull out two by two an' 'fore you know it they gone too. Fin'ly we see the director man come outa the buildin' down there an' he go to one a the Self-Wareness cats an' he tell him to break it up, dem'stration it over. Then we get back in the buses an' come home.

You know, Ninety-three dog, you a big dis'pointment to me. All the time I in here tryin' to keep you company by talkin' with you, an' all you done is go off to sleep on me. Well, if that be the way you goin' to do things, I ain't goin' to hang 'round here. I goin' to check out Fifty dog an' then I goin' out to get me a paper an' have a look at what kinda jobs they have. If an' I can find me somethin' good to be doin' maybe then I don't get me on the Unemployment or the Welfare. Maybe I find me somethin' cool to be doin'.

THURSDAY

Dig, Ninety-three dog. Dig, dig, *dig.* Just dig, man, *all* the way. Now if an' you knew how to be givin' a cat the palm, man, you be doin' it to me the whole day. An' you know what I got for you here, dog, right here in this package all wrapped up nice like? You better believe what I got for you. I 'spect from the way you jumpin' 'round, man, that you can smell it. It a good thing that a boxer dog he have a small tail like 'cause from the way you movin' you rear end, dog, if an' you tail it be long you beat youself to death with it. So you think you know what it is, huh? Yeah, you be right. Two pounds a ground round. I have the man make it up special this mornin' an' it fresh as anythin' you have in you life. An' you goin' to have youself some other kinda cel'bration. Come on, man, I give you a pound now an' then maybe a pound 'fore I goes home tonight. None a that dry food today, dog. You goin' first class, man, 'cause you a friend a mine. Dig it all the way, Ninety-three, I pass my G.E.D. I say *dig IT!* Yeah, baby, oh, *yeah.* I so happy I don't know what to be doin' with myself. But I got me my high school *e*-quiv'lancy diploma an' I a diff'rent cat from now on, I tell you that. An' last night, man, I fly so high on the wine I think I never comin' down. But I ain't got me no trouble or pain today 'cause I still flyin', but I ain't flyin' on nothin' 'cept thinkin' that I a high school graduate. This here high I got goin' for me now it be the best an' longest high I ever have in my life.

Here, Ninety-three, you eat up you ground round, an' dig what kinda life be the good one. I don't know what make you fly high, dog, but I know that what you been diggin' for food it ain't been the best, an' I thinkin' s'mornin' comin' down here that they must be some way I turn you on like me. Look to me like from the way you eatin' that a pound a ground round it do the job.

Course a couple a things happen yesterday that I got to tell you 'bout an' then I got to get me on over to the hospital an' look up the big white doctor.

When I go to take my G.E.D. yesterday I just don't care 'bout it, see, an' that be 'cause I know deep inside a me that I ain't never goin' to be gettin' the math'matics. Now I tell you one thing, dog, an' that be the math'matics man he done his job good, all right. He done a job on me I don't think no cat never do. What happen it be this. I just sittin' at the desk an' the lady she come down to me an' she give me the math'matics part a the 'xamination. I just puts it front a me' an' I know I ain't goin' to be doin' nothin' with it. I lookin' 'round the room to see if they be any other cats there from NEW, or any from the neighb'hood. I don't see nobody I know. Then after like a few minutes I takes me a quick peek at the 'xamination, an' all sudden like the first problem, that the addition one, it look like I know the answer. Then quick like I looks at the next one, which be the subtraction thing, an' I sees I know how to do it without no mistake. All sudden then I starts to get me a bit worked up. I puts down the answer for the addition problem an' then I does the subtraction one an' checks it to like make sure, an' then I moves on to the fraction-dec'mal thing. An' I see I knows how to do that one. That be when I looks over the whole 'xamination an' it look to me that maybe I already took the thing maybe sometime back. Right then I thinkin' to myself that I gots a chance to be passin' it 'cause I know some a them problems. It ain't goin' on in my head that I *thinks* maybe I knows how to do them, I knows for sure. An' they be a big diff'rence in that, dog.

So I keeps workin' on through 'bout seven, eight a them problems an' I just knows them, man—knows them cold. An' when I get to the first tough mother, an' that be the first word problem, I see what up, all right. These here problems they the ones the math'matics man he tell me I got to know by heart 'fore he let me take the 'xamination 'gain. Only the math'matics man he tell me I learnin' only kinds a problems, you know, when all the time he been teachin' me to memrize what goin' to be the problems on the 'xamination. He don't give me like every problem, an' they ain't in no order. But after I catch on to what goin' on I just looks 'bout the paper for the ones he taught me up an' I just sits there an' works them through so cool like. An' when I know I got me down like 'bout twenny-fi' a the mothers I all sudden get excited 'cause I know the thing it in the bag now. But I haves me some trouble findin' all the ones he give me. Some a them problems they look like others an' you got to be a sharp cat to know which one the man taught you an' which one he ain't. He only give me thirty, like I told you, an I s'pose he figure I get me the other nine I got 'fore on my own. He close to bein' right 'bout that.

Sorry I have to cut outa here a little while 'go, Ninety-three, but when I come in this mornin' I called me up the big white doctor 'bout the job he say he get me if I haves me my diploma. He give me a number to call an' I been tryin' it all day like.

The doctor I tryin' to get he ain't been there all day but they say he be back in 'bout a hour.

So I tell you what happen after I finish up the math'matics 'xamination. I figure I pretty close to passin' the thing, you know, but I ain't 'xackly dead sure I make it. So I heads on up to NEW to dig up the math'matics man so he can call for me to make sure I got a 35. But when I walks in the door at NEW I see right 'way that somethin' goin' on an' it don't look good. They's a whole mess a cats movin' all kinds a stuff here an' there, an' desks they travelin' 'bout on dollies an' chairs is bein' moved so fast it look like they flyin' 'bout the place by theyselves. An' right in the middle a the big old hall the director man is just standin' there with his arms folded like maybe he the king a everythin' that goin' on.

I look at him an' he look at me for a second an' we can both tell we don't like what we lookin' at. But I just goes right on by him an' up the stairs to where the teachers' offices is. But when I open up the door that lead to where them offices is they's the same kind a traffic goin' on there that was downstairs. An' when I walk down to the math'matics man's office I looks into some others an' I see the teachers with piles a books on they desks an' big old trash barrels in there an' it look like they throwin' everythin' they own into them. But all the offices that ain't happenin' to, you know. Some a them offices they haves the teachers in them behind they desks just like always. An' when I get to the math'matics man's office I see he be one a the teachers who cleanin' out everythin'. The door it open, you know, but I knocks on it anyway. Math'-matics man he don't look up or nothin', he just say kinda like through his teeth, "Come in." I step into the office an' I sees right 'way that the mother he have one long hair 'cross his ass. After like a second he turn 'round an' when he see me his face it ease up a bit.

"How'd you do?" he say quiet like, an' I don't do nothin' 'cept make a little nod at him. Then he smile a bit like maybe he know somethin' I don't know, an' then he look 'way from me. He move over to the window an' he say easy like, "Do you want me to phone for you?"

"I got a lot ridin' on bein' sure," I tell him. He don't waste no time, an' he go right to the phone an' he call the lady down at N.Y.U.

He ask her what I make an' when she tell him he write it down an' hand it to me. It say, Math: 42. An' when he hang up he look at me an' he say, "What are you going to do now?"

"See 'bout gettin' me a job that pay me some more," I tell him. He nod at me an' then I say to him, "Can you tell me what goin' on here s'evenin'?"

"Retrenchment," he say, an' he look at the pile a math books he got on his desk an' then he put his hand on them like maybe they somethin' special to him.

"What retrenchment mean?" I ask.

"It's a nice word for being fired," he say quiet like.

"That what happenin' to all the other teachers?" I say.

"NEW is being cut back at the staff level to economize," he say, but he don't say it like he much care 'bout it.

"So the director man he get the money from the City?" I asks.

"Half of it," he say, "and consequently half of the staff is being let go."

"So where you goin' to teach next?" I ask.

"I don't know," he say, an' he look out the window.

"You don't have youself no trouble gettin' a job," I tell him. He nod, but what I sayin' it don't seem to make no diff'rence to him.

We just sits there for a bit an' neither a us is talkin'. Fin'ly I gets me up the courage to ask him how he know what them problems on the G.E.D. they be. He give a short little laugh an' he say, "It was a process of absorption. I suppose that during this year I've sent about a hundred or so trainees down to take the G.E.D.," he say, "and when they've come back I just asked them what problems they remembered." He look out the window an' he smile an' say, "I guess I know the whole exam by now."

"So how come you only give me thirty problems an' not the whole thing?" I ask.

"I guessed that would be all you'd need," he say, an' he dead right 'bout that. What the man done, see, was to give me 'nough to help me by, but he still make it so I got to get like ten, twelve on my own. I don't know if what he done was right or not, but I know that what he done was good. Ninety-three, I haves me my high school diploma, an' they ain't no way no cat he ever take it 'way from me. The way I lookin' at it that a good thing, all right.

Man, that there hospital it a spooky place, all right. They's tunnels an' tunnels an' passageways an' things that don't never make no stop. An' the traffic an' commotion goin' on in the place it just got to be somethin' else. Peoples runnin' every which way with tanks a stuff an' other peoples on stretchers, an' cats in wheelchairs an' on crutches. That whole place it somethin' else, man.

When I fin'ly call that doctor who lookin' for somebody he tell me I won't have no trouble findin' the place he at, an' then he give me a whole bunch a jive directions. Man, I lost from when I take the first turn he say I s'posed to, an' the only way I find out where the man is it be 'cause some securi-ty cat he stop me over there an' he ask me my business. When that security cat do that I just stands there an' I looks him up an' down like who he think he is anyway, an' then I tell him, "I the Spec'men Supervisor for the Research Center."

He raise up a eyebrow at me like I jivin' him, an' I is jivin' him. I only the Spec'men Supervisor for the big doctor's part a the Center here. I ain't like the cat who in charge a the whole thing. But the security cat he buy my boo an' then he ask me if he can be a some service to me. I tell him who it be I lookin' for an' then he give me a whole mess a directions that ain't no ways like what the doctor done give me. But fin'ly I finds me this here tiny el'vator with a sign over it that say, "To First and Second Sub-basements Only." I push the button an' the doors they open up nice.

They ain't no cat runnin' the car, an' I looks over to the panel thing they got there an' I pushes me off the button that say, "Second Sub-basement." The car it start to hum up so easy like an' then the ride down it begin. Now I tell you one thing, Ninety-three, an' that be that either that little el'vator be the slowest thing ever made or the second sub-basement it 'bout a thousand feet down. I don't know like which it be, but it take me like three, four minutes to get down there. An' when them el'vator doors open up they ain't nobody in sight. They just this here kinda blank wall that all white an' the floor it ain't nothin' but concrete painted black. An' the only thing that be in sight it be a big arrow-like sign that pointin' to the left. On the arrow is writ in big old black letters: PATHOLOGY. That where I s'posed to be goin', an' I tell you, dog, I relieved to be on the right track. So I starts off to walk where the arrow it pointin' an' I tell you I walks an' I walks till I beginnin' to think that this here it got to be a tunnel that maybe go under the river to Brooklyn. It twist an' it turn an' it keep on goin'. An' at every turn they got a sign just like the one that at the el'vator so you can't lose you way.

Fin'ly I comes to a couple a tunnels that leads off from the one I in an' they's a whole mess a signs there. I stops an' I looks for the one that say PATHOLOGY. It 'bout the sixth or seventh down an' it tell you what tunnel to be takin' from there. So I walks down it for a piece an' pretty soon I comes to a place where the tunnel it widen out an' stop. Right then I see all the doors they got that lead to a whole mess a what look to me like doctors' offices. So I go from door to door lookin' for the name a the doctor I there to see, an' when I comes to that door I knocks on it an' waits for a few seconds. When I don't get me no answer I knocks 'gain, an' then I hear this big old voice shout out, "God gave you hands, open the goddamn door yourself."

So I do 'xackly what the voice tell me, but 'stead a findin' me a office where a doctor s'posed to be I see I walkin' into this big old room that all white. An' the first thing I see it be the back a the doctor an' he bendin' over a table like we use on you, Ninety-three. Only they ain't no dog on this here table, man. They's two white legs stickin' out from 'round the doctor.

"What is it?" the doctor say without lookin' up.

"You told me to come over to see 'bout the job," I say to him, an' it be when he turn 'round that I see what goin' on. The cat he got a dead body on the table there an' he got it cut open from his throat to his privates. An' half the cat's insides is hangin' outa his body.

"Oh, yes," the doctor say, "you're Mr. Peoples."

"Yes, sir," I say to him, but I ain't lookin' at him. I lookin' at the poor cat who all laid open. The doctor he see my mouth it hangin' open 'bout a foot an' he say, "I take it you've never seen an autopsy."

"You take it right, doctor," I tell him, but then I get to thinkin' that if I want the job from the man I best to close my mouth an' get my eyes back in my head an' start actin' cool, you know.

"Well," he say easy like, "once you've gotten past the first couple the rest come easy."

"That so?" I say, an' cool like I start to look 'bout the place. Then he tell me that I come with some good rec'mendations from the big white doctor.

"He told me that you've got a good ability with instruments," he say, "and that you're extremely reliable."

"Ain't been sick a day all year," I tell him.

"Exactly what have your duties been over in the Center?" he ask.

"I been the Spec'men Supervisor for a whole mess a dogs," I tell him. "An' I done a whole lot of splenectomies, an' operations where I got to get the heart all exposed for the doctor to be workin' on the valves."

"I see," he say.

"But I didn't never mess with no heart myself," I tell him.

"I understand," he say, an' then he shut up for a little while an' I look the place over 'gain. Then after a bit he say to me, "Frankly, Mr. Peoples, I need a man with your kind of experience."

"What kinda job you got here?" I ask.

"The exact nature of it is hard to determine," he tell me. "There are a good number of different duties." When I ask him what they be he tell me one a them be takin' charge a the bodies when they come down from upstairs an' that each one got to be numbered 'xackly right an' then put in a big old book, an' then you got to make sure that the body it go in the right drawer in the morgue. When he say that he tell me it be a good idea if I have me a look at the place where I be spendin' a lotta time. The morgue it be 'tached to the room we in then, you know, an' we walk through a door near the end a the table where the cat is laid out, an' when we go inside the morgue I tell you I get a bit uptight, all right. But once you inside the morgue for a few minutes it ain't nothin', you know. Ain't but like three walls with a whole mess a big drawers that come outa them. An' they's a little table over in one corner with a light on it an' all the paper an' stuff to be recordin' the bodies when they come in. Once you in the place you gets used to it.

So what the morgue doctor he do next is he show me how you check a cat in an' how you puts him in a drawer an' all the rest a the boo. An' then he show me a couple a bodies, an' when he do that I figure the man he tryin' to check me out on how I take all this business. I figure that right 'way, an' I steel myself up good an' I don't show him nothin' when he pull out a drawer an' show me this here dead cat. So he do it only one more time an' then I guess he satisfied that I can take whatever come my way. It be right then that he turn 'round an' he start to go back in the other room. I say to him, "This here it don't look like it be a job that take up all my time."

"There's more to it," he say, an' we go back into the other room an' he tell me that the rest a the job it have to do with helpin' him an' some other doctors when they be doin' autopsies. I ask him how I s'posed to help out an' he tell me I be doin' everythin' 'cept the cuttin'. I be in charge a all the instruments, an' gettin' the bodies outa the morgue an' gettin' them set up for the doctors, an' I be takin' spec'mens to the pathology place an' then doin' what cleanin' up got to be done. An' when he finish up that he say to me, "Well, Mr. Peoples, are you interested?"

"Yeah, I be interested," I tell him. "What the job pay?" I ask, an' I tell you that be 'portant to me 'cause after tomorrow I don't get me no digit no more from NEW. I be on my own. Then he ask me what I been makin' over here in the Center, an' when I tell him he think for a while an' then he lay some heavy dust on me, man, like I think I never make in my whole life. He goin' to pay me like a whole lot more than I been gettin' here. When he tell me how much he want to pay me he see my eyes get big in my head an' he ask me, "Is that sufficient?"

"All the way," I tell him.

Then he ask me when I can start an' I tell him on Monday. He say good, an' then he walk me to the door an' he give my hand a little shake like an' he ask me if I can find my way back out. I tell him I know the way, but I get lost anyhow on the way back out 'cause I ain't payin' no 'tention to the signs. I thinkin' 'bout the bread I goin' to be gettin' come Monday.

You know, Ninety-three, I just went an' saw me the big doctor an' I told him that I all set up with my new job, an' then I ask him if an' I can cut outa here 'cause they ain't nothin' more for me to be doin'. The cat don't hardly look up or nothin', man. He just tell me that as far as he concern my time it be my own. I don't know what goin' to happen to you, dog, but I figure if an' you able to make it this far you goin' to make it all the way.

Now I just goin' to turn me 'round an' walk me on outa here just like this be any other day.